THE ONE
THAT GOT AWAY
WITH MURDER

THE ONE THAT GOT AWAY WITH MURDER

TRISH LUNDY

Henry Holt and Company
New York

Henry Holt and Company, *Publishers since 1866*
Henry Holt® is a registered trademark of Macmillan
Publishing Group, LLC
120 Broadway, New York, NY 10271 • fiercereads.com

Our books may be purchased in bulk for promotional, educational, or
business use. Please contact your local bookseller or the Macmillan
Corporate and Premium Sales Department at (800) 221-7945 ext. 5442 or
by email at MacmillanSpecialMarkets@macmillan.com.

Library of Congress Cataloging-in-Publication Data

Names: Lundy, Trish, author.
Title: The one that got away with murder / Trish Lundy.
Description: First edition. | New York : Henry Holt and Company,
2024. | Audience: Ages 14–18. | Audience: Grades 10–12. |
Summary: Teenage Lauren must confront her dark past when
she gets pulled into a murder investigation involving her new
fling and his brother.
Identifiers: LCCN 2023048878 | ISBN 9781250292162 (hardcover)
Subjects: CYAC: Murder—Fiction. | Brothers—Fiction. |
Interpersonal relations—Fiction. | Mystery and detective stories. |
LCGFT: Detective and mystery fiction. | Thrillers (Fiction) | Novels.
Classification: LCC PZ7.1.L8495 On 2024 | DDC [Fic]—dc23
LC record available at https://lccn.loc.gov/2023048878

First edition, 2024
Book design by Aurora Parlagreco
Printed in the United States of America

ISBN 978-1-250-29216-2
1 3 5 7 9 10 8 6 4 2

For my daughter

ONE

My mom doesn't need to know the real reason I visit her at work.

I slip her a venti iced chai latte as she's charting her patients, and she gives me a quick kiss of thanks before her eyes dart back to the computer screen. She thinks I'm a good daughter, treating her to her favorite drink at dawn. In her eyes, I'm her little pick-me-up. In reality, she has no idea why I'm here. Why I visit her at Valley Hospice every Saturday morning with her chai; why I haven't missed a Saturday for the past six weeks. And like so many things in my life, it's easier if she doesn't know the truth.

I leave the nurses' station and head into the oldest wing of the hospice center, the Crestmont wing. Soft, battered floorboards creak underneath me as I pad down the hall. The rising sun makes the faded photos hanging on the walls come to life again. The largest one is of Carmichael and Rosemary Crestmont, the wing's namesake. A pair of scissors glints in Rosemary's gloved hand as she cuts the ribbon on opening day in 1973. She's dressed in a floor-length fur coat and stands in three inches of snow. Carmichael has his arm around her, a huge diamond bracelet dangling off his wrist.

I turn the corner, finding myself in the hallway with supplies. Dust coats everything like a thick layer of frost. I stride past each dark door until I reach the one at the very end. I grip the cold brass handle and push it open, my insides already softening. How I always feel right before I see him.

I find him leaning against one of the storage shelves. His volunteer T-shirt is untucked. His dark hair falls around his pale face.

"Hey," Robbie says, his voice still warming up for the day, all throaty and tired.

"Hey," I say back. I drop my keys onto the threadbare couch. Then he's in front of me, and the best part of my week begins.

His lips find the back of my neck, the place no one ever touches except for him, at least for now. I close my eyes and I'm back in my old bedroom, a taller body on top of me that smells like sun and salt. I pull off his shirt to bury the memory, and he's slipping my practice jersey over my head. The faster we do this, the faster he helps me forget. Luckily, he smells like cedar and musk with a tinge of menthol and the slightest hint of tobacco. His bad habit. He kisses me as we fall together onto the couch. He makes his way down my body, past my collarbone, my stomach. I want him more than anything and pull him closer, savoring the way he tastes. I surrender to the way his teeth graze my lips, the way his hands find my jaw. He strokes my cheek and his touch is smooth and careful. I shut my eyes tighter, imagining a calloused hand instead.

"You're a little tense," Robbie says, breathless. I open my eyes. His lips curl into a hungry smile. "I can fix that."

He pins my legs down. I close my eyes again. I try not to picture anyone this time. Just darkness. Nothingness. Because Robbie knows exactly what to do. I lose myself in it. The warmth returns. Then it builds and builds and builds until it can't build anymore and I collapse.

He rises and I unbuckle his jeans. He reaches for the condom in his pocket before I slide them all the way off. I run my fingers through his hair, pulling him even closer. I wrap my legs around his waist and kiss him, hard, pressing myself against him until he shivers and lets go. The two of us are left sprawled on the couch, hearts still racing.

I will give myself a few minutes to catch my breath, then get dressed and tell him I'll see him next Saturday. This is our routine. The same one we've had ever since I first crossed paths with him in the hallway. He'd asked me if I wanted a tour. When I saw the way his eyes focused on me so intensely, I knew. I knew what I wanted. What I needed. I've done this enough to know how it works. And I knew he wanted it, too.

As I'm slipping my jersey over my head, I catch Robbie staring at me.

"What?" I say.

"I just like looking at you," he says.

I feel my cheeks flush. "You can look all you want next Saturday," I quip back, turning the other way.

"About next Saturday," Robbie says, sliding on his jeans. "I'm going to be at my lake house for Labor Day weekend."

"Oh," I say. I can survive one weekend without hooking up with him. "Right."

A curious look emerges on his face. "I could text you so you won't miss me so much," he says.

I bend down to grab my shorts. "I'm not big on texting," I say.

The less connected we are, the better.

I slide on my shorts, then my socks. When I turn around to pick up my keys, I find Robbie. His head tilted slightly from looking down at me. He smiles. "Don't forget this," he says, pressing my phone into my hand.

Warmth spreads from my throat down into my stomach. I have to throw it on ice.

"Thanks."

Then I'm gone, fixing my messy hair into a ponytail. A few strands fall out of place, and I can't help but notice how well they hold his scent.

TWO

Coach makes us run a mile on the track before practice. It's already so humid I can feel the eggs I doused in hot sauce fighting for a way out of my mouth. I'm not used to it at all, being from California. I'm not used to a lot of things in Happy Valley, Pennsylvania, where we just moved so Mom could take things to the next level with Mark, who she thinks is her soulmate. And partly so I could have a "fresh start." Or maybe mostly so that I could have a fresh start.

This is my shot to not entirely screw up my life like I did back home. I need to maintain at least a 3.5 GPA to make up for the disaster that was my junior year. Getting into a semi-decent college is doable. I'll stay focused. I'll go to school, play soccer since it's the only thing I've ever been good at, and study. Robbie is a nice bonus. He told me he also goes to Valley High. As long as things stay exactly the way they are, we can keep seeing each other on weekends once school starts next week.

It's perfect. A no-feelings arrangement. Because seeing him helps me forget, and forgetting is the only way I'm going to move on from everything that happened in California. Things are going to be different here.

They have to be.

I don't think my legs can pump any faster. Then I see the dark swoosh of Mara Kumari's hair in front of me. I force myself to pick it up, just a little bit more. Mara's left forward, and she's not in love with the fact that I've joined the team. Even after I sent three perfect corner kicks her way during tryouts. I kind of get it. I'm breaking into a circle of teammates who've played together since seventh grade.

I have to earn my place to start as right midfielder. That means getting a mile time that beats Mara's.

I sprint down the straightaway of sun-soft rubber, but have to slow up around the curve of the track. This pace is actually killing me. I need to catch my breath if I plan on going all out for the last stretch. Just as I'm about to race down the next straightaway, there's a smell. The one that makes my stomach go cold even when it's 85 degrees out.

I look out, beyond the track. Plumes of smoke rise up from the farm on the other side of the road. A farmer carries a torch, deliberately stoking the flames on a small area of her land. It's just a small fire. A contained fire, to burn weeds and decaying crops. But then every logical thought I have is over-ridden by panic.

Suddenly, everything around me is on fire. I lurch forward, stumbling because I'm drunk. Sweating because it's hot as hell. The smoke is black as night and I can't see anything. Then I feel his hand, gripping mine. Leading me out.

Until something crashes down around us, and he's screaming. I inhale ash. His burning skin. His burning hair. It suffocates me.

I cough and it's like I'm hacking up a lung. Another pony-tail whips by. *Shit.* I give it everything I have.

I'm relieved when I cross the finish line near the front of the pack. Nice to know my legs still work even in a state of panic.

"Six thirty. Not bad, O'Brian," Coach Holliger says, glancing at his watch. He's wearing a faded Penn State Soccer 2014 T-shirt, the year he graduated. The sleeves are tight around his tanned arms.

He flashes me a quick smile. "Those long legs carried you ten seconds faster than yesterday."

I narrow my eyes at him. I've only had women coach me my entire soccer career, and they've never commented on my body. Not even a little bit.

I try to shrug it off. It's probably his version of an awkward compliment since we barely know each other. Coach had been surprised when I was the only person he didn't recognize at open practice sessions in July. Who transfers schools—let alone coasts—right before their senior year?

Sometimes it doesn't feel real. I live here now. I can never go back to California. There's nothing left for me there, anyway.

Rachel was my last tie to home. We grew up together, playing soccer since we were eight. I'll never forget the first day I came back to practice after it happened. My teammates were surprised to see me. It had only been a few days. But I was losing my mind, staying in our apartment. Being alone with my thoughts. Dry heaving whenever I thought about Clint, because there was nothing left in my stomach to throw up.

It felt amazing to exhaust myself. It was a Friday. Rachel and I always got dinner after practice on Fridays.

"I can't wait to inhale a McFlurry," I told her.

She looked at me and blinked. "Oh, I made plans, Laur. I'm really sorry. I didn't think you'd be back so soon."

It was the first time in three years she told me she couldn't. But I could tell by the hesitant look in her eye that it was more like she wouldn't. That was the end of that.

I may not have to win Coach over, but my new team is another story. If I'm starting, that means I'm taking Taylor Covington's spot. That means I have to beat her record for assists.

No pressure.

I guzzle down half my water and I'm trying to catch my breath when I feel a strong pat on my back. I turn around to find Alexis Okada, one of our team captains.

"Good run, Lauren," Lex says. She isn't even a little bit winded, and I know she came in first.

"Thanks," I say, still huffing.

Lex is all muscle, with quads that can send a ball halfway across the field. She plays center mid, and is already committed to Penn State. She bends down next to me, pulling a roll of white prewrap out of her bag. She tears off a piece with her teeth and ties her short black hair back. "My parents are in Hawai'i visiting my grandma so I'm having a kickback tonight for a little team bonding. You can spend the night, too."

I cap my water and shove it back in my bag. All my teammates need to know about me is that I'm dedicated to helping us win on the field. I'm not interested in making friends here.

It's for their sake as much as mine.

"I have plans actually. But thanks."

I jog over to our field, kicking up tufts of freshly cut grass. Then Coach blows his whistle. Time to work my ass off.

I take a seat on a locker room bench. After practicing all morning, my shin guards are ripe. I peel them off and stick them in the sides of my bag, then slide on my sandals. I check my phone. A new text from Mom.

Hi honey! Mark is coming over tonight. I'm thinking we could go out since it's Saturday. There's a noodle house downtown. How does that sound? He's really looking forward to spending more time with you.

I let out a groan. Mark's been over three times this week.

It's not that I hate Mark. He makes Mom happy. But sometimes I get sick of being their third wheel. Sometimes I just want to go to dinner with Mom. The two of us. Like we used to do.

Just then, a sharp laugh shocks me out of my bitching. When I look up, I see Mara keeled over laughing while she and Lex exit the locker room together. As the doors close behind them, and the sliver of light from outside vanishes, I think about how pathetic it sounds to spend the last nights of summer third-wheeling my mom and her boyfriend's dinner.

I chuck my phone in my bag.

I could show face at Lex's. Show everyone I'm a team player. I'll leave before anything has a chance of getting out of control.

I race out the door to catch Lex.

"My plans canceled," I lie. "What's your address?"

Damn, I probably look desperate. But I kind of am.

THREE

I eat a late lunch of radioactive-orange mac and cheese to make sure I'm not a lightweight tonight. I'll have a couple of drinks instead of explaining why I've been trying to stay sober. If they're anything like my team back home, they like to party. I'm not trying to draw even more attention to myself by pretending like I'm better than everyone else.

I shovel the last of the macaroni into my mouth and my phone lights up with a new text. From a number I don't recognize. My stomach drops. I changed my number right before the move to put an end to the constant messages from Donovan and the rest of his teammates.

I take a deep breath and slide open the text.

I'm one step ahead of you

Blood rushes to my head. What the hell does that mean?

But then Mark and Mom are here, their arms full of groceries. I darken my phone. Maybe if I just ignore the text, whoever it is will leave me alone.

"Hey, babe," Mom says.

I tried to let her down easy for tonight's dinner, telling her I had mandatory team bonding. It's not a total lie. Still, my heart twinges a little bit. I know it hurts her feelings that I'm not obsessed with Mark.

"I grabbed a couple things for you to bring to Lex's," she says. She pulls out a huge bag of barbecue chips and bag of peanut M&M's.

Damn, she really does know how to make me feel bad.

"Aw, thanks, Mom."

"Team bonding sounds like a whole lotta fun," Mark says, unloading a bag of groceries.

I grimace. It kind of annoys me that his caramel almond coffee creamer and calcium-fortified orange juice have taken up permanent residence in our fridge. As long as he hasn't officially moved in with us, I can tolerate it. I guess.

That was the deal I made with Mom. I agreed to the move as long as it meant not living with her long-distance boyfriend she met on eharmony. She can wait to live with him until I'm in college. It's less than a year away.

Mark folds up the paper grocery bag and makes eye contact with me. His blue eyes crinkle as he smiles. "How are you liking Happy Valley?" he asks.

He's always tried to engage with me, ever since I first met him in California. Apparently, the headquarters for the company he works for are based in Silicon Valley. Mom would see him when he was in town for work trips. He came over to our apartment once and I told Mom I approved of him. Which is true. I just don't want to spend every second with him.

Mom looks at me expectantly, as if she's saying, *Please don't be bitchy.*

"It's a little boring," I say honestly. I can just feel Mom tense up as she opens the dishwasher. "But I'm warming up to it."

"The sunset tonight will be beautiful, you can bet on it," Mark says. "There's nothing like a Happy Valley sunset during the last days of summer."

"I mean, I think watching the sun set over the Pacific Ocean in Santa Cruz is pretty hard to beat."

I can't help myself. Then I catch the look on Mom's face, which is pure disappointment. A hot flush of guilt rushes through me. Mom would have never even started dating Mark in the first place if her last relationship had worked out.

It didn't. Because of me.

"But I guess I'll never know until I see it," I add, flashing a quick smile in Mark's direction.

Then I catch the time on the microwave. Six thirty. Lex's kickback starts in an hour.

I sequester myself in the upstairs bathroom. I haven't worn makeup in months, but figure I should at least put some mascara on. I rummage through the cardboard box of my toiletries and find my stained makeup bag at the bottom of it. I find something else, too. My old flask.

I pick it up, hearing liquid slosh inside.

Then Rachel's voice is in my head.

You've been drinking way too much.

I shouldn't.

But there's probably not *that* much left.

I unscrew it and the smell of vodka singes my nose hairs. I take a swig and it burns. In the best way. I drain the flask and take the mascara wand to my lashes.

Before I leave, I can't help but glance at the text again. They haven't sent me any other messages, which is a good sign, but I decide to google their 773 area code. Chicago. Weird. None of the messages I got back home had Chicago area codes. Maybe it really was the wrong number.

I delete the thread and pop a piece of gum in my mouth. Then I slip out the front door before Mom can smell the alcohol on my breath or Mark can give me some of his famous "advice" about being a teenager in Happy Valley. Once I'm outside, I notice there's a small Penn State flag staked into the fresh mulch. Now our house is just like every other one in our neighborhood. The university is the lifeblood of this town. People are obsessed.

Lex lives just a couple of neighborhoods over, which makes for a short walk through some fenceless backyards. I guess that's a perk of living in a small town. Everything is within a ten-minute radius and they've never had to deal with a little thing called traffic. One thing I don't miss about California.

And as much as I want to compare the setting sun to the beauty of back home, I have to admit, it's pretty, like sherbet melting over rolling green hills.

I sigh, taking in the heavy, slow way my breathing feels any time I'm a little tipsy. God, I've missed this feeling. It's like the only thing that stops the constant flow of panicked thoughts. I briefly went to therapy back home. Mom thought I was falling apart. She wasn't wrong. But it's not like I could tell my therapist even a sliver of the truth. I'm a minor. She's a mandated reporter.

I could never tell anyone the truth. That was always the problem. That's why I fucked up so badly in the first place.

The door to Lex's house is unlocked. I take a deep breath. Here, in Pennsylvania, I remind myself, no one has to know about my past. No one will ever know. I'm just the new girl.

I notice everyone's taken their shoes off and left them near the doorway, so I do the same. SZA's new song pulses in my ears. I follow the source of the music down into the finished basement, where the bass makes everything shake. Most of the team is already here. I set the chips and M&M's on a table with pizzas and wings. I find Lex behind the bar counter, mixing drinks. Mara comes up behind her and steals her for a kiss.

Maybe it's the alcohol coursing through her veins, but when Mara sees me, she smiles. I smile back. Something glints against her brown skin, near her collarbone. A gold necklace.

Lex whips around the bar and gives me a hug. She smells like grenadine and whiskey. "You made it! Let me get you a drink."

She hands me a cupful of whatever concoction she's just poured. For the first time, I notice her eyebrow's pierced. She never wears her piercing at practice.

I take a sip of the drink she made. It's strong as fuck.

More bodies fly down the stairs. Andrea Moreno, our goalie, with Gwen Solomon, a forward, and Sophia Hughes, our right defender. They didn't come alone. A handful of guys I've never seen before follow closely behind them.

I check them out. They're tall, with muscular calves. Rough hands. And enough cockiness to fill a room. Lax bros. I can spot one from a mile away.

That's why Robbie's refreshing. He's not my usual type.

"Can we have just *one* party without them?" Mara says, rolling her eyes.

"Sorry to break it to you, but half our team's straight," Lex says, filling up more red Solo cups.

"The least they could do is bring the soccer guys," Mara says. She migrates to one of the speakers and turns up the music. "I actually have something in common with them."

My phone vibrates in my jeans. I take another swig of my drink before I check it.

It's a text from an unknown number. The same Chicago one, actually.

Shit. I was hoping that wouldn't turn into a situation.

I find an isolated corner near the food table and pop a

handful of chips into my mouth. I crunch them in between my teeth and glance down at the text.

You're not going to leave me on read, are you, Lauren?

I'm in no mood to bullshit right now. If I entertained every anonymous text I got back in California, I would have actually lost my mind. I start typing a reply.

Blocking you

The next text comes through before I have a chance to do it.

It's Robbie

My heart does a little thump in my chest.
I'm more relieved than annoyed. Not that I'm going to tell him that.

How did you get my number?

He texts back instantly.

I called myself on your phone while you were changing ;)

I grab another handful of chips and text him back, unsure of whether I'm surprised or mad, or both.

> **I'm wondering how exactly you did that since my phone was locked.**

I've seen you press 1 1 2 2 for the last five weeks . . . C'mon, Lauren. You're practically begging someone to hack your phone.

My cheeks burn.

> **Why do you have a Chicago number? I guess you were hoping I wouldn't find this whole you-hacking-my-phone-thing creepy?**

Typing bubbles instantly.

I had to get a new phone one summer. I was in Chicago at the time. And ouch. I guess I'm failing miserably at trying to impress you?

I feel myself smile, and quickly suppress it.

Andrea's standing in front of me. Up close, I'm surprised to find I'm taller than her, since she's such a presence on the field. She's wearing a low-cut crop top and sweats. Her bare arms have two sets of brown tan lines from alternating between her long-sleeved goalie jersey and her short-sleeved practice jersey. Her dark brown hair is tied up into a messy bun instead of her usual braids.

She glances down at my phone and raises an eyebrow. "We're starting the bonfire," she says. Her voice is clear as a bell, even as the bass thumps through my chest.

Behind her, I notice everyone is headed for the door that leads outside.

"Oh, cool," I say.

I have no plans to join them. I'll keep the food table company and then I'll slip out as everyone's getting wasted.

Andrea locks eyes with me. "It's team tradition," she says. "We write one thing we're going to leave behind in the old season and then we burn it. We start off every year with a clean slate."

Of course it's team tradition. The last thing I need is to make enemies with our keeper.

"Got it," I say.

I quickly save Robbie's contact and take a step toward the door. Andrea points to a basket filled with brand-new Adidas slides. "Grab a pair of those, too. We always get new ones at the start of the season."

First I grab the closest bottle from the bar and refill my drink. Then I reach into the basket. I find my size of the customized blue-and-white Adidas slides. Our team colors. I throw them on and walk outside.

I gulp down what must be cheap vodka. I need liquid courage if I'm actually going to walk over to the fire pit in the middle of Lex's backyard. The flames are a couple of feet high. It takes me a few seconds to breathe again.

I try to psych myself up. This will all be over in a matter of minutes.

I make my way toward the small table by the fire pit. Andrea hands me a slip of paper and a permanent marker.

"Get ready to burn it," she says, her smile lighting up her face.

Right.

"Can't wait," I say.

I rub the soreness that tugs at the base of my throat. Being this close to the flames makes me want to tie a plastic bag over my head.

I need to get this over with already.

I chuck my empty Solo cup into a garbage bin and pop off the marker cap.

I write **EVERYTHING.**

It's vague. But truer than anything else I could have written.

I roll my paper into a ball and throw it into the fire. Except I miss, because I suck at anything involving hand-eye coordination. It lands on the ground.

Then someone picks up my paper and drops it into the fire for me. It disintegrates instantly.

"I got you," Mara says.

"Thanks."

"You miss your team in California?" she asks.

The firelight makes her necklace glow. This close, I can see the pendant. A crescent moon.

"Yeah. I do," I say honestly.

I miss how everything was before. Before I blew up my life. I don't miss the way those last few practices went. The way I couldn't find a warm-up partner. The way even Rachel kept her distance from me in the team huddle.

I shove my hands into my pockets so Mara won't see the way I'm coming undone. I find my phone. My crutch. I never had bad social anxiety before everything happened with Clint, but now it rears its ugly head at the worst times.

I have a missed call from Robbie. Now he's calling me, too?

I look up to find Mara's eyes glued to my phone. "Are you tight with a Robbie back home?" There's an edge to her voice. One I don't like.

"Um, why?" I ask.

"Tell me that's not Robbie Crestmont saved in your phone," she says.

I blink, trying to catch up.

Robbie's a Crestmont. Of course he is. That's why he volunteers at Valley Hospice when every other volunteer there is like seventy years old. His family is the reason why it even exists.

I meet Mara's gaze. I'm not trying to get on her bad side.

"We just met," I say. "He volunteers at my mom's work."

"You'd better stay the fuck away from him," she says.

I laugh nervously. "Wow, why do you care so much—"

"It's not funny," she says, her floral perfume suddenly nauseating.

I'm tipsy and my filter quickly goes out the window.

"Okay, what the hell is your problem?"

"Come on, babe," Lex says to Mara, beelining for her from the other side of the fire pit. "How could she know—"

"*Know what?*" I ask.

"Please don't infantilize me right now," Mara tells Lex. Her eyes don't leave mine.

She leans in, making sure I hear every word. "Every girl the Crestmonts date winds up dead."

FOUR

The entire party stares at me. A look I've only ever seen on the field at this point. My body goes rigid. I realize I have no idea who Robbie is. Who Robbie *Crestmont* really is.

He told me he's hooked up with both girls and guys in the past. He failed to mention that any of them were dead.

"What do you mean?" I ask, sounding more desperate than I want to.

Then a voice breaks through the thumping bass.

"My sister Victoria died at his lake house."

Andrea.

She takes a step toward the fire, tossing a ball of paper inside. The flames hiss ash into the night sky.

"Robbie claims he never heard her drown," she says.

Her gaze is so intense I have the urge to look away, but I wouldn't dare. "He claims he had no idea how she got that wound on her chest. Yet he was the only other person with her that night. He's a fucking liar."

All I can hear are the crackles and pops of the wood and

papers. The awful sound of things burning. I might vomit all the alcohol in my stomach.

"Jess Ebenstein dated Trevor, Robbie's little brother," Gwen says. She tosses her paper into the fire. I jump as sparks fly into the air. "He was the last one to see her alive after a party homecoming weekend."

Holy shit. Brothers with a dead girlfriend each? What are the chances?

And what are the chances that I immediately fell into something with Robbie? I chose him, among all the other random Valley High boys I could have picked to feel me up this summer.

I mumble something like "That's messed up," but I can't be sure, because I'm not sure of anything right now.

Then some lax guy has a bottle of something dark and strong and I'm taking a handle pull, and then another. Maybe they'll chalk up my grave mistake to me being the new girl. The naïve new girl.

But the thing is, I'm not.

The ground sways underneath me as I back away from the flames, which seem to be growing taller by the second.

Me and Robbie, I'm realizing, aren't so different after all. We're both damaged goods. Different kinds of damaged, but damaged nonetheless.

But my team doesn't need to know that.

FIVE

I try to peace out before the rest of the girls wake up. If I could pump my own stomach and give myself an IV of badly needed fluids, I would. After I learned about Robbie's deep dark secret last night, I overdid it. Maybe overdid is an understatement. I took every shot that was offered. I tried to forget about everything they said and now I'm paying for it.

But before I can make my escape, a voice calls out to me.

"You can't leave yet."

It's Lex. She's followed me into the foyer. She peels off a shiny sheet mask from her face and looks way too refreshed for someone who hosted a rager last night.

"I have bagels," she says. "And I think you need one."

She's not wrong.

I shrug, following her into the kitchen. Lex has a spread of bagels, cream cheese, fresh fruit arranged on a platter, a pitcher of iced coffee, and a pitcher of light orange liquid that must be either Gatorade or Pedialyte. Given everything I know about her, it tracks that she's not only team captain but team parent, too. I help myself to the orange liquid and gulp it down. Gatorade.

"You're saving my life right now," I tell her.

I slide onto a barstool on the island and reach for a bagel. I take a bite and chew.

She watches me eat. Then she grabs a bagel for herself. Cuts it in half.

"I know last night . . . must have been a lot," she says, spreading cream cheese on one side.

It makes my head spin.

I've been on the other end of this before. When everyone wanted to know what happened with me, Clint, and Donovan. What really happened. Like my teammates. They needed the details so they could choose whose side they should be on. It's like they were listening and judging me at the same time.

Even Rachel. Especially Rachel.

I may not have known Victoria or Jess, but Lex did. I try to be respectful of that.

"If it's not too much for you, can you tell me what happened to them?" I ask.

Lex whispers. "Mara was best friends with Vic. Andrea's sister."

Oh. That explains why Mara came in hot.

"Vic had played on varsity since eighth grade. She started dating Robbie freshman year. They were obsessed with each other. It kind of annoyed Mara that Vic spent every free second with him."

Lex leans against the countertop. "That summer, before sophomore year, Vic went to Robbie's lake house for Fourth of July. The next morning, he said he found her floating in the lake. He said she must have gone for a late-night swim."

Every muscle in my body tightens.

"Mara never thought she drowned by accident," Lex says. "Vic was a great athlete. Andrea didn't think so, either. Especially because of the cut she had on her chest."

Lex's eyes dart away from mine. "Vic was found topless. Maybe her bathing suit top got caught on something sharp in the lake, and came unraveled after she drowned. That's what the Lake Monarch police went with, anyway." She hugs her arms across her chest. "Or maybe someone attacked her."

My arms prickle with goose bumps. In my stomach, the sickening feeling that I know so well surfaces. I take another sip of Gatorade, making sure the bagel stays down.

Lex shakes her head. "They never found anything that could have explained her wound. No one saw either of them that night, because it was just the two of them at his lake house. No one could confirm Robbie's story. He turned into a totally different person after that."

"Like how?" I ask.

"Robbie played varsity soccer, too. He was good. Phenomenal, actually, just like Vic. After she died, he quit. He started getting into music, wearing black, all that. I don't know if it's because he feels guilty or he wants to just punish himself, or what."

I fold my napkin in half, then in half again, and again. "Or maybe he was grieving."

"I don't know," Lex says. Her brow furrows. "He hasn't come to any of the vigils for her that we've had since then. If he really had nothing to do with it, he's not acting like . . ."

Like the perfect victim.

Like a guy who'd just lost his girlfriend.

There's a code of conduct when it comes to tragedies. Fuck it up, and everyone thinks you're guilty.

I unravel the napkin, squeezing it in my hands. "Did they charge him with anything?" I ask.

"No," Lex says.

I soften my voice. "What about Jess? What happened to her?"

"After last year's homecoming dance, Jess and Trevor went to a party, and he found her passed out. Except she wasn't passed out. She had overdosed from a speedball."

I bite my lip. He found her just like Robbie found Victoria.

"People think he drugged her," Lex says quietly. "But there was also dirt under her fingernails and her arms had scratches on them. Like she'd been struggling with someone."

"Jesus."

Lex glances over her shoulder even though the only thing behind her is the stove. Then her eyes are back on me.

"The Crestmont family has more money than they know what to do with. Their dad, Lionel, is an attorney. He's a powerful person here in Happy Valley. I'm not sure that we'll ever really know what happened to either of them."

I sip my Gatorade, my stomach gurgling. I hear rustling

from the living room, and that's my cue to get out of my seat. I don't want to be here when everyone else wakes up. I've had enough attention on me to last the whole year.

"Robbie's never even mentioned Vic to you, has he?" Lex says.

I bring my glass to the dishwasher, trying to dodge her gaze. Trying to let myself off the hook. "Look, we're just hooking up," I say.

When I turn to face her, Lex is still looking at me. "Maybe it's time to end things," she says.

I sleep for most of the afternoon, only waking up to eat Mom's leftover prawns and chow mein. When I check my phone, Robbie's missed call from last night glares at me.

I've been dreading it. Calling him back.

Maybe, if last year had never happened to me, I would automatically believe what everyone said. That he had something to do with his girlfriend's death. That Trevor had something to do with Jess's. I wouldn't question it.

But last year did happen. Rumors are powerful. The truth is usually more complicated than anyone wants to believe.

I type *victoria moreno happy valley* into the browser on my phone. Her varsity soccer photo is the first thing that comes up. She has golden-brown skin, wavy brown hair, and amber eyes. She faces the camera with a huge, braces-filled smile. I find an article from the local paper, the *Centre Daily Times*, about her. Varsity soccer since eighth grade, like Lex said. She also ran track and her mile time set a school record: 5:02. Shit, she was like preternaturally fast.

My eyes skim the article. The next thing I read makes my stomach turn. *After her father passed away, Victoria became a teen volunteer at Valley Hospice, where she spent Saturday mornings assisting nurses and families.*

My hands are suddenly clammy and I wipe them on my shorts.

Robbie must think of her every time he's on top of me in the storage room.

Not that I have any reason to judge him. Because I do the same thing.

I glance back to the article.

The star athlete's body was discovered in the early morning hours of July fourth in Lake Monarch by her boyfriend, an incoming sophomore at Valley High, who has been cooperative with the local police. She is believed to have drowned.

A chill runs through my entire body. Finding her like that must have been devastating.

I read through more articles, but they all say the same thing. No charges were ever filed against Robbie. Against anyone.

All of this feels all too familiar.

I close out of the articles and lie back on my bed.

It doesn't matter how I feel about Robbie, I realize. Whether I think he's innocent or guilty. What matters is that my teammates think he's guilty. I can only imagine how the rest of Valley High feels. Being associated with him could ruin my chance at a fresh start.

Lex was right. It's time to end things.

I press his contact on my phone.

"Lauren," he says.

I picture the way his mouth curls up ever so slightly when he says my name.

"Hi."

"I missed your voice," he says.

I miss when you could be my escape.

"You heard it yesterday."

"Guess I'm getting Lauren withdrawals," he says, and there's a tugging in my lower belly.

"Why did you call me?" I ask.

"Do you have plans Labor Day weekend?" he asks. "Because if you don't, you should come to Lake Monarch with me."

I don't say anything. I don't even know what to say. I rub my neck and my fingers leave a sweaty film on my skin.

He's inviting me to the lake house. The place where his girlfriend took her last breaths. If he was really guilty, he wouldn't do that.

Would he?

"I'm thinking a real bed would be nice for once," he quips.

I sink deeper into my pillow and close my eyes. He's right. This would be an upgrade from the couch in the Valley Hospice storage room.

Why am I still thinking about him like this? I can't do this. This is supposed to be the beginning of the end.

"Lauren?"

Unless we spend one last weekend together. One last weekend of forgetting where his body ends and mine begins. One last weekend of pretending like we're not haunted by the things we can't even speak to each other about.

Technically this would be before school starts. My teammates won't even know.

But Mom could be a problem.

Unless I lie to her.

"Maybe," I say finally.

"Maybe?" he asks, like he's not used to hearing a non-definitive answer.

Then there's a long pause before he says, "I heard the varsity girls had a party last night."

He's fishing. He's wondering whether or not I know about him and Victoria; if the team scared me off last night, when everyone was drunk.

"That's why I'm incredibly hungover today," I tell him. He doesn't need to know anything more than that.

"Rough," Robbie says, his voice sounding suddenly terse. "Well, let me know if your maybe changes to a yes."

Before I can reply, I realize he's ended the call.

SIX

Friday after practice, I hear Mom laughing, and Mark's laugh echoing after hers. I find them in the kitchen, making a pizza together. Mom splashes some sauce a little too hard on the dough and some of it splatters onto Mark. He over-exaggerates a gasp, and she tries to rub it off. I don't think I've ever seen Mom attempt to cook something other than pancakes or grilled cheese. We're more of a takeout family.

I clear my throat so they don't start making out or something.

"Oh, hi, Laur," Mom says, practically batting her lashes at Mark. I fight the urge to roll my eyes. Instead I tear off the prewrap that's too tight against my scalp. I remind myself he makes her happy. She turns on the sink and sticks her hands underneath the running water. "If this is inedible we can always get Domino's."

"I'm sure it'll be good," I tell her.

I take a deep breath. I've been putting this off ever since Sunday. My game plan has been to wait to ask Mom about going to Robbie's lake house until the very last minute. Then it won't seem like such a big deal to her.

Or me.

We've texted a couple of times, but Robbie hasn't mentioned anything about this weekend. He knows I have the upper hand.

It's only one weekend. The last weekend of summer.

It's now or never.

I relax my jaw and try to channel my most charming self. "I was wondering . . . Could I go to a friend's lake house tomorrow? For Labor Day weekend?"

"Who?" she asks.

"Lex," I lie. "Some of my teammates are going. The senior girls."

I haven't lied like this to Mom in months. It doesn't exactly feel amazing. But she's not about to let me go to a boy's lake house alone. Not with my track record.

She briefly looks up at me, and it's like her eyes widen. Like she's wondering if I'm telling her the truth.

"Where is the lake house?" she asks.

"Lake Monarch," I say.

"Where is that?" Mom asks.

"Just north of here," Mark says. "A lot of folks in Happy Valley grow up going to Lake Monarch."

"Is it safe?" Mom asks.

"I'd say it's pretty safe," Mark says, slicing up some black olives.

I bite my tongue, hoping he doesn't mention anything about Victoria. That's one way to ensure Mom doesn't let me go.

Mark adds the olives to the pizza in neat circles. "There was a drowning a couple years back."

Great, thanks, Mark.

"A girl from Happy Valley," he continues. "She was a soccer player like you, Lauren. But they were never able to determine if her boyfriend, Robbie, had something to do with her death."

"Robbie Crestmont," Mom says bitterly.

She already hates him. I made the right call in lying.

"He volunteers at my work," she says. "Not sure how much he actually helps us, but it's not like we can let him go. I'm sure he's the kind of kid who has never had to be accountable for his actions."

She turns and looks at me. "I think you should stay here and have a quiet weekend."

I try not to deflate on the spot.

Mark slides the pizza into the oven and gently closes the door.

"Lake Monarch is a beautiful place," he says. "It could be a peaceful weekend away before your senior year."

"You'd let Ainsley go?" Mom asks Mark.

The moment of truth. Mark glances at me. "I would."

I give Mark a small smile. He's trying to win me over. "Ainsley loves it there. We stay at my uncle's cottage whenever we go."

Mom locks eyes with me. Then her gaze softens. "All right," she says. "You could use a little getaway before your last year of high school."

I stare at her, making sure I heard her correctly. "But I want you back no later than Monday afternoon," she says. "You need a good night's rest before your first day of senior year."

"Thank you," I say, my fingers already itching to text Robbie.

When I reach for my phone, I can't help but notice the way Mom frowns as she wipes down the counter.

SEVEN

This will be my last weekend with Robbie. My last weekend of being able to numb myself before senior year. Come Monday, I'll break it off with him. I'll start Valley High without ties to anything complicated.

Are you going to do it or not? I remember Rachel saying, when Clint and I had gotten into another one of our fights. It was just a couple of weeks before the fire. I thought that if we broke up, then I wouldn't be around the lax guys anymore. I hoped Donovan would finally leave me alone.

But I loved Clint. I couldn't bring myself to do it.

If I had, maybe I'd still be living in California.

After I told Robbie I was down to go to his lake house, he texted me:

This just made my day. More than you know

My face burned as I read it. Then the thought briefly crash-landed into my head that maybe I shouldn't go.

But it's only three days. Three days that will help me forget about the worst day of my life.

It's worth it.

I'm shoving my bathing suit and beach towel into a duffel bag when there's a knock on my bedroom door. Mom.

"What time are you leaving?" she asks.

I glance at my phone. It's nine forty-five. I try to pack faster.

"Ten," I say quickly.

She sits down on my bed as I rummage through a cardboard moving box for a clean pair of underwear.

"You still take your birth control every day, right?"

I toss the pair of underwear into the duffel. I meet her gaze.

"I've never missed one. Why?"

"If there are boys going—"

"There aren't," I say quickly. I turn my attention to a pile of socks so she can't see how red I'm getting.

Mom is kind of always in my business about birth control. She had zero sexual health education and got pregnant with me at eighteen, and she had no one to talk to about her options. My bio dad hung around for a couple of years, but then he met someone else and started a new family. We don't really talk. How I prefer it.

She sighs, as if she can finally relax knowing the odds of me remaining unpregnant are still ever in her favor. "I know I was on the fence at first, but I think it's great you have a group of girls that could be your friends. I know it isn't easy to forget about—"

I immediately cut her off. "I'd rather not talk about it."

"Okay."

She leans over toward me and gives me a kiss on the head, like she used to do when I was little. Something about this, about the tenderness she's showing me, makes me want to curl up in her lap and cry.

"Thanks for letting me go," I rasp.

"You deserve to," Mom says, and I have the sudden urge to confess everything. "Text me this weekend, okay?"

"I will," I promise.

I hug her tight, smelling the honey-scented oil she puts in her hair to keep the cranberry color from fading. She's worn her hair in every shade of red—from Ariel to Lindsay Lohan—since I was little.

"What are your plans with Mark?" I ask.

"Ainsley is coming over. It's the first time I'm meeting her."

Mom lights up every time she talks about Mark. Like she used to do about Andrew.

I'll never forget walking into our apartment after school and hearing sobbing from her bedroom. She'd just broken up with Andrew, after the news got out about the fire. I cracked her door, finding her curled up in the fetal position on her bed. The same exact position I had left her in that morning.

I never want to see her like that again.

"We can all get dinner or something when I'm back," I suggest.

Mom beams. "I'd love that."

Then I'm grabbing my duffel and heading downstairs. I told Robbie I'd meet him a street over from mine, on the cul-de-sac. He agreed to it without even asking me why. I'm sure he could guess.

I spot him from a few feet away, popping the trunk to his car. He's not alone. Two other people are in his car. They must be Trevor and John. Robbie mentioned they'd be joining us. His insurance policy against slander.

As I get closer, the guy in the front seat gets out. He's tall, with deep brown skin, wearing leather boots, tight black jean shorts, and a Bauhaus T-shirt. He has a nose ring and when he puts out his hand, I notice his fingernails are painted glittery black.

"I'm John. You must be Lauren," he says.

I shake his hand. His grip is firm. "You sure you want to join this group of degenerates all weekend?"

The way he says it, it's like it's a challenge. As if he's daring me to join them.

"I think she's pretty sure," Robbie says, squeezing my shoulder.

John lets go of my hand, then Robbie's grabbing my duffel. It's the first time I've seen him outside of volunteering. His uniform has been replaced with black jeans that are almost as tight as John's, and a black tank top tucked into them. My eyes dart to the white pack of Marlboros sticking out of his pocket.

Then it's like a younger version of Robbie glances back at

me from the rolled-down window of the car. Same pale skin, same dark hair, same intriguing brown eyes. But the animated features aren't there.

"Hey," Trevor says in my direction. I can't help but notice the way he gives me a once-over.

"I call shotgun," John says, hopping back in the front seat.

I'm intensely aware of my place as an outsider in their little group.

I open the door to the back seat and slide in. Then we're leaving my neighborhood. Robbie puts on something alt-J-esque, and I fight the urge not to glance over at Trevor too often. He wears AirPods for most of the ride, and only takes them out when we stop at a Dunkin' Donuts drive-through.

We get back on the highway, and then Robbie takes an exit that leads us onto a two-lane country road. We pass falling-apart houses and rusted farming equipment next to an abandoned barn. The sunlight disappears completely. With all the trees and cloud cover, it's like the temperature drops ten degrees.

Then the dark clouds move in, and a downpour hits. Robbie slows the car, turning on the windshield wipers. We crawl along the country road as it turns to mud.

I glance out the window just as the entire forest lights up. I can make out the edges of a body of water before everything goes dark again. Thunder booms overhead.

"Finally. My kind of weather," John says. "This goth swelters in the summer heat."

"The humidity here is next level," I say, but he doesn't say anything in response.

He's going to be tough to win over this weekend.

I turn back toward the window, hoping I'll see more lightning. We almost never get thunderstorms in San Jose.

Unfortunately for my amusement, it's a fast-moving storm. The sun peeks out of the clouds. I roll down my window, taking in the damp, earthy scent of the fresh rain. Then Lake Monarch comes fully into view, blue-black and still as glass. Cottages line it on all sides like little white snowcaps.

Robbie veers left, onto the gravel driveway of a lakeside mansion. It's massive, with sleek wooden beams and dark windows. He parks behind a black Porsche Cayenne. Perks of having generational wealth, I guess.

Then we're out of the car, unloading our stuff. I crane my neck toward the backyard, spotting a state-of-the-art dock suspended above the water.

"Dad must have taken the boat out," Trevor says, removing his earbuds. It startles me, hearing his voice. It's so similar to his brother's.

Robbie flashes me a smile. "Welcome to Lake Monarch," he says.

As I grab my duffel, I'm in awe of this lake house. I wonder what their actual house looks like.

"Pretty modest home," I say under my breath. I hear John stifle a laugh.

"The understatement of the century," he says easily.

I hope he's warming up to me.

Robbie opens the front door, and I carry my things inside. As we enter the foyer, I crane my neck to look up at the floor-to-ceiling windows with an incredible view of the lake. A huge telescope is positioned in front of it. I walk toward it, noticing a fish the size of a dinner plate carved out of quartz on a side table, next to a large candle in a mercury vase. Liquid wax pools on all sides. It's been lit for hours. I have the sudden urge to blow it out. Instead I dig my nails into my palm, stifling it. Not like I want to start off the weekend by showing Robbie all the ways I'm messed up inside.

"Let me show you your room," Robbie says.

I spin around, leaving the candle behind.

We head upstairs, where there's probably five or six bedrooms, at least, judging by the number of doors. Robbie opens one. "This one's yours."

Inside, everything is dreamy and white. I set my duffel next to the queen-sized bed with a fluffy duvet. There's a dark wooden nightstand, a sunrise carved into it, complete with a shiny, pearlescent orb for the sun. One of the mercury-vased candles sits on top, but thankfully this one's unlit. A black-and-white family photo of Robbie, Trevor, and who I'm guessing is their dad is framed next to it. No sign of his mom. I wonder how she fits into the picture.

My eyes drift to the large window on the other side of the bed. I go toward it, taking in the view of the lake. I spot the bright cap of a swimmer. A few docks across the way, people are fishing. Kids play on the sandy bank. Then the clouds come in, casting a shadow over everything.

"This room has my favorite view," Robbie says, taking up the space on my left side.

His eyes dart out to the water. I wonder if he's thinking about Victoria. If she still takes up as much real estate in his brain as Clint does in mine.

He turns to me, half his face shadowed. Then he leans in, kissing my neck. I close my eyes and lean against the coolness of the window.

"We're going to have fun," he says.

We will. At least for one last weekend.

I open my eyes, and by then he's already moved for the door. I hear John call out from downstairs that he's starving.

"Hey, Trev, can you help me set up the bonfire?" Robbie asks.

He says those words, and my blood turns to lead.

Summer is bonfire season. I should be used to it by now, the way people are obsessed with them. Even if it's something I'll never be able to relate to again.

Trevor adds another log to the fire and I brace myself as sparks fly into the fading golden-hour sky. I keep my eye on where they land. Into the brush. Onto the stone edges of the makeshift bonfire pit. Too close to the side table with food for my comfort.

John takes his roasted hot dog and sets it into a bun. He douses it in ketchup and mustard.

"This is a delicacy," he says, popping it into his mouth.

It looks incredible, but I have no desire to go anywhere near the flames. I'm content with cold buns and stealing Hershey's chocolate with graham crackers to round out my dinner. It seems like Trevor is, too. I watch him reach for the pack of hot dogs, then pull his hand away like he's decided against it at the last second.

Robbie opens the cooler, fishing out a beer. He offers me one.

"Thanks," I say.

My plan of trying to be sober isn't going so well.

I pop it open and take a few gulps. The buzz will deaden my nerves.

Robbie tosses a beer to Trevor and hands one to John. John takes it from him, and his fingers graze Robbie's during the handoff.

I blink, wondering if I imagined it.

Then my attention moves on, to a glowing white boat pulling up to the dock. Robbie trudges down the small hill we're on to meet it, and Trevor follows.

Which means I'm left alone with John. He quickly types something on his phone before darkening it again.

"I'd be tripping if I had to leave California," he says.

He never takes his brown eyes off me as he sips his beer.

"I'd imagine it's *far* from ideal to transfer schools right before senior year."

He's fishing for the real reason why I moved.

"My mom was in a serious long-distance relationship," I say. "We decided to move here, where her boyfriend's from. We can actually afford a house for once."

It's the same thing I told my soccer teammates.

"So then you're a saint," he says sarcastically.

"To be honest, I'd just gotten out of a traumatic relationship right before the move. I was ready to leave everything behind."

John crosses his arms and mulls it over. I've given him just enough hints of the truth to satisfy his curiosity, I hope.

"Did you grow up here?" I ask, trying to deflect.

"Born and raised," he says.

He wipes his mouth on a napkin, balls it up, and tosses it into the fire. I manage to keep my cool.

"Will you leave home for college?" I ask.

"My mom is a physical therapist at Penn State, and her tuition discount is incredible, but I'm not letting that limit me," he says. His eyes dart to the flames and back to me. "Wherever I go, I plan on studying abroad. I visited Germany with my ex-boyfriend and his family last summer, and I fell in love with Berlin."

John purses his lips. "Even if it made me realize I didn't love him."

"I feel like you could totally have the Berlin artist vibe thing going on," I say.

John smirks, like he might consider my compliment. Then he's standing up.

"Lionel likes a formal welcome committee," he says.

I follow his lead, already dreading it. Impressing parents has never been my forte.

Lionel steps onto the dock, and in the dying light of day, I glimpse him for the first time. The first thing I notice is that his teeth are neon white. He wears a crisp polo and khaki shorts, with Sperry's on his feet. He puts his hand out, offering it to a much younger blond woman wearing a black bikini, a see-through cover-up draped over it. She's maybe half his age.

"The stargazing is going to be incredible tonight," Lionel's saying. "Stace and I got a nice preview."

When Lionel glances my way, I try to hide my judgment.

"Lionel Crestmont," he says, sticking out his hand.

"I'm Lauren. Nice to meet you," I say. His handshake is like a death grip.

He turns to the woman standing beside him. "This is my girlfriend, Stacy."

She smiles demurely at me. "You have amazing hair."

The humidity here makes my light brown hair look like I got electrocuted. That's why I almost always have it up in a ponytail.

"Thanks."

Seeing Stacy up close, no way she's over twenty-five. Her skin is like porcelain.

Lionel gives John a hug.

"My man, you smell amazing," Lionel says. "What cologne is that? I need the rec."

I'm cringing inside.

"It's Replica Jazz Club by Maison Margiela," John says. "It's going to be my autumn scent."

"It's a perfect fit," Lionel says, flashing his teeth.

He puts his hand around Stacy's waist, gripping her like a trophy wife. He leads her down the dock, toward the house. "I think it's old-fashioned o'clock," he calls out. "Robbie, can you mix us some?"

I guess he has no issue with four underage people drinking. Which, obviously, I'm fine with. But still. I kind of expect parents to at least *pretend* to follow the rules.

Then I think back to what Lex said. The rules don't really apply to Lionel Crestmont.

As I leave the dock and head toward the house, I think of Victoria. It's impossible not to. This was the last place she was alive. Robbie must have walked down the same dock I was just on moments ago and seen her in the water. Or maybe he couldn't find her and he took the boat out. Or maybe he jumped straight into the lake.

I wonder if it's triggering for him, being back here. He's good at hiding it, if it is.

Then again, that's a skill set I have down pat, too.

I'm so in my own head, I don't notice that Robbie's caught up to me. When his hand finds my lower back, I almost jump out of my skin.

"Didn't mean to scare you," he says.

"You didn't," I say.

I try to put Victoria out of my mind.

"Fun fact. Stacy used to babysit us," he whispers.

Ew. Lionel went for his kids' sitter?

Robbie must see the disgust flash across my face because he laughs. But I can still feel the nervous energy in his fingertips as he grazes my spine. "When my mom started dating her younger coworker, my dad had to outdo her. They still compete with each other, even though they've been divorced since I was ten."

Ah. He does have a mom in the picture.

That means not only does he have to deal with one parent's romantic partner, he has to deal with two.

"I wish they knew we don't care about their partners even half as much as they do," I say, meeting his eyes.

"But that would break their fragile little hearts, Lauren," he says.

His hand leaves my back as we head inside.

EIGHT

Robbie makes drinks for everyone, and Stacy puts together a charcuterie board. Lionel asks me all about California. He tells me he's invested in crypto and has made several trips to Silicon Valley. I learn Stacy is also a lawyer, and that's part of the reason why she and Lionel reconnected. She's twenty-six, so I was only a year off.

After we graze, Lionel lets us all take turns looking at Saturn through the massive telescope I spotted when we first arrived. When it's my turn, I find myself holding my breath looking at the rings. Pictures don't do it justice. I also glimpse the Big Dipper and the Little Dipper, which is basically the extent of my star knowledge.

By the time I climb into bed, it's nearly midnight. My belly's full of expensive cheeses and two old-fashioneds. I turn, facing the open window, toward the sounds of crickets and lake water lapping at the shore.

Then I notice a small glow. And a cloud of smoke, blowing out over the lake.

Robbie.

He's at the edge of the dock, smoking a cigarette.

My stomach twinges. A thought crosses my mind. I could meet him outside. And I kind of, sort of want to. Like in some weird way, I want to be closer to him and his trauma, because it makes me feel better about mine.

I slip out of bed, grabbing my hoodie. I throw it on, and open my door as quietly as I can. I creep down the stairs and unlatch the side door.

Robbie greets me with a tired-drunk smile. "You found me," he says, taking a drag.

I watch the way his mouth takes in the cigarette, the way he holds on to the taste.

He notices me watching him. He pulls out his pack, offering me one.

I feel itchy all over.

"No thanks."

"I know it's a gross habit," he says, putting the pack back in his pocket.

"I quit actually," I admit. Surprise flashes across Robbie's face. "It was affecting my cardio."

It's a good enough lie, something that comes to me easily.

He takes another drag, then stubs out the cigarette under his foot.

"I only picked it up after I quit soccer," he says. He stares at me. "I'm sure you know my story by now. Or at least, the version your teammates want you to believe."

My bare legs shake. We're doing this. We're addressing the elephant in the room.

"I don't necessarily believe everything I hear," I say.

Robbie looks out onto the lake. "Two days ago was the full moon in Pisces," he says. "Are you into that stuff?"

"Into what?"

"Astrology. Moon phases."

"Other than looking at horoscope memes, no. Not really."

"Victoria got me into it," Robbie says.

Her name hangs there in between us. It's the first time he's ever mentioned her. His eyes meet mine, as if this is a test. "She loved using my dad's telescope to gaze at the moon."

"What would she say about the full moon?" I ask, taking his challenge in stride.

He looks up at the night sky.

"She'd say it's been making me nostalgic. Making my dreams more intense than they already are. Pisces is an emotional sign."

He turns toward me. "Ever since she died, I've only been back here in the winter. When the lake is frozen."

My heart thrums inside my chest. This is the first time he's been back here? With me?

"What changed your mind?" I ask.

"Meeting you," he says.

I feel my pulse in my ears.

Then he's right in front of me. His hand grazes my cheek,

and I smell the tobacco stained on his fingertips. "I don't think we're all that different from each other, Lauren," he says.

I pull away, unsure of what he means.

"Me with Victoria," he says, "you with Clint."

I can't feel my body. I can't remember how to breathe.

He knows.

I have no social media. My name isn't in any of the articles, because all of us were minors.

I thought I was careful.

"Wait," Robbie says, but I can finally feel my legs again. He's running to catch up to me, but he has a smoker's lungs and I've been clean for months. I reach the door and then I'm inside, bounding up the stairs. I slip into my room and shut the door.

My whole body's shaking. I hate this, that this is how my body still responds. All someone has to do is name-drop my ex-boyfriend and I'm a mess.

The door creaks open.

"Don't," I whisper. "Don't you dare come in here."

"Lauren, I'm sorry—"

I clench my fists to keep from exploding. "Was this your game plan? Corner me just to make yourself feel better?"

"No," he says, stepping inside and closing the door. "It wasn't. I only looked you up to protect myself. I found a Reddit thread."

Yeah, that makes perfect sense.

I've been on those message boards. They call it the Winter-green Fire. I've seen the disgusting lies they've spread.

"I should have asked you up front," Robbie says.

"Yeah, you should have. But I guess you didn't need to, since you got all the information you were looking for."

"It wasn't my best moment, okay?" Robbie groans. "I'm sorry. I . . . with the full moon, I thought it might be the time to . . . bring it up." He swallows. "When I met you, I knew we shared some of the same darkness."

I sit down on the edge of the bed. I don't want to admit that he's right. There's been this mutual, unspoken under-standing between us. Because we both came out on the other side of something that irrevocably changed us, and we're both still desperately trying to find our footing. We feel closer than we actually are, because we've both been through the unimag-inable.

That's why I couldn't resist being with him one last time. And now he's the only one in Happy Valley, apart from Mom, who has any idea of who I really am.

"I didn't come to the lake with you to dig shit up about your past, much to the disappointment of my teammates," I say. *I came here because it's going to be our last weekend together.* "They don't even know I'm here right now."

He sits down beside me and holds my gaze with a pleading look. "Please, can you forget I ever said anything?" he asks.

"Can you forget about everything you saw on Reddit?" I challenge him.

"Yes."

He says it like he means it. How is this so easy for him? "I know how quickly things can turn away from the truth," he says. "And I trust you."

You don't even know me. You don't even know what I'm capable of.

"You shouldn't," I tell him, all my armor going up.

"I don't think you can scare me off that easily."

When he looks at me, everything feels charged.

Part of me wants to tell him to fuck off. But the other part of me still needs him because I don't have anyone else. This is why I came here. I need to feel something. Something other than the numbness I've been feeling ever since I heard Clint's screams.

This weekend is my final chance.

I kiss Robbie, pulling him onto the bed. Everything is kinetic. We're moving fast, even faster than normal.

I briefly open my eyes so I won't be tempted to think of Clint.

NINE

"Trust me, the temperature's perfect," Robbie says.

I narrow my eyes, seeing gooseflesh travel up and down his body.

"Yeah right."

It's supposed to be overcast all day, and there's a chance of rain again this afternoon. I wrap a beach towel around my body and perch myself on the back end of the boat.

John lays out on the deck, his skin shimmering with oil. The breeze picks up the tropical scent.

"Aren't you freezing?" I ask him.

"I'm coaxing the sun out," John says. "She's being shy but the deck's warming up. I can feel it."

I look out toward the water, seeing boats anchored all around us. They must all think the same thing. Coolers overflow with cans of beer. Kids cannonball into the water, laughing their heads off. A Jet Ski speeds by. A boat passes us with someone water-skiing off the back.

My eyes find Robbie again. He floats on an inflatable chair. Water beads up on his skin, across his pecs. I flush, thinking back to last night. And for a moment I ease into a relaxed state of mind. I feel calm for the first time in weeks. Then, as if my brain could sense my brief second of vulnerability, I'm struck with a fear from the night before.

He knows. He knows what happened with Clint.

Robbie surprised me. On purpose. He wanted to have the upper hand.

I take a breath. Deep down, I know it was smart of him. Find someone equal to or worse off than you, and suddenly the guilt, the grief, doesn't seem as heavy anymore.

John's method works, because the sun finally breaks through the clouds. I let my towel fall from my makeshift cocoon as sweat gathers across my torso.

John sets his sunglasses in a drink console. He grabs his phone, but when he catches me glancing at him, he decides against whatever it was he was going to do. He places it underneath his sunglasses and dives into the water, making a splash. He swims over to the other inflatable chair.

"I thought you'd never join me," Robbie tells him.

He reaches his arm out and John floats over, grabbing on to it. Robbie reels him in closer, until their chairs are right next to each other.

Another boat cruises by. The motion sends a sizeable wave underneath ours. The guys bounce up and down on their chairs, floating farther away. I notice the sun's already dried Robbie's board shorts. That's my cue to put on sunscreen. The only parts of my body with any sort of semi-tan are my legs and arms, from soccer. The rest of my pasty white skin is fair game for a burn.

I reach into my tote bag, rummaging around. I find ChapStick that's soft as putty, a stray tampon, and a hat. No sunscreen. I put on the hat, at least. That's what I get for failing to unpack all my moving boxes.

I open the boat compartment closest to me. Inside is an expensive bottle of tanning oil. I'll use that as my last resort. I try another compartment, in the middle of the deck, but find only a handful of red Solo cups. I move toward the front of the boat, searching underneath life vests. Sweat gathers across the back of my neck. I am actively burning.

I try the compartment underneath the steering wheel. I find a fire extinguisher and some old magazines. And a small bottle of Coppertone sunscreen in the far back corner.

I arch, reaching for it, but it's still too far away. I get down on all fours, wincing as the hot wood hits my skin. I just grasp the bottle when something else catches my eye.

Something blue and white. Tie-dyed. It's tucked behind a ripped floatie.

I drop the bottle of sunscreen and reach for it.

It's a bathing suit top. Just a top. No bottoms. Maybe it's Stacy's. But it's too Target-esque when her brand is more like Saks.

My hands shake. All I can think about is what Lex told me. That the top Victoria was wearing when she died was never found.

No fucking way this is it.

I should leave it. Pulling it out is like opening Pandora's box.

But I've already seen it. It's too late. I have to know. I have to know as much about Robbie's past as he knows about mine.

I grab the bikini top. The first thing I notice is how stiff it feels. It smells like something sweet and rotten. Like Malibu Rum gone bad. The pattern is warped and sun bleached.

Then my fingers feel something on the underside, something old and crusted. When I turn it over, I suck in a breath.

It's a brown-red stain. The size of my fist.

Holy shit.

Victoria had a wound on her chest.

A boat cruises by. I huddle over the bikini, trying to hide it from view. Then I hear John's laugh, closer than before. I shove the bikini back to where I found it and grab the sunscreen. I'm closing the compartment and getting to my feet as fast as humanly possible.

I try to pry open the bottle of sunscreen but my hands are shaking so badly I can't. The boat rocks and I'm losing my balance. I grab on to the nearest railing, watching as Robbie swims to the side. He hoists himself up and over the edge.

He cannot know I found her top. I dump a handful of sunscreen into my palms and chuck the bottle into a different compartment before he can tell where I got it from. Then I go to work, starting with my legs first.

"Want me to lather you?"

Soon he's behind me. His fingers graze the top of my shoulders. A shiver rockets down my spine.

"Yeah," I say. "Here."

I wipe some of the white goop into his palms. He starts with my shoulders.

"You have a big knot right here," he says, working his fingertips into my flesh.

"I slept weird," I say.

"Or maybe you hardly slept," he teases.

If I think about us being together last night, I might pass out. All I can focus on is the image of that bloodstain.

I open and shut my eyes. His hands massage their way down my vertebrae. I clench my jaw.

Robbie works his way around me, coming to stand in front of my face. I try to relax my jaw and smear the last dollop of sunscreen into his palms. He rubs his hands together and finds my arm, blending sunscreen into my skin. I catch him looking at me. At all of me.

"You look so hot," he whispers.

My tongue is like sandpaper. "I already did my legs," I say. The thought of him touching my inner thighs is something I can't handle right now.

I wipe my hands off on my towel. When I look up again, Robbie's grinning at me. Before I have a chance to react, his arms are around me. I'm screaming as he launches us over the side of the boat.

I sink into the lake. Sediment swirls around me. My hand

catches in a tree root and I yank it away as my other hand brushes against something slimy. I instantly recoil. Then I make out Robbie's shape in front of me. His dark hair, his pale skin.

He smiles. Bubbles pour out of his mouth like foam. Then he's swimming toward me. I kick myself upward.

I finally break the surface. Fresh air hits my face. Then John's there, pushing a floatie toward me.

"Come on in," he says. "The water's fine."

I hoist myself onto the floatie, my heart still racing. Robbie surfaces a few feet away.

"Sorry," he says. "I know that wasn't the holiest of baptisms."

I can't paddle away fast enough.

As soon as the boat touches the dock, I'm off it. I try not to race toward the house, but once I'm inside, I take two stairs at a time until I'm back inside my room. I lock the door behind me. I'm not taking the chance that Robbie's going to take me by surprise again.

I jump onto the bed and grab my phone off the nightstand. My hands are clammy even though they're sunburned.

I deleted all my actual social accounts last year, but I still have a Finsta. I search for Victoria's profile.

It's public. Her last post from that weekend. At Lake Monarch. She's posing on the dock.

There's no denying it now. She's wearing it. The top I found on the boat. In this photo, there's no sign of anything on her chest. No fresh or healed wound. No blood. Nothing.

I gape at the photo.

How has no one found this? Was their boat never searched? Or did someone put the bikini top there after the fact?

There's a knock on the bedroom door and I jump so hard my phone slides out of my hands, landing on the floor.

"I hope you like salmon burgers," Robbie's saying from the other side.

"I'm not feeling great. Going to take a nap," I call back. There's no way I can go out there right now. I have to get a grip on things first.

If that's even possible.

The door handle turns, but the lock keeps him from entering.

"You okay?" he asks, his voice filled with concern.

I catch myself wondering how genuine it is.

"Yeah. Started my period."

"Oh, sorry. Let me know if you need anything," he says.

"I will."

I hear his feet step away from the door. Once they're on the stairs, I find my phone again. I open up Instagram and stare at the photo of Victoria.

She poses with one long leg in front of the other. Her glistening abs are front and center. Her hair is wet, like she just emerged from the water.

Robbie must have taken the photo of her.

I click on the comments. The latest ones were made just weeks ago. People say how much they miss her. They wish she was here for senior year. I go in reverse order, scrolling up through the oldest comments. I find one from Mara.

My best friend is so hot

Victoria replied to her.

Even hotter when I get my braces off next week!!!

I close my eyes for a second. It's a gut punch. Seeing her comment. Knowing she'd never get them off.

I sigh out a deep breath. I open my eyes and scroll down. Another comment from Mara.

Tell me this is just a nightmare and I'm going to wake up from it. I miss you so fucking much.

And one from Andrea.

We lost today's game. No surprise since you weren't with us. I hate it here without you.

I wonder if and when he'll make an appearance.

It takes me a couple more seconds, but my eyes finally find it. From Robbie's now-defunct account.

I love you. Forever.

I know what it's like, to love someone and hurt them.

Maybe Robbie didn't have anything to do with her death.

Or maybe he did. Maybe he hurt her but he didn't mean to. And he didn't know how to explain it without seeming like he did it on purpose.

I know how fast things can spiral out of control.

TEN

I only have to make it through one more night and the drive home tomorrow. Then I'm free. Free of pretending like everything is completely fine, like I didn't just find evidence of Victoria's probable murder.

Coming here was a colossal mistake. I should have listened to Mara and Lex and the rest of my teammates. They knew better, much better, than I did.

When Mom texts me asking me how everything's going, I fight the urge to ask her to pick me up. Because then she'd know I lied.

It would break her if she knew I was going behind her back again.

But more importantly, I don't want anyone here suspecting that I found what I found. I just want to fucking get out of here and get as far away from all of them as possible.

I finally open the door to my guest room because it's been hours since I peed. My heart races, hoping I can creep to the bathroom and back without having to interact with anyone.

But to my surprise, I find a heating pad and a handful of Dove chocolates outside my door. A note sits on top of them.

We went on a hike around the lake. Hope you feel better xx

I can't stomach the sight of his handwriting. I gather up the stuff and take it back into my room, chucking it into the garbage bin from Anthropologie that probably costs two hundred dollars.

"You're lucky he didn't see you do that."

All of me tenses. I spin around, finding Trevor. He leans in the bedroom doorway. His eyes are locked on mine.

How long has he been standing there, watching me?

My voice isn't as steady as I'd like it to be. "I didn't even hear you."

"I didn't want you to hear me," he says. He looks at me like I'm a stain that needs removing. "Why did you stay behind?"

"Excuse me?"

He takes a step closer to me. Suddenly, this room seems way too small. I have nowhere to go but the window behind me, and that's a fifteen-foot drop. At least.

"You know exactly what I'm asking," Trevor says. "He's too trusting. Good thing I'm not."

"He can hold his own," I find myself saying, inching backward. "Robbie can always blackmail me if I piss him off."

"I know," Trevor says, scowling. "I'm the one who told him about you."

My vision tunnels for a second, and then I'm against the window, the cool glass pressing against the backs of my arms.

"I'm good at finding things out," he says. "One day I'll be able to prove his innocence. And my own. Each day I'm getting closer."

Not if you found what I found.

Then there's a voice from the hallway. Suddenly, Lionel peeks his head in.

"Trev, I hope you're making Lauren feel welcome," Lionel says, stepping inside.

There's a huge pair of binoculars around his neck and a thick book in his hand called *The Birds of Lake Monarch*. He laughs and pats Trevor's back, but I notice that when he grips Trevor's shoulder, it's a little bit too hard. Like he's pulling him backward. Away from me.

"Only the warmest welcome," Trevor says, his eyes flitting up to mine.

"Our bird feeder is almost out," Lionel says. "How about you take Lauren down to Holliger General Store? You can show her around a bit and pick up some birdseed for me. The goldfinches can't get enough of that blend."

Holliger? As in Coach Holliger?

Then Lionel looks at me, flashing his bleached grin. "Lauren, you have to try their kettle corn, too. It's a Lake Monarch staple and it is *addictive*, let me tell you."

My stomach sinks. I force the muscles of my mouth upward. "I love kettle corn," I lie.

"Really, it's sublime," Lionel says. He winks at me. Then he pats Trevor's back one more time before he's gone.

I inhale, biting the inside of my cheek until I taste blood.

I can still feel the knotted, soft spots in my mouth from when I used to do this all the time. When Clint was still in the hospital. When I was trying to give up smoking. The scars from my past life. Tasting them again is like salt in the wound.

I bite down harder.

"Well," Trevor says, his brow raised in amusement. "Shall we?"

I swallow the tangy metal of my own blood.

"I'm not going anywhere with you," I say.

"Fine. Stay here. Be my guest. But I'll have to tell Robbie what Donovan told me over the phone."

Blood pools in my cheek and I wince. Is he bluffing?

"We should leave now if we want to be back before sunset," Trevor says. "And I'm taking it that you would."

ELEVEN

It's a half-mile walk to the general store. We round the bend and pass a quaint little cottage with a small painted sign on its mailbox that says *The Lowrys*. Two kids carry a canoe down from the house, and a group of adults look on. I can hear the ice in their cocktails clinking. Never in my life have I so badly wanted to be a part of something so normal.

Trevor's the first one to break the silence.

"Why are you so interested in my brother?"

"I'm not 'so interested,'" I say, keeping my eyes on the adults. "I didn't know he had the past he has or I never would have gotten involved with him."

"Then break it off," Trevor says.

I'm going to. But I'm not going to give Trevor that satisfaction. I need to find out if he was bluffing about Donovan or not.

We pass by a red cottage with a sign that says *Welcome to the Mitchells' Cottage* and I catch the eye of a parent helping a half a dozen little kids put their marshmallows onto long sticks. I get a wave from behind a white picket fence. Then they notice Trevor and frown.

"Why are you obsessed with me?" I ask.

"If we're talking obsession," Trevor says, "you have quite the list going for you, Lauren. First there was Donovan. Then Clint. Now Robbie. The question is, what are you planning on doing to fuck up Robbie's life? We already know what you did to Donovan and Clint."

I want to dig my nails into the meat of his cheeks.

"Tell me exactly what I did. Or you're bluffing."

Then Trevor does something I don't expect. He pivots, stepping in front of me.

"I'm not bluffing."

He's taller than Robbie. Broader. He's so close to me I can smell the lake water dried on his skin. There's something else, too. Something cool and familiar. Maybe they use the same soap. It makes my chest tighten.

"What did Donovan tell you?" I ask, not backing down.

"He said none of it was an accident."

My stomach clenches.

"That's vague," I say.

"He told me you disfigured his best friend."

It's like Trevor has both his hands around my neck and is squeezing as hard as he can.

I hate that word. *Disfigured.* That's what they all said. That Clint was going to be disfigured forever. That I did it on purpose, to make sure no one else could have him. No one but me.

My tongue grazes the scars inside my cheek and I

remember how I couldn't get rid of the sour taste of vomit. I threw up my first day back at school after the fire. I threw up that whole first week back, hugging the toilet in the girls' bathroom like it was my one and only true friend.

"I told you I wasn't bluffing," Trevor says, pulling me back to the present. "Robbie deserves to know who he's getting involved with."

I can't help myself.

"Is that because he needs to be able to cover his tracks?"

Trevor's face darkens. "You're just like the rest of them."

I stare him down. "Like who?" I ask. I know his button, and I'm going to press it. "The rest of your dead girlfriends?"

For a moment, he's silent. The veins in his neck surface.

"You have no idea what you're saying—"

"I know that you've stalked me," I say.

"I didn't *stalk* you—"

"It's not far-fetched given what everyone in Happy Valley thinks you did."

His pupils swell. "Wouldn't you like to know," he says. Then he moves. Quickly. His hand is on my bicep. "You have to be careful."

"Are you threatening me?"

"I'm warning you."

Behind him, Holliger General Store looms with its old-fashioned saloon doors. Out walks a family with a loaf of bread. Their young daughter licks an ice cream bar and their son puts at least three sticks of gum into his mouth. When the parents turn to look in our direction, Trevor drops his hand from my arm.

I can't get away from him fast enough.

I push open the doors to the general store and find myself in front of a fishing supplies display. Neon fishing lures sway from the breeze that I've just let in. I walk past it, into the snack aisle. Old-time candies in wax wrappers are stacked neatly beside a cold fridge with vintage sodas. I pretend to peruse them, glancing behind me.

The saloon doors open. In walks Trevor.

I grab a Coke and walk down the aisle. I look up and spot the old-fashioned cash register. I know Trevor isn't careless enough to pull anything shady if there are other people around.

I walk up to the counter and find a guy ahead of me, leaning across it. He's tall, with tanned legs, wearing a tank top and swim trunks. He's pretty engrossed in conversation with the girl behind the counter. A girl with short blond hair.

A girl I recognize. Gwen. As in my teammate Gwen. Wow, could this place get any more small town.

Gwen's eyes light up at whatever the guy is telling her.

Then I'm wondering if she's going to question what I'm doing here. And who I'm with.

I go to turn around when I hear my name.

Shit.

I spin around, coming face-to-face with the guy Gwen was talking to, who is not just some guy. He's Coach Holliger.

Were they just hard-core flirting?

"First time at Lake Monarch, Lauren?" he asks.

"Yeah," I say. I glance over at Gwen. She nods in my direction, but can't distract herself fast enough. She empties the tip jar into the register.

"Whatever you want, it's on the house," Coach says. "Player discount."

"Thanks," I say.

"Cool if I take off for the day?" Gwen says to Coach, closing the register.

"Yeah, of course. Thanks again for helping out. My family really appreciates it," Coach says.

Gwen smiles, then disappears through the employees-only door.

"We've owned this store for generations," Coach says. He sighs. "But it's the end of an era. My dad's selling it. This summer season was our last."

"Sorry to hear that," I say.

"Yeah," Coach says. There's a heaviness in his voice that I don't expect. "I've tried to get back here any chance I can. Lot of memories in this old place. It's too bad we can't keep it in the family."

He pulls up his tank top to wipe the sweat off his face, and I briefly catch sight of his abs. Coach is ripped.

Then it's like he notices me noticing, and I blush.

Because usually I'm quicker than that. He lets his shirt fall back down.

"Well, I hope you have a good weekend," he says, giving my shoulder a little squeeze. "Enjoy that Coke."

He goes behind the counter, and that's when I see Trevor, the bag of birdseed Lionel mentioned in his hands.

"That all for you?" Coach says tersely.

Trevor sets the bag on the counter a little too forcefully. I turn to leave. If I hustle, I can make it back to the house before he catches up to me.

I walk in the door out of breath, since I basically ran back. I find Robbie's and John's muddied shoes and socks abandoned near the doorway. They're back from their hike. Hopefully I can sneak up to my room before they spot me.

I climb the stairs as quietly as I can. Thankfully this is a brand-new house and the stairs don't even let out a sigh, let alone a creak. I'm a few steps away from my room when I hear whispering. I pause for a second, hearing Robbie's voice. Then John's.

I'm too far away to hear what they're talking about.

Ignore them. Go to your room.

But the image of Victoria's bikini top is all I can think about.

I want to know what they're saying when they think no one else is around.

I creep closer toward the sound of their conversation, which is coming from the Jack and Jill bathroom that connects between both of their rooms. Steam escapes from the doorway that's ajar.

I tiptoe even closer. Then I finally see them.

John's bare back is to the door, nothing but a towel tied around his waist. Robbie is right in front of him, his hand on John's bicep. Then Robbie reaches up and cups John's face in his hands.

A warm curiosity burns in my belly as I watch something I know I'm not supposed to see.

I step away from the door, away from the steam. The sudden coolness of the hallway makes me shiver.

This must be why, I realize, John has stuck by Robbie's side, all this time.

I wonder if that made things complicated with Victoria.

I wonder if there was only enough room for one of them.

TWELVE

"I feel like you've been avoiding me," Robbie says. "Or am I just reading into things?"

Everyone else is still downstairs, eating dessert. I made a careful point to sit with Stacy during dinner, since Trevor and Robbie seemed to want nothing to do with her. I asked her about her career and tried to pretend like I wasn't keeping a full-on panic attack at bay.

A sourness tangs my throat when I look at Robbie, and it's like he can sense it. His expression twists into one of regret. "I shouldn't have pulled you over the boat," he says. "I'm sorry."

I flex my clenched fingers. He thinks I'm acting weird because of a play fight. Not because I found his dead girlfriend's bloodied bikini top and then caught him and John having a moment.

I try to bring myself back to the present. Back to Robbie. His skin is suntanned from a weekend of boating. A pack of cigarettes sticks out of his pocket. The menthol scent clings to him like cologne.

"I liked it," I lie, and then I'm slipping inside the door

to my room and closing it. I don't think I could fake my way through a hookup tonight if my life depended on it.

He waits there, I can tell, for a few seconds, before he finally gives up.

I wonder if he'll pay a visit to John tonight.

Just when I thought I was about to finally get some relief, this weekend changed everything. Now the only thing that can keep me sane is my own bedroom.

During the car ride back to Happy Valley this morning, I felt like I was going to break down. Sitting one seat over from Trevor was just the cherry on top. This time, I noticed, he didn't have his AirPods in. He listened to every single thing I said as I made small talk with John and Robbie, pretending like I wasn't one fake sentence away from spiraling.

I've been in Happy Valley for less than two months and I couldn't even manage to have a casual hookup without it turning into a disaster.

There was a time when I really thought my friendship with Rachel might survive everything back home. Even after she broke our Friday dinner plans. I told myself it was just a rough patch. But after Clint's first surgery, she couldn't even meet my eyes, like she was embarrassed to be associated with me. I spared her the work of having to friend-breakup with me. I didn't think I could handle any more rejection. Instead I distanced myself, going off campus for lunch, becoming a hermit on weekends. Lauren the partier was no more. As much as I wanted to numb myself, I got how bad it would have looked. I kept my head down. When Mom proposed moving to be closer to Mark, I got a fast-track ticket out of town.

Now I'm wondering if I was better off in California. If I had just stayed there and faced my own shit, I wouldn't be in this situation.

I find Mom with Mark, drinking wine on the couch, watching an old John Wayne movie. One of Mark's favorites. I'd rather gouge my eyes out then have to sit through it. But Mom seems to enjoy it. Or, at least, she's pretending to. She's like a chameleon when it comes to dating. She adapts to whatever her current partner likes, which makes me feel unhinged, but I've already told her as much. All it did was hurt her feelings.

"How was the weekend, honey?" Mom says, turning down the volume on the TV.

I mentally prepare to sell the hell out of this weekend. If Mom catches one whiff of bullshit, she's going to call me on it.

"The Okadas' house is beautiful," I say, emphasizing all my consonants. "They're very generous. We had some amazing charcuterie boards."

"Oh, I love a good charcuterie board," Mom says. "Mark and I just chowed down on ours."

"It was delicious," Mark says, sipping his wine.

"What else did you guys do?" Mom asks.

I list off as many things as I can to make it all the more convincing, and then I tell them I'm exhausted. Which is true.

I head upstairs and take a shower, trying to wash this entire weekend away. But when I towel off I feel just as bad as when I got in it.

I'm about to crawl into bed when there's a knock on my door. Mom peeks her head in. "You're not asleep yet, are you?"

"No."

I don't actually know how it's possible for me to get any sleep tonight. Just like last night. I feel like I ran a marathon but my brain won't shut off.

Mom sits on the edge of my bed.

"Mark still here?" I ask, looking behind her.

She shakes her head. "He just left."

"How was your barbecue?" I ask.

"It was very relaxing. I like Ainsley. She's a soft-spoken girl. She stayed for an hour and then headed to her mom's. I had to pick up a last-minute shift beforehand and Mark prepped for the barbecue all by himself. We have plenty of leftovers for this week. But enough about that. Tonight is about you."

She reaches around behind her back for something that I've just now realized has been hidden this entire time. "Tomorrow is a big deal—"

"I don't want to make it a big deal—"

"It's the first day of your last year of high school. You're doing it at a brand-new school, in a brand-new town. That's not lost on me. So I got you a little something."

She hands me a small box wrapped in sheer white ribbon. "Go ahead and open it."

I untie the soft ribbon. It falls away, coiling like a snake on my bedspread. I open the lid of the box and empty out the tissue paper. Inside is a necklace. A black satin choker, with a heart-shaped purple gemstone placed in its center. The light from my bedside lamp hits the stone and it glitters like stardust.

"It's beautiful, Mom. Thank you."

Although I'm not really sure that it's my aesthetic. Then again, I don't really know what my aesthetic is. I used to try hard to look good all the time. White tops paired with neutral tight skirts and chunky platforms were my go-to for school. Once Clint told me it was his favorite outfit, that's all I wore. I did my hair in waves almost every day, and spent at least an hour putting together a no-makeup makeup look. Now if I manage to brush my hair, I call it a win.

"I used to have one just like it," Mom says. "But I saw this at one of the boutiques downtown the other day and I thought amethyst was perfect because it's your birthstone. And if you don't choose to wear it, at least it can be sort of your good luck charm for starting school."

I gently set the box down on my bed. I reach across to give her a hug, taking in her honeyed scent.

Mom pulls away first and holds my gaze. "I know you must have a lot of nerves and that's okay. But is there anything else you want to talk about?"

"No. I'm excited," I say quickly. There's no universe in which I tell her what I found this weekend. I try to convince myself with my own words. "I'll get to start over."

THIRTEEN

The amethyst necklace dangles on my key ring as I walk through the doors of Valley High. It's straight out of the fifties, all brick buildings and stained yellow floors. Everything is indoors, which is different from my old school. My locker is candy-apple red and the lock is sticky. I have to do my combination twice to get it open.

I notice a couple of stares in my direction as I put my things inside my locker. I'm sure there aren't many new seniors at Valley High. I'm sure I'm the only one.

I'm already over it.

I slam my locker closed and head to physics. As I round the corner into the science hallway, I spot a guy in a faded green Lake Monarch shirt. I wish I hadn't seen it. My body's not cooperating anymore. My heart skips a beat, then another. The bell for first period rings and all I can think about is the way Vic's bathing suit felt in my hands. The stain of her dried blood, flaking off like lead paint from an old house.

I fumble for my water bottle in my bag. Maybe I should

just tell Robbie about what I found. Listen to his explanation. He must have some kind of explanation.

Or maybe he'll deny everything and make sure no one else finds her top ever again.

The warning bell rings and I shuffle into physics. I slouch into an empty seat and take out my notebook and pen.

"This seat taken?"

Lex slides in next to me, flashing me a grin. I find it in me to smile back. It's comforting to see a familiar face.

I could tell her. About Vic's top. But then she'd know I was with Robbie after she told me to stay the hell away from him.

Then everyone would know.

There's something that's suddenly distracting. A distinct smell. Cool menthol. Heat rushes into my stomach.

He's in my first-period class. Of course he is.

Today he's wearing tight jeans, and a black band T-shirt. His hair is slightly styled, still falling over his face, and he's clean-shaven.

We lock eyes, but he doesn't smile. I don't, either.

Robbie takes a seat up front, not even trying to be remotely close to me. Not wanting to stain my reputation the way his is already stained. I notice the way people look at him. The disdain flashes across their faces. I was the subject of those glances once upon a time. I don't ever want to be that person again.

Lex leans into me. "How'd it go?" she whispers.

I pull my eyes away from Robbie and back to her.

"What?" I ask.

"Breaking it off?"

I tell her it was fine. When our teacher walks into the room, I have never been so relieved to dive into the laws of thermodynamics.

———————————

Robbie texts me as I'm cleating up in the locker room.

Saturday feels too far away.

I suck in a halted breath.

I avoided him after physics, and thankfully we didn't have any other classes together. But John and I did. AP Lit class. The one and only AP class I'm capable of taking. I sat behind him and he asked me if I was coming to their show this weekend. I guess he and Robbie are in a band together. I said I wasn't sure.

I wish I could go back in time and shake the version of myself who decided to go to Lake Monarch. I'd shake her until she woke the fuck up.

I try to push him out of my mind in the jog over to our field. Coach has us warm up for a half hour before we scrimmage. Lex and I are on the same team, and she gets the ball after kickoff. I run up the side of the field. I shout that I'm open, and she passes me the ball. I weave it around the other midfielder, but then Mara's in front of me. But she's a striker, not a defender. I slide the ball through her legs, easily, then cross the ball to Gwen. She sends it to the back of the net.

Pride rushes through me. Gwen just gives me a look like, *Yeah, that's what you should be doing.*

I'm going to have to work a little harder to wow them, that's all. I have to make them forget I ever hooked up with Robbie.

I have to make myself forget.

I catch Mara's expression as I jog back to our side of the field. She's pissed. Hungry. Because now my team's up 1–0. Carly gets the ball after kickoff and passes it to Mara, who takes off like a racehorse, but then Lex is there. Mara plays dirty. She feels for Lex's jersey, yanking it down to the side. But Lex is an equal match. She elbows Mara, getting the ball, then Mara steals it back and sprints past her, dribbling through the sweeper. She grounds it to the right, past Andrea.

By the time practice is over, I feel like I could collapse. It's the best I've felt in days. I'm the last one in the locker room, and the last one out. But just as I'm about to leave, I hear a voice from behind me.

"We have this tradition," Mara says.

She comes into view, and I look up at her from my seat on the locker room bench. A gold pendant dangles from her fingers. Her moon necklace, the one she wore at Lex's kickback. "Each of us takes a turn wearing it on game day for good luck. The captains decided it's your turn, since you're new. It'll officially make you one of us."

"Uh, thanks," I say, and she drops it into my palm.

"I'm sorry about the other night," she says, frowning. "I was drunk and I just wanted to warn you about Robbie. I'm . . . maybe a little too passionate about it."

I should have listened to you.

"I . . . appreciated the warning."

She smiles. "Wear that tomorrow," she says, then she's gone.

It takes me three tries, but I finally get it clasped around my neck.

The house is quiet when I get home. Mom's in bed before an early morning shift.

I bring a Tupperware of leftover enchiladas up to my room. I glance at my open physics textbook in between each forkful, then over at my phone. At Robbie's unanswered text.

I push the Tupperware out of the way and pick up my phone, testing out a few different iterations before coming up with the best thing I can think of.

I can't make it this Saturday. Sorry

But I hesitate before I press send. Because a new thought crosses my mind: What if he suspects I found the bikini, since all of a sudden I'm giving him the cold shoulder right after being at the lake?

Maybe I shouldn't break things off so abruptly, just in case he freaks or something. I don't know who he really is. Who his family really is. I don't know what they're capable of.

I'll ease into ghosting him. Let him down gently.

Not sure if I can make it yet

I send it. I sigh, relieved to not have that text hanging over me anymore. At worst, Robbie will think I'm just playing mind games.

I grab hold of the pendant around my neck. My fingers run over the cool, smooth moon as I try to focus on my homework. I manage to get a few pages done before I'm back at Lake Monarch. The smell of the water hits my nose, cold and sediment-heavy. My feet blister against the boat deck. My hands brush against the hardened, mildewed fabric of Victoria's bikini.

I shut my textbook. My concentration is ruined for the night.

I change into sweats and brush my teeth. I plug in my phone and check if Robbie texted me back. That's when I notice I have a missed call. From an unknown number.

They left a voice mail.

They called just a few minutes ago. When I was in the bathroom.

I haven't gotten an anonymous voice mail since I changed my number. I can still hear Donovan's voice, calling me from a burner phone. Something that could never be traced back to him. Because he knows what else burned in that fire.

As soon as Clint recovers, I'll tell him everything you did to me. Every place you kissed. Every position—

I didn't let myself listen beyond that.

Now I press PLAY.

At first, all I hear is heavy breathing.

I tell myself it's bullshit but it still makes the hairs on my arms stand up. Then comes the voice, all muffled and warped, like it's been put through a synthesizer.

I know you're a good girl, Lauren. Don't tell anyone about what you found on the boat. And I'll keep you safe.

FOURTEEN

I grab a bottled Frappuccino from the Valley High cafeteria and chug it. I didn't get any sleep last night. I don't know that I'll get any sleep ever again.

It's real now. Someone knows what I found.

Someone like Robbie.

Or Trevor.

Or John.

I sink into a beanbag in the library and crack open my physics book. I'm already behind in my goal of keeping up my GPA. The old me would say screw it. The old me wouldn't bother turning in this assignment.

I skim the chapter, if only to prove the old me wrong. I search for keywords with the hopes of finding the right answers to the assignment that's due tomorrow. I have to graduate with decent grades.

"Mind if we join you?"

I already know it's his voice from the way my body responds.

I look up and try to conceal the nerves running through

me right now. It's Robbie and John. They just happen to be in the library at the exact same time as me.

Because maybe they're watching me more closely than ever.

I unclench my fingers from my physics book.

"Yeah. Sure," I say, trying to seem like I'm unbothered and wondering just how well I'm succeeding.

They take the beanbags opposite me. I glance back down at the chapter, flipping to the next page. Then I reach up and grab the pendant Mara gave me, toying with it as I jot down notes in the margins.

"Where did you get that?"

I look up at Robbie. His mouth tightens. "The necklace," he says. His voice is like ice. "Are you trying to mess with me?"

I glance over at John. He sinks deeper into his beanbag, his eyes wide, mouth agape. I'm not used to him being this quiet.

"What are you talking about?" I ask.

But Robbie gets up in a rush and disappears into the bookstacks.

John looks over his shoulder, then back to me. For the first time, it's like he's not putting up a front with me.

"He gave that necklace to Vic," John says.

My pulse slows, like all of the blood is congealing in the pit of my stomach.

John leans toward me. His voice goes so low I can barely hear it. "How did you get it?" he asks.

I think back to Mara in the locker room. The way she looked at me. How sincere she looked as she pressed the small pendant into my palm.

Suddenly, it feels like I'm wearing someone else's skin. I reach around to the back of my neck and struggle to unclasp the pendant. Some small sense of relief washes over me as it finally falls from my collarbone into my hand.

I never noticed it when I was looking through Vic's recent Instagram pictures. Maybe she'd taken a break from wearing it before she died.

"Mara gave it to me," I say, closing my fist around it. "She said it was a team tradition, like they pass it around before games for good luck."

John shakes his head. "None of the girls would dare to wear it," he says, his voice gravelly and soft. "It was such a huge source of contention between Robbie and Mara. He wanted to keep it after she died, but Mara fought him on it. He still isn't sure how she got ahold of it."

I slump deeper into my beanbag, wishing it could absorb my entire body. I should have known. It's a moon, after all. Robbie said that was Vic's thing.

"Are you saying Mara stole it?"

John grimaces. "There was one day where Robbie just couldn't find it. He thought she might have taken it out of his bag when he was swimming for PE."

Mara knew if I wore this, and Robbie saw, it would get under his skin. Because he'd see it if I was still seeing him.

This was some sort of test. And I just failed it.

But what she doesn't know is that I'm walking on eggshells after what I found. Especially after that voice mail.

I could even be sitting across from the person who left it on my phone.

"I have to ask you something," I say. "Did you . . . always believe Robbie was innocent? Even from the beginning?"

I cock my head, curious as to how John's going to respond.

John tugs on the ankh earring dangling from his ear. It's a while before he says anything. The bell for next period rings but neither of us moves.

"I hate that question," he finally says. "I wish I could say I always believed him one hundred percent, but I had my doubts in the beginning."

My shoulders relax. I feel like he's being real with me.

"None of it ever made sense," he says. "Vic was a great swimmer. She'd gone out on solo night swims before, usually to cool off from a fight. They were fighting a lot that week before she died."

Clint and I were fighting a lot before everything went to hell, too. Which didn't look good for me.

"What did they fight about?" I ask.

"Where do I even begin? Look, Lauren. I'd be lying if I said I was thrilled when Robbie told me he was hooking up with you."

I hold his gaze.

"Because you have history together?"

My statement hangs there. John purses his lips. He doesn't say anything. "You don't have to answer that," I say quickly. "But I saw the two of you. I didn't mean to, but I was coming up the stairs and—"

John's brow furrows. "You *saw* us?" he asks. "And what exactly was it that we were doing?"

"You were in the bathroom . . . after the hike. Robbie was touching your face . . ."

"If you had observed, or *spied*, rather, on the rest of that *moment*," John says, "I think it would have unfolded a little differently than you imagined." He sighs. "There's no way you would have known this, but the past couple weeks have been torture for me. I was waiting for my mom to text me with good news. She finally did after we got back from the hike. Her labs and imaging from her appointment confirmed she's still cancer free. I was overwhelmed in a good way. Robbie was supporting me through that."

Oh.

Right. I'm actually scarlet now.

"I'm sorry," I say awkwardly. "And I'm glad to hear the good news for your mom."

"Thanks," John says. "Though, I mean, I know me and Robbie have some chemistry." A curious look emerges on his face. "I'd be lying if I said I didn't lean into that this weekend. I had to vet you, okay? Maybe I was seeing if you could really stick it out."

John twists his nose ring. "We hooked up once. Robbie

and Vic were on a break. They took a lot of breaks. Typical them."

Okay. I wasn't exactly *wrong*.

"Robbie was leaning into figuring out his sexuality, and he was comfortable with me," John says. "And of course, my best friend's hot. I was down."

I wonder if it's possible that John is downplaying his feelings for Robbie at all. If he ever had them. "But let's just say the boundaries of that break weren't exactly clear to both parties," John says. "I almost stopped talking to him after that. Vic was hurt. She thought they weren't going to hook up with other people."

"That's messed up."

John buckles one of his leather boots tighter. "Oh, I mean, it's beyond. He's lucky I forgave him. But I couldn't imagine not having him in my life. He was the only one of my friends who really supported me when my mom was going through her treatments. He apologized to me and to Vic. I forgave him."

"And what about her?" I ask.

"She didn't hold a grudge against me, but it was never completely the same afterward between us. Like everything was just way too messy. And I mean, it *was*. She got back at him by hooking up with Trevor."

"Wait. *What?*"

"Trevor had always had a crush on her. She leveraged it."

That could give Robbie one hell of a motive to kill Vic.

"She told Trevor she was broken up with Robbie. He had no idea she was cheating. When Trevor found out the truth, he was enraged. It nearly cost him his relationship with Robbie."

That means Trevor could have a perfect motive, too.

I don't know if John realizes how damning all of this sounds.

"Did Vic and Robbie get back together after all that?" I ask.

"They were in the process of it," John says. He bites his lip. "Originally I was supposed to be there, too. That weekend at the lake."

My eyes dart to his.

"I was with my mom, at one of her appointments," he says. "Besides, I told Robbie he and Vic needed some alone time. They really needed to figure things out."

John has made it a point to tell me he has an alibi.

His eyes glance out the window, at the cross-country team running by outside. "Then that weekend turned into a nightmare. If I would have been there . . . maybe I could have seen something. Maybe Vic would still be here. Or at least, I could have proven that my best friend didn't hurt her."

John's phone lights up. He glances at it, then slips it into his pocket. He grabs his leather jacket off the beanbag, sliding it over his slim frame. "I asked him to walk me through that night. He said they'd fought. He'd gone to bed in his room, which doesn't have a lakeside view, and chugged a six-pack of beers, because he was pissed. Then he passed out, and when he woke up early in the morning, she hadn't come to bed."

He looks at me with his deep brown eyes, rimmed with thick eyeliner. "I saw how much he grieved for her. How much he loved her. I *know* Robbie. To believe someone or not is a choice. I've never been more confident in mine."

I wish I could say the same.

FIFTEEN

When I enter the locker room at three thirty, I stride past rows of girls tying up their cleats, throwing up their hair into braids, and pulling on their shin guards. Then I get to Mara, mid-bite of her protein bar.

I dangle Victoria's crescent moon pendant from my palm. But before I can utter a word, her face melts into a look of complete shock.

"I've been looking everywhere for that!" she says.

Every single head in the locker room turns to look at me. At the pendant I'm holding on to. The pendant *she* gave me. "Robbie asked you to take it," she says. "Didn't he?"

For a second I can't find any words; I'm just bewildered. Stunned.

She can't actually be doing this right now.

"You gave this to me. Yesterday, after practice—"

Lex pushes her way through the sea of faces watching us. "What's going on?" she asks.

"This is what's going on," Mara says, snatching the necklace out of my hands. "Lauren stole Vic's necklace from me."

Lex does a double take, glancing from Mara and back to me. "Oh no—"

"No I fucking didn't," I say. I can't believe she's pulling this. "You said it was team tradition to wear this—"

"Why would she ever give that to you?" Andrea interrupts, snapping on her goalie gloves. Disgust is written all over her face. "That'd be careless. We barely know you."

I meet Mara's eyes, but she doesn't back down. She's fully committed to selling this. "I thought you were better than this," she says. "But it's clear he's had his influence on you already."

I start laughing. I can't help it. This is completely ridiculous. All of it. The bikini. The phone call. Mara framing me.

This cannot be actual reality.

"I didn't steal it from you!"

"You've been making a mockery of my sister's death," Andrea says. "You should be ashamed."

I stand there, speechless.

Then Coach's voice echoes into the locker room from outside, calling us to hustle up.

I pull on my cleats, and a huge knot forms in my right shoulder. Stares follow me as I jog out onto the field. I keep my head down during our warm-up drills, since it's mostly individual skills, but by the time we get to scrimmaging, I feel like I'm back in California.

It's January. My first game since everything happened with Clint. With Donovan. We're playing a team in Golden Gate Park, and the fog is so thick I can only see our center mid and one of our forwards. I've been yelling *I'm open* for the last five plays, but no one will pass me the ball. Even the girl defending me seems confused.

Then something hits me from behind and I'm back in Happy Valley.

My nose hits the ground first. The grass smears against my face as my body buckles underneath me.

I hear Coach's whistle and groan as I try to sit up. The grass underneath me is wet and crimson.

I hold my head forward so I don't swallow mouthfuls of blood.

"What the hell was that?" I hear Coach say, his feet jogging toward me.

Then Mara's voice. "She was in my way."

A hand is on my back, helping me up. Lex.

"Don't you dare," Mara says.

Once I'm on my feet, Lex drops her hand.

I feel a bruise blooming on the side of my thigh from where Mara clocked me. My nose gushes blood. I pinch the bridge, hoping it'll slow the flow.

"Maybe I should bench you for our first game," Coach tells Mara as he slips an elbow through mine.

"Nah, Coach. Lauren deserved it," Gwen says, meeting my gaze. "She's hooking up with your favorite. Robbie Crestmont."

Gwen definitely saw Trevor enter the store after me, then. She could put two and two together.

Coach looks at me, disappointment in his eyes.

"Everyone get water," he says, and then he turns to me. "Let's take a little walk."

I trudge alongside him toward the perimeter of the field. The blood slows down a little bit.

He looks at me, frowning, his thick eyebrows almost meeting together in the center. "That's who you were with at the lake."

I shrug, tracing a circle on the ground with my cleat.

Coach leans in closer and I can smell his breath. It's sweet and fruity, like watermelon gum. "You know what he did, don't you?" he says.

I narrow my eyes at him. "You're okay with the fact that Mara just bodychecked me because of who I slept with a few times?" I say.

His cheeks flush. "No. How she handled it wasn't okay. But I need to know if you're loyal to this team or not."

I try to wipe away the crusted blood from my nose but it's pointless. Almost as pointless as trying to explain myself. Coach has no idea what I've been through this week.

"I'm loyal to the team," I say with about as much enthusiasm as I can muster for this entire conversation.

He squeezes my arm. "That's what I'm talking about. You're a great player, O'Brian. Don't jeopardize that. Take the rest of the day off, all right? We can start fresh tomorrow."

We can start fresh.

I'll never hear the end of it.

I tie my cleats to my bag, slip on my shoes, and peace out. I don't know if I feel like crying or screaming or both.

"Lauren."

Lex's voice. Calling after me. I ignore her, charging toward my car.

"I believe you," she says.

I spin around, finding her less than five feet behind me.

"She never takes that necklace off. Ever," Lex says. "She tapes it underneath her jersey so the refs won't see. You would have had to steal it off her body, and I know you didn't do that."

"You knew but you didn't say anything?" I say.

"I wasn't going to confront her about it in front of everyone," she says. "Vic's death is still really raw for her. I know she was trying to warn you in her own way."

I hike up my bag higher, feeling righteous. I'm still pissed. I want something to dangle over Lex. My old tendencies rise to the surface.

"She has no idea what she's doing," I say, and all my words come out fast and hot. "If she knew what I know, she wouldn't try to mess with Robbie."

Lex stares at me, her blue-black hair slipping out of her headband. "Why do you say that?"

My face grows hot with instant regret. "No reason."

I turn, headed for my car, but Lex is a center mid so her stamina is beyond, and then she's in front of me. She crosses her defined arms. "When you're bullshitting, your eyes dart to the left. Just like they did in physics. You did it again just now."

I wish she was just an ounce less perceptive.

"I went to Robbie's lake house this weekend," I sputter.

Her eyes search my face. "I know," she says finally.

The fucking general store.

"Let me guess. Gwen told you."

"John posted an Instagram story and Mara thought the girl in the photo was you. Then Gwen confirmed it."

The thought crosses my mind that John could have posted that *just* so Mara would see I was there.

"That's why she gave me the necklace," I say, putting the pieces together. I brush my fingers against the soft leather of my cleats.

"What happened this weekend?" Lex asks.

"You were right. He doesn't miss Vic at all," I say, lying out of my ass, because I have to give her something. "He never brought her up all weekend. Not even once."

I catch my reflection in my car window. Dried blood has collected under each nostril. My shirt is splattered with it.

Lex shifts next to me. Her fingers play with the braided bracelet on her left wrist.

"We're protective of each other here," she says finally. "And you're one of us now."

"I don't think everyone feels the same way as you."

"Think of this like your initiation. They'll come around," she says.

I bite my lip. I'm not as optimistic as she is.

Lex heads back up the hill. Once I'm inside my car, I pick up my phone. I find my text thread with Robbie.

Because he's all I'm thinking about. Because I still don't know if he's the one who saw me find Vic's top. If he's the person who left me the voice mail.

Or if it was his brother. Or his best friend.

Or someone else.

I could officially end it right now. Tell Robbie we're done. Pretend I never found what I found. Keep my head down, just like the caller wants me to. Graduate from Valley High without another life-ruining scandal. Because that's what I do. That's what I'm used to doing, what I'm good at doing. Evading capture. I ran away from Clint and everything that happened between us.

My thoughts drift to him. I know it'll make me miss him even more, but I look him up on my Finsta. Sometimes I stalk him to see if he's in a new relationship. Part of me wants him to be. I want to know he's moved on. Because maybe then, I can, too.

His latest post is a photo taken at one of his lacrosse games. He seems even taller than he was last year. His quads are full-on Hercules status. His face may be scarred but he's still beautiful.

I'm sure he's deciding on which lacrosse scholarship to take right now. I remember a scout from Penn State watching one of his games sophomore year. He always talked about going to an East Coast school. I wonder if he'll post about his decision.

I close out of my Finsta, rubbing the knot in my shoulder.

I can never change what happened with Clint. I can never go back and undo all the hurt. The regret. But maybe I can do things differently this time.

I'm the one who found Vic's top. Maybe I can find answers. Find out what really happened. Or didn't happen.

And if Robbie's the one who has them, I have to keep him close.

Closer than ever.

Hey. I'm sorry about the necklace
Can we talk?

He replies almost instantly.

Can you come over? Tonight

My fingers sweat as I type a reply.

Yes

I'm really doing this.

SIXTEEN

The Crestmont house gives me Manderley vibes. Or maybe that's only because we're reading *Rebecca* in AP Lit. Or because I'm already on edge about being alone with Robbie. I get chills just looking at it. It's white and sprawling, with black shutters on thirteen massive windows. Roses in deep shades of red and purple bleed their petals as I walk to the front door. Two copper lanterns flicker on either side. The flames are real. I pull the drawstrings on my hoodie even tighter.

The doorbell chimes out of tune three times before the pitch-black door opens.

The woman who greets me is tall and striking. Her hair is tied back into a severe bun.

"Robbie's upstairs. Second door on your right," she says kindly.

I breathe out, relieved she's not a real-life Mrs. Danvers. At least at first glance.

Then she's gone, her heels clicking down the foyer. She looks too conservatively dressed to be a fling of Lionel's, and besides, she's young but not young enough for him. She probably manages the house.

I step inside, floorboards creaking beneath me. Their lake house may be new and modern, but their Happy Valley house sags with age. It smells like coffee and stale champagne.

I look up into the high vaulted ceilings. A chandelier with yellow crystals hangs above me. I notice a few of them are chipped.

I head toward the staircase. I grip the banister and the oily residue of lemon polish sinks into my skin. As I climb the stairs, my eyes drift to the huge still life paintings that decorate the wall. They're rich and vibrant, nothing like the neutral ones from T.J.Maxx that Mom has framed around our house.

Then I sense I'm not alone. The hairs on the back of my neck stand up as I spy someone at the top of the landing, looking down at me.

Trevor.

I brace myself for a confrontation, but something about his energy seems softer tonight. For a second, both of us just stand there. Then I hear the clattering of dishes echo from the kitchen, and it sends us into motion again. He grips the banister, and it's like my signal to keep moving, too. I hug the wall next to the paintings. When I pass him, I can just barely hear his words.

"Don't hurt him," he says.

Every part of me feels on edge until I reach the landing. I wonder what lengths someone like Trevor might go to protect his brother.

I tuck his words away. I can't dwell on them now.

I find Robbie's room, the second door on the right. There's a faint glow underneath his door.

I knock more rapidly than I mean to. "It's Lauren."

"Yeah," he says. "Come in."

I push open the door. His room is freezing. The window's open. Long, discolored curtains sway with the breeze. A towering bookcase is in one corner, half filled with records. Peeking out from behind them are dozens of shiny objects. Medals and trophies. Relics from Robbie's past life as a soccer player.

A dim lamp sits on a wooden nightstand, next to a photograph inside a tarnished frame. The boy inside the frame is one I'll never know. His dark hair is lighter. His skin is sunkissed from hours of playing on green fields. His smile is bright, and his arm is around Victoria. She kisses his cheek.

Then there's the Robbie I do know, sitting on the edge of his taffeta-soft bed. A pen and journal rest in his lap.

He casts them aside and looks up at me, half his face hidden in shadow.

My stomach turns with the sensation that I shouldn't be here.

Maybe I shouldn't be injecting myself into this messiness. Into a mystery that I don't know I'll ever make sense of.

I dig my heels into the soft carpet as his eyes move over my face. He drinks me in like the first time we met. "You didn't know the necklace was hers," he says. "I realize that now."

If I'm doing this, I have to be vulnerable. I have to make it convincing.

I have to forget what I found on his boat.

I leave the safety of the doorway and the room closes around me. I count the steps it takes to reach his bed. One. Two. Three. Four. Five. Six.

I push any thought of Victoria down as I sit on the edge of the bed. I have to forget her right now if I want to help her.

The lie spills out easily.

"I never wanted to hurt you," I tell him. "Mara—"

"It's okay," he says.

He reaches up and moves the hair from my half-fallen ponytail out of my face. My insides turn as cool as the menthol that clings to his skin. Everything in me screams *Run*.

I try to exhale as he shifts next to me.

"Mara was closest to Vic," Robbie says. "She never forgave me for . . . certain decisions I made."

I wonder if he's referring to him and John. "When she didn't believe me after everything that happened, I felt like I was losing Vic a second time."

I notice the top two buttons of his shirt are undone. "The harder I tried to convince her, the less it worked."

Something I'm familiar with, too, as much as I don't want to be.

But the difference is that I was never accused of murder.

"Ever since she died, it's just been me and Trevor and

John," he says. "I know they didn't exactly give you the warmest welcome this past weekend."

"I picked up on that," I say.

"Since Vic died, I've barely looked at another person. But when I saw you that first day, I just thought, I don't know. I don't think I was thinking straight, actually, because I hadn't felt that feeling in a long time."

He bites his lower lip and it makes my cheeks burn. "Then I saw her necklace around your throat and I thought what we had was over."

What we had.

But we're just hooking up.

Or, we were.

I haven't been able to bring myself to touch him, let alone kiss him, since I found what I found.

That has to change, if I want him to keep opening up to me.

I shift my weight on the bed, feeling the tenderness of the fresh bruise on my leg. I reach for his hand. His fingers tremble in mine like he's nervous, and it takes me by surprise.

"I think you're the only thing getting me through," he says.

I lean in to him. I pretend the voice I hear is deeper, huskier. A voice that used to call me to tell me good night for almost two years. A voice that used to whisper my name as we hid underneath my bedsheets.

I close my eyes and imagine it's his hard body next to

mine instead. I lose myself in the feeling, in his touch. A touch I haven't stopped dreaming about since I left him behind.

But then I taste nicotine, and my stomach twists. My memory flashes to the boat, to the decaying fabric I held in my hands. The smell is overwhelming, must and mildew and decades-old pennies. The smell of death. I'm losing control.

I shudder, and he feels it.

"Are you okay?" Robbie asks, his breath quick and labored. He immediately drops his hands from me.

My eyes flash open. "I was thinking," I say quickly, willing my body to cooperate, "about Victoria."

Robbie peers at me, his cheeks reddening.

"Since wearing her necklace," I explain. "I just . . . I wondered what you think happened to her that night. I've never asked you."

He almost flinches away from me.

My armpits dampen with sweat. I shouldn't have asked about it so soon. Maybe I just fucked this all up. I still don't know if he's the one who left me the voice mail. I don't want to piss him off.

His left hand brushes against his jean pocket. Where he keeps his cigarettes. A tic I used to have, too. Something I did when I was nervous.

"I guess I owe you that, at least," he says finally. "I didn't ever bother explaining because for so long, I tried to prove myself to everyone. Except everyone thought I was doubling down."

His fingers flit from his pocket to the moonstone and onyx rings he never takes off. He twists them, gathering his words. Another nervous tic.

"I'm willing to hear you out," I tell him, trying to encourage him.

"I tried to convince myself it was an accident for a long time," he says.

It's like he braces himself for what he says next. "I should have protected her and instead I slept through it all."

Are you lying through your teeth right now?

"She'd gone out before on midnight swims," he says. "I'd wake up to feeling her skin all cool from the lake. That night, I never woke up. Never woke up to her climbing into bed. Never felt the sheets dampen with lake water. The sun was rising by the time I opened my eyes. Then it was too late."

My ears burn.

"Do you think she drowned?" I ask, keeping my voice as steady as possible. "Or do you think someone killed her?"

A vacant look comes over his eyes. "I don't think her death was an accident," he says.

"Who do you . . . think it was?" I ask.

He slouches forward, his shoulders knitting together. I wonder if I've gone too far.

"I don't know. I think they were stalking us. Waiting for the right moment," he says, his gaze faraway now. "Fourth of July is one of the busiest times of year at Lake Monarch. But it's also when everyone parties the hardest. Everyone goes boating and day drinks until they pass out. They must have known that. They knew no one would come to her rescue. Especially not me."

I sit on my hands so he can't see that they're on the precipice of shaking.

"I even did hypnotherapy sessions to see if I could remember any sounds or anything subconsciously from that night," he says. "But I'd been drinking and I passed out like the pathetic piece of shit that I was back then. If I had just apologized to her the right way she wouldn't have gone out for a swim. She'd still be alive."

He shuts his eyes and opens them again, like he's trying to banish the memory. "I know how convenient it is, the way everything unfolded," he says. "It will always haunt me. I was the only other person there with her. Our lake house had just been built and there were no security cameras up yet. That's what everyone kept saying. *It's really fucking convenient, isn't it, that Robbie was there but that he didn't hear anything, that he let her go out on the lake that late. What kind of boyfriend lets his girlfriend take a midnight swim alone?* But Vic always did what she wanted. She was badass."

Robbie takes the pack of cigarettes out of his pocket, but he fumbles it and it falls to the carpet. He bends down to pick it up.

Is he flustered right now because he's guilty?

The cigarette package crumples inside his grasp. He talks faster than I've ever heard him speak. "They could never explain how she got that wound on her chest or why her top was missing. I don't think they wanted to admit that there could be an actual murder in their sleepy little town."

He dumps a cigarette into his hand and pinches it in between his fingers. "There was so little evidence left behind. Nothing could implicate me, but nothing could clear my name for good in the eyes of Happy Valley."

He just confirmed it. No one ever found the bloodied bikini top during the investigation.

Did Robbie hold on to it until all the searches were completed, then put it back on the boat? Did he keep it because he just couldn't bring himself to part with the only piece of Victoria he had left?

I look at Robbie. His shirt clings to his frame. I try to picture him losing control of his emotions. I try to imagine the kind of violence he could be capable of. The kind of violence Vic had to endure.

Being drunk would have made it easier for him to justify everything.

Just like it made it easier for me the night of the fire.

Maybe he kept her top just to be able to relive the night she died.

Robbie latches the curtains to the side of the window. He lights up and the craving hits me in a way I haven't felt in months. I feel like ants are crawling over my skin.

"Sometimes I wish you didn't go to Valley High," he says.

Me too.

I inhale the smoke that escapes into the room. I suck it down into my lungs and clench my teeth.

"Sometimes I wish you only existed in those Saturdays I used to see you before volunteering," Robbie says.

He ashes his cigarette in the small tray on the windowsill one too many times and I think *You're wasting it.* "That way I could pretend to be someone else. Someone who this never happened to."

I wonder if Robbie's pretending right now, in this very moment, to be someone who he isn't. The same way that I am.

His eyes pierce me. "Would you have ever told me about Clint?" he asks. "On your own?"

I answer in a heartbeat. It's the one thing I'm sure of.

"No," I tell him.

He nods in a way that tells me he understands.

I hate the way it feels, that he can understand me.

SEVENTEEN

Five minutes into Friday's game, I swipe the ball from the girl who's guarding me and cross it. It goes straight to Mara. She's got too much ego not to use a perfect ball and she launches it into the back of the net. One goal for Mara, one assist for me. She looks at me and then she looks past me. No one else besides Lex gives me a high five. I try to shake it off but busting my ass for nothing is starting to get old. By the end of the first half, we're only up by one. It's 3–2 and they've been keeping the ball in our half more often than not.

I sit on the bench, chugging water as Coach addresses us.

"I want us to try a few different plays in the second half," he says. "They've been on Mara like flies to honey and that's going to make it harder for us to score."

Then he eyes me. "Lauren. Try taking it up yourself."

A few scoffs escape from the girls beside me. That's all I need to officially light my fuse.

"I mean, I could stay on the bench and we could lose this game, but that's up to you. I guess it depends on if you want to win states senior year or not," I say.

"Hey—" Coach starts.

"We don't need you to win states," Mara says.

"If you do get your hands on that trophy you'd better lock it up because I just might be tempted to steal it," I say, and Mara's jaw drops.

"Enough," Coach says. "This is not the time."

Lex has us huddle up, but when I go to join, the team shifts away from me, like I'm a virus they don't want to be anywhere near.

"Come on," Lex says, creating space for me. "We're a team."

"Have a fucking backbone, Lex," someone says under their breath.

"Lauren is one of our best players," Lex says. "Whether you like it or not."

"She's the one who started shit," Gwen says.

I'm tempted to spill about the closeness I saw between Gwen and Coach at the lake. But that wouldn't exactly win me any fans right now.

Then the ref blows his whistle, and we break.

Newton Township has the ball first. They kick off and make it past our strikers, and our center mid, all the way to our defensive line. If we don't keep them out of our half, they're going to score. I panic for a moment as I keep up with their other midfielder, but then Sophia clears them out, taking the ball up herself. I take off, sprinting up the side of the field.

I'm open. She sees me and sends the ball flying.

I trap it just before it goes out-of-bounds, and then I'm past number eighteen. I sprint up the sides, dribbling with as much control as humanly possible. I hear Mom's voice break through the crowd, cheering me on. I fake a pass to Mara, then take it past a defender. Another finally catches me. But she's winded. I've been watching her all first half. I cut toward the middle, and before she can shove me, I briefly look up, spotting the goal. I don't have time to debate. I fucking go for it.

I send the ball toward the left corner. Just out of the goalie's reach. The ball slips by her, kissing the back of the net.

And that brings us to 4–2.

"GO, LAUREN!!!" Mom yells.

I beam. I can't help it. I scan the crowd and find Mom. Something inside me deflates as I watch her kiss Mark. As if that's how she's celebrating *my* goal.

I jog back toward our half. Lex runs over to me, squeezing me. She's the only one who does.

"I need you to tell them you believe me," I tell her, catching my breath. Her eyes dart over to Mara. "You haven't talked to her, have you?"

"I'm working on it, okay?" Lex says, and then she's jogging across the midline.

Every single one of my teammates besides Lex ices me out. As if I just scored against my own team. It's a miracle Sophia even gave me the ball.

I keep my head down and try to focus on playing. Toward the end of the game, after Lex puts it in the back of the net and it's likely we're going to maintain our lead, Coach subs me out to give Taylor time to play. She won't give me a high five as we switch off and I feel like telling her *You're only getting playing time because of me.* I fight the temptation to not be a total asshole.

Coach pats my bicep. His hand slides down to my elbow. "You were incredible out there," he says.

I look up at him as he readjusts his hat, a swoop of light brown hair falling across his forehead. "Way to keep the drama off the field."

"It's not *drama*," I say, rolling my eyes, as if Mara and I were fighting over something as trivial as a crush. Which we wouldn't be, anyway, since I am, unfortunately, straight.

Coach puts his hands up. "My bad," he says. "I'm proud of you, that's all. We're on the right path now."

Maybe you shouldn't be that optimistic.

Once the game ends, I shake hands with our opponents. Coach debriefs, and as soon as he's done, I grab my stuff and head toward Mom. And Mark. Who's basically her shadow at this point.

"You were amazing, honey," she says, hugging me. Then she leans in closer. "But what's up with the rest of the team? They seemed . . . subdued after your goal."

"It'll blow over, okay?" I say, and Mom's face sags with concern. "I have to earn my place on the team. Don't worry."

"I'm sure it'll all work out. You're an excellent player," Mark says.

Mom squeezes his arm. She hangs on his every word.

"You're right, Mark."

God, she's so earnest sometimes.

"Thanks," I say. "I'm starving. Can we do McDonald's tonight?"

Back home, Rachel would always get a Quarter Pounder with cheese and a side of chicken McNuggets with sweet-and-sour sauce.

I'm an addict, I swear, she'd say, dunking a nugget into the sauce.

We'd recap our game, if we'd had one. If it wasn't soccer season, then we'd plan out our weekend. When I first got together with Clint, I'd tell her every single juicy detail and we'd be squealing and laughing as we shoveled hot fries into our mouths.

Tonight I want to think about the before. Before we stopped talking. Before everything bad happened.

Before I found Victoria's bikini top.

Mom glances at Mark and then back to me. "Well, actually, Ainsley is free tonight, so I thought I'd cook for the four of us and you can finally meet her. What do you think?"

I feel my shoulders slump. I know she's been dying for me to meet Ainsley. Ainsley also goes to Valley High, but she's a junior, so we've never run into each other. Not that I would even know what she looks like.

I swing my bag to my other arm. Every muscle in my body aches.

I try to put some energy behind my words. I have to meet her sooner or later, I guess. "Sure," I say.

Mom claps her hands together. "Great! I have the steaks marinating."

———————————

Ainsley's not exactly talkative. She's been at our house for almost two hours and has barely said a word, other than *Please*, *Thank you*, and *Can you pass the ketchup?* Maybe she wants as little to do with Mom as I do with Mark, which I get. Her skin is porcelain white, and her hair is curly and strawberry blond. She wears a knee-length dress that's giving *Little House on the Prairie* vibes. She looks way too innocent to be only a year younger than me.

Mom peppers her with leading questions, asking how school is going, what activities she's in. Ainsley gives her short answers. It kind of annoys me. Mom is trying to connect with her. Ainsley could at least throw her a bone.

For dessert, Mark serves up an apple crumble. Apparently, it's his specialty. I've never been much of an apple-anything person, but I scarf it down, browned butter and soft apples and all. It helps quiet the gnawing feeling I've felt in the pit of my stomach ever since the end of tonight's game.

I offer to wash dishes to make this night end faster, but Mark says he'll do it. Mom goes to help him, and that leaves me with Ainsley. Her eyes dart to the living room, like she's searching for her escape.

"Wanna hang in my room?" I ask.

Anything's better than sitting at the table and watching Mom and Mark steal kisses in between drying dishes. I can't wait until their honeymoon stage is officially over.

"Sure," she says. As I lead her up the stairs, she asks if she can use my bathroom.

"Yeah, it's that one," I say, pointing to it.

I plop down on my bed, unwrapping the prewrap hair tie from my wrist. When Ainsley enters my room, I notice her entire demeanor has shifted. There's a spark in her blue eyes, the same color as Mark's.

She eyes me with a snarky grin. "Do you want to murder my dad yet for overstaying his welcome?" she says.

I'm shocked that this is the same girl who sat at our dinner table moments ago. She seemed so sheltered.

"I'm thinking that's a yes."

"If it was up to my mom," I say, "he'd already live here."

"Your house beats his apartment. His dream is that I'd live with him but my mom got the better end of the divorce deal. I have a bigger bedroom at her place."

Ainsley plops down beside me. She tugs at the first few buttons of her dress. "He made me promise I'd 'dress up' for tonight." She rolls her eyes. "He still thinks I'm twelve."

"Is your mom any better?"

"Oh yeah," Ainsley says. "I don't have to hide this from her."

Then Ainsley hikes her dress up, revealing a tattoo the

size of a dinner plate on her thigh. It's black and white, in a sketch style, of a bat hanging upside down in a barn, blood dripping from its mouth. "Jess drew it. It was one of her last ones," Ainsley says, running her fingers over the smooth ink.

Jess, as in Jess Ebenstein?

Ainsley's bright blue eyes meet mine. "I'm sure you know about her and the Crestmonts by now."

Oh, shit. She did mean Jess Ebenstein.

"Yeah, I do," I say.

I catch myself staring at the haunting tattoo until Ainsley rolls her dress back down.

"My dad would lose his mind if he found out I got this. If you could keep it to yourself, that'd be great."

I nod, pulling my legs underneath me until I'm sitting cross-legged. "Were, um, you and Jess close, then?"

"She was my best friend," Ainsley says.

"I'm sorry," I say.

"Me too. Life is insanely unfair."

"I ran into Robbie when I first moved here," I tell her, trying to keep things unassuming. "He volunteers at my mom's work."

"He's a real do-gooder," Ainsley says. Her voice drips with sarcasm. She looks up at me, her face hardened. "Or maybe that's just the guilt talking."

"Seems like everyone here is convinced he's guilty," I say, sitting back on my elbows. I glance up at her, trying to judge how she reacts.

"Almost everyone," Ainsley says. "I think both of the Crestmont brothers are entitled pieces of shit who flip out if a girl doesn't do what they want them to."

Heat radiates from her body. The anger she's been holding on to for the past year. "What happened to Jess shouldn't have ever happened," she says. "I was at that party and I couldn't even stop it from happening."

I sit up a little straighter, my heart beating faster. "You were?"

"My entire class was. It was homecoming. I was drunk, hooking up with one of the theater boys. I didn't think Jess would mind because she had her own thing going on."

"With Trevor."

"Yeah. With him."

Ainsley's eyes dart to the stack of cardboard boxes I still haven't unpacked. She rubs her shoulder.

"He strikes me as kind of creepy," I say honestly.

"He is," she snaps. "Jess's art was always better than his. She was gifted. That's how we all first met. In eighth-grade art class. She started winning local competitions and he never even placed. I knew he was jealous of her talent."

"And you think that's why he killed her?"

"He didn't like her going places without him," Ainsley says. "She said he was just protective but I think he was controlling."

Ainsley digs her nails into her thighs. "And that night . . ."

She swallows, like it's suddenly hard for her to talk. "I saw the EMTs running into the backyard. I thought some freshman who crashed our party needed to get their stomach pumped. It didn't even register that it'd be her. That she'd be dead."

Ainsley releases her nails. Little red half-moons are imprinted on her pale skin. "If I'd been sober that night, she wouldn't have died. I know it."

I curl my fingers into my comforter. It still smells like my old room. If I'd been sober, everything that happened to Clint could have been prevented.

"Wasn't Trevor the last person to see her alive?" I ask.

"He told me he found her passed out on a lounge chair by the pool," Ainsley says, "and when she wouldn't wake up, he called 911."

Ainsley rubs her thigh. "Well, turns out he lied. He didn't call 911 first. He called Robbie first. Seconds and minutes make a difference when someone is dying. He could also never explain the scratches on her arms."

My stomach sinks.

"Jesus."

"Her family was planning on moving to Florida when Jess went to college, since her older sister was already away at school. They ended up moving a month after she died," Ainsley says. "I know the druggie rumors broke their hearts. Neither of us did drugs, that's why I *know* Trevor drugged her and he waited until she was already dying to call for help. No fucking way she overdosed on her own. She'd never touch that kind of shit. I promised her at her grave site I'll never try them either after what happened to her. I promised her I'd always keep her memory alive."

Then there's a knock on my door, and Mark's voice is on the other side. "Ains? You ready?"

Ainsley gets up. "Time to be a Puritan again," she says.

After she leaves, it takes me a while to move from my bed. I'm still processing everything she said about Trevor.

I finally will myself to reach into one of the cardboard boxes and fish out a pair of pajamas. Seems easier to keep using these moving boxes since I'm just going to be moving again for college in less than a year.

I bring the pj's with me to the bathroom and wash off the grime from today's game. My big Friday night plans are going to be googling Jess Ebenstein and finding out what I can about her and Trevor while everything Ainsley said is still fresh in my mind.

But it's like as soon as I slip under my comforter and pull my laptop into my lap, my phone lights up. And it keeps lighting up.

I don't have enough self-restraint to just let it go.

There's a text from Robbie.

I just want you to know that everything posted on that account is bullshit. You okay?

What the hell is he talking about?

I start to reply, but then I see Lex has sent me a Snap, too.

I saw this on my Insta feed

She's sent me a screenshot. Of a photo of me. Posted on an account called the Unhappiest of Valleys.

Except it's not just any photo. It's the photo of me being escorted out of the police station last year. A photo that was leaked to Reddit by Clint's mom, even though I was a minor. The photo already has 439 likes.

I feel the blood drain from my face. My phone is slipping from my grip.

This is not happening. This is not happening *again*.

I brace myself for the caption, but then my vision's tunneling. It's like I'm shutting down, like my body's remembering everything from all those months ago, when everyone wished I'd been the one burned in the fire.

I didn't disagree with them.

EIGHTEEN

I stare at the popcorn ceiling above my bed and mentally run through the caption. It's the only thing I've been able to do all weekend.

Did you know Valley High's newest student is an arsonist? Sure you didn't, because she's worked hard to keep the biggest mistake of her life under wraps. Hell, that's why she moved all the way from California to our little town right before the start of her senior year of high school. The reason? She started a fire that led to her boyfriend having second- and third-degree burns on his face and body. And I mean, he recovered, but not one hundred percent. He'll never get his perfect face back. Did you know charges were never filed, and that her mom was dating the local DA at the time? Hm, talk about privilege. Here's the thing, Lauren. You can never escape your past. Especially not in Happy Valley. The past is everything here. It's our identity. And if yours has a mistake, you can kiss your life goodbye.

Soon bright pink light fills my room. The alarm on my phone goes off. I still can't move.

Whoever posted this wants to humiliate me. As if wearing Vic's necklace wasn't humiliating enough.

Maybe it wasn't enough for Mara. Maybe she's the one behind this account. Maybe she researched me just as much as Trevor did.

My second alarm goes off.

Could it be Trevor?

I've debated ditching school all weekend. But if I don't show up today, then I'm only giving the post more power. Especially because today's the first pep rally of the year. My entire team is expected to show up.

I moved across the entire country to get away from this shit and look how well that worked out.

I swing my feet over the edge of the bed. My body is as heavy as dead weight.

I reach for my phone. I text Lex.

Can you skip first period?

————————

Don't look down at your phone. Keep your resting bitch face on and take a sip of your triple shot like you don't give a damn, like none of this actually bothers you.

The lies I tell myself. That I have to tell myself in order to survive today.

It's an out-of-body experience. I glimpse the swivel of every head turning my way as I enter the senior hall. Conversations hush as my tennis shoes squeak against dirty tile. The sound of my own name pricks my ears.

Lauren O'Brian.

Yeah, the girl from California.

She's a pyro.

I bite my lip and I'm back at Wintergreen High. My cheeks are ruddy, my eyes swollen. No amount of makeup can mask the trauma I'm carrying. I swear smoke still clings to my hair, even though I washed it three times with vanilla shampoo. Then I smell something familiar. The faintest hint of weed layered underneath something warm like cinnamon. I refuse to look at Donovan, at the sneer on his face. But then his hot breath is in my ear, against my neck. *I'm going to make your life a living hell.*

I gulp down another sip of my latte and I'm back at Valley High. I catch the stares of a couple of football players. They shrink from my gaze as soon as my eyes meet theirs. *Good. Be afraid of the resident arsonist.*

I finally reach the door that leads straight into Valley High's basement. When it shuts behind me, I can exhale for the first time today.

I find Lex where she said she'd be, sitting on one of the rusted sinks in the abandoned girls' bathroom. Her legs swing back and forth. She's wearing our home game uniform just like me. Her hair is shiny, slicked back with pomade that smells like coconut. Her green captain's band is tight around her arm.

We have twenty minutes before the pep rally starts.

I chuck my coffee cup into a trash can that might not ever be emptied.

"I promise you, Mara doesn't run that account," she says. "The way they've talked about Victoria in the past, trust me. She would never do that to her."

"Just like she'd never take off Vic's necklace?" I snap.

"That's different," Lex says.

"I'm not sure it is."

"No one actually knows who runs the account. It's always been anonymous."

"You think they're a troll."

"Yes," she says. "An influential troll." Lex sighs. "I wish you would have . . . told me about all this before. I could have helped you. I can still help you—"

My pulse quickens. "Right. Let me just casually bring up the most traumatic night of my life to someone who doesn't want to tell the team about the deranged lengths her girl-friend will go to."

Lex looks like I just slapped her across the face. "I told you I'm working on it."

"What's there to work on?" I say.

My fingers brush up against the moldy tile of the bath-room walls. "She needs to tell the team what she did. She framed me for stealing Vic's necklace."

"I have to get her to admit it to me first, okay?" Lex says. "She hasn't done that yet."

"What kind of relationship is that?"

It's out of my mouth and then I can't take it back.

"You're one to give relationship advice," she says, crossing her arms, but the look on her face tells me she's hurt.

"Sorry," I say.

I know I'm being unfair. This is why I don't have friends. Why I shouldn't try to make new ones.

After the fire, I tried to explain everything to Rachel. She finally agreed to meet me at McDonald's, something we hadn't done in weeks. I thought she'd understand. But the way she looked at me as each word tumbled out of my mouth made me realize she had already made up her mind. It didn't help that our friendship had already been shaky those last few months before the fire.

My nicotine addiction had reached scary new heights after everything that happened with Donovan. I was up to almost a pack a day, which I couldn't afford. But cigarettes were always at parties. Which meant my partying was of control. When I wasn't drunk, I was hungover. Only part of me was present because I hated being sober. I could barely offer words of support when Rachel was dealing with her pregnancy scare because I was so out of it.

My recklessness got away from me. I was hardly aware of how much it was affecting my life. How numbing my feelings led me to be three hours late to her seventeenth birthday. I'd pregamed it with Clint and lost all track of time.

Rachel knew I was a time bomb, waiting to explode. I

just happened to do the worst damage to someone other than myself. I could see in her eyes that she thought the same thing as everyone else: She wished it'd been me instead of him.

"If you want to do this on your own, fine. Be my guest," Lex says. "I'm someone who keeps my word. If I say I'll do something, that means I'll do it." She hops off the rusted sink. "We have to go."

The pep rally. How could I forget. It's like one of Valley High's holy days.

"I think it'd be best if I didn't go."

"If you're not guilty of anything, then why would you let them win?" Lex says, giving me a cutting glance on her way out.

Because that's how it works here. Guilty until proven innocent.

I trail behind her, dodging old stacks of textbooks and cases of forgotten trophies. I make my way toward the end of the hall, where the stairs lead back up to civilization.

Maybe she's right. Maybe I should show up. It would be a big *Fuck you* to everyone.

I put one foot in front of the other, trudging up the stairs. Then I'm in the east wing of the school. The ground shakes underneath my feet as pump-up music blares from the gym.

I peek inside. It's packed. Every single student at Valley High is in festive blue-and-white outfits. The athletes, the pride and glory of the school, sit together in the front rows. I watch as Lex takes her seat with the rest of our captains. The music fades to a rumble, and then the walls of the gym start closing around me.

I step back, knowing in my body I can't do this. I turn around. I take the hallway that leads back to the west wing of school. Every single person is in that gym, beaming with Valley High pride.

Every single person, that is, except me.

And the person walking toward me with broad shoulders and a polo shirt tucked into his khakis.

Shit.

Coach.

"Where are you going, O'Brian?"

"Home," I say truthfully.

He frowns. It's the look he reserves for refs who make calls he doesn't like. "We need you at the rally—"

"Do you really think that?" I ask sarcastically.

"Yes. You're a valuable asset to the team."

"I'm pretty sure everyone else would disagree."

"I can't, as a faculty member, just let you walk out of school," he says. He puts his hands on his hips.

Please don't go full dad mode on me right now.

"You can pretend like you didn't see me," I say in the nicest way I can. Not like I need to piss off Coach more than I probably already am by skipping the rally. I glance behind me. "It's not like anyone else is here."

He sighs, like he's given up on trying to convince me. "I

hope you know that I'm here for you," he says. "Do what you need to do."

The tension eases in my shoulders.

"Thank you."

I pick up my pace in case I run into anyone else. Thankfully, the rest of school is deserted.

I push open the doors to the outside, wrapping my arms around myself. I'm still not used to anything below 70 degrees in September. But it feels good to get out of the stale heat they pump through the school halls.

My phone vibrates in my pocket.

I pull it out. Mom.

She never calls me at school. I'm sure one of her colleagues' kids saw the Instagram post and showed her. I'm sure she's already called Andrew, the DA, because the photo posted to the Unhappiest of Valleys account was supposed to be scrubbed from the internet. Mom broke up with him as soon as everything happened, because she didn't want his career to suffer. From being associated with us.

She loved him. She gave him up for me.

I really need to be nicer to her and Mark. She deserves to have one normal relationship in her life.

"Hey," I say gruffly. I round the corner toward the parking lot.

"Honey," she says, "I just heard the news. Word travels so quickly here—"

"I'm fine," I say, gritting my teeth.

If there's one person I don't need to take on this burden, it's Mom. It's better if I just let her think it doesn't bother me in the slightest. "I mean, it was only a matter of time, right?"

I hear her suck in a breath.

That's when I notice the flashing blue and red lights. Four EMTs. Loading someone into the back of an ambulance.

Someone I recognize.

"I'm not sure we're talking about the same thing, Lauren," Mom says. "One of my colleagues also works in the ER and just texted us about a call made from Valley High—"

His face looks all wrong, because it's too pale, because his eyes are too lifeless.

Trevor Crestmont.

NINETEEN

"**I need you to cooperate with** me, okay?"

I'm shaking. That's what the officer said to me when they questioned me after the fire. My keys jangle in my hands with every breath I take.

"Did you see anything else?" the police officer says.

"No."

Then I spot something dark and yellow and wet all over the asphalt where Trevor and the ambulance once were. Vomit.

"Can I have your name, please?" the officer says.

Mom's voice shouts through my phone's speakers. "I don't consent to you asking her any more questions."

The officer shrugs and walks away.

I bring the phone up to my ear. It feels like it weighs a hundred pounds. My voice cracks when I speak. "I don't know what's going on."

"I know this must be really triggering, honey. I'm coming to get you."

I close my eyes. Sirens blare in the distance. The chaotic cheers of the pep rally echo from the gym.

I want to burn it all to the ground.

TWENTY

Mom's black Honda Accord pulls up to the curb. Somehow, I manage to drag myself inside.

She reaches over and touches my face. Her purple eyeshadow creases in her lids. She's still in her scrubs. Her red hair is piled on top of her head in a messy bun.

"Did you get an update?" I ask Mom.

I try to get a handle on the way I'm falling apart inside. Mom doesn't even know that I've been involved with Robbie.

It takes a while for her to answer. I finally turn to look at her but she won't meet my gaze. She stares straight ahead, unblinking. "I know that family . . . I know they're complicated, but . . . ," she's saying as I start seeing spots along the dashboard.

I brace myself for what she says next, because she pauses, because I know that's not the end of her statement. "But he coded. They tried to save him . . . He took a lot of drugs, honey."

They tried to save him.

Her words hang there. An impossible statement.

Mom puts a hand on my shoulder as I struggle to process what she's just told me. "The dose he took . . . it might have been intentional."

The drugs, the puke everywhere.

Then it suddenly makes sense, everything she's saying.

Trevor overdosed.

"You haven't been doing any—" she asks me.

"No."

It comes out like a bark.

She drops her hand and exhales. "Okay. I know. I'm just a little shocked by this."

I look out the window as our neighborhood blurs by. Then we're pulling into our driveway. Mom parks. She opens her door.

"I just need to sit here for a second," I tell her.

She can't know the real reason why I'm this upset. Why all of this is incredibly confusing for me. "I just thought . . . ," I try to explain, "if we moved away, no more bad things would happen."

I want Mom to tell me everything's going to be okay. I need her to tell me that.

Instead all she says is, "Me too, Laur."

This morning the biggest thing I was fixated on was a stupid Instagram post. Now someone else is dead.

TWENTY-ONE

It's been one day since Trevor overdosed. I drafted about a hundred different versions of a text to Robbie but ended up saying *I'm so sorry* this morning. It felt trivial and not enough but nothing else sounded better.

I sneak my phone into my lap during math and stalk Instagram stories on my Finsta account. Everyone's talking about Trevor. They're shocked. Given all the speculation surrounding him and Jess, it's not a grieving kind of shocked. It's a spectacle.

Ainsley's profile is public. Her Instagram story is a photo of her and another pale white girl. Her strawberry-blond hair is curled, and her round blue eyes light up her face. I strain to get a closer look, because she could be Ainsley's twin. But her face shape is square, whereas Ainsley's is round. Bright pink lipstick is painted on her lips. She has kind of a rockabilly vibe.

The girl is Jess.

Thinking of you today. I'll never stop. You always deserved better. #JusticeForJessEbenstein

My stomach sinks, in spite of everything. I get the feeling

that no one's going to grieve Trevor except for Robbie and John. It just feels so heavy.

Maybe that's because if I had been the one in the back of that ambulance, I'm terrified no one would grieve me, either.

I get a text from John, just as I'm leaving practice for the night.

Could you come over? Robbie's place. He could use the extra support right now.

―――――――――

Huge vases of white flowers, draped with all sorts of sympathy banners, crowd the Crestmonts' front porch. Mourning bouquets. Even if Valley High isn't grieving Trevor, at least some people are.

The front door's been left open. I carry some of the vases with me inside. I wonder where the house manager is. Probably dealing with more important things than deciding where flowers will go.

I glance up at the daunting staircase and my chest aches. I don't know how to do this. How to console the boy I'm hooking up with. The boy who could have murdered his girlfriend. The boy who just lost his baby brother.

I don't know where the truth starts and ends. I don't know what to believe, or who.

Then a familiar voice slices through my thoughts. John.

He's dressed in an all-black sweatsuit, with an iced coffee in one hand and his phone in the other. He gives me a hug, and I feel the coldness of his drink through my clothes. Then he pulls away, but not before I notice his entire body seems to deflate.

"Damn," he says, whispering. "I can't even believe it."

I bite my lip. I don't know what to say.

John's phone lights up and his eyes dart to it and back to me. "Robbie's upstairs," he says, unlocking his phone with one hand. "It's good you're here."

It hits me that we're all Robbie has now. Me and John.

I don't even know if I count.

I put one foot in front of the other. A shudder goes through me as I remember Trevor passing me by on the stairs.

Don't hurt him.

I wish I'd answered him that day.

I think you have it backward. I think I'm the one who has to watch my every move around you two.

I pass Robbie's room but it's empty. I keep going, until I reach the one with a light shining under the door. I knock.

His voice echoes from the other side. "Yeah."

I hold my breath and open the door.

My eyes drift to the mess of Trevor's room. Heaps of dirty clothes are piled up on the floor. Bags of half-eaten Doritos and empty Sprite bottles clutter the desk. Behind the debris is a plastic picture frame, of a younger Trevor, cheesing hard, with Jess sitting in his lap. She's grinning from ear to ear, her lips painted in bright lipstick.

A chill runs through me as I think of the photo in Robbie's room. Of him and Victoria.

Now three out of the four people in those photos are dead.

My eyes travel to the bed in the middle of the room. There's a huge open binder, stuffed with so much shit it resembles an accordion. Thick papers bulge out in every direction, like someone saved every single assignment from their entire high school career.

Except, that's not what's inside. My eyes skim the open page. There's a string of printed-out text messages tacked up underneath a large font that reads:

TIMELINE—JESS

11:03 P.M. Trev, I'm in the kitchen!

11:08 P.M. Thanks be there in five babe

11:12 P.M. Where are you? I'm in the kitchen.

11:20 P.M. Jess?

11:25 P.M. Jess where tf are you

Next to it sits Robbie.

I don't know what to say to him. I can't tell him about the ambulance. I can't mention Trevor's lifeless face.

Instead I go to him. I take his hand in mine. I try to forget all the theories and rumors and devastating evidence I came across.

Because right now he's not a potential murderer. Right now he's just a boy who's grieving. That much, at least, I know is true.

He hunches over. I find myself rubbing his back.

When he looks up at me, his eyes are wet.

"This town did this to him," he says finally.

He picks up the binder and shows me the open page. "I found this under his bed."

There's a desperation in his voice I've never heard before. "I've been looking through it all evening. He thought there was more to Jess's death. More to Vic's. He was trying to prove we had nothing to do with them."

Robbie flips to another page. "People will think he killed her and the guilt ate him alive. They'll be so wrong. So fucking wrong. He died of a broken heart."

He looks at me and I feel myself shrink.

"Trevor had nothing to do with Jess's death," Robbie says. His arm brushes up against mine and his skin is hot to the touch. "I need you to know that. Just like I had nothing to do with Vic's."

I choose my next words carefully.

Because there's still the impossible question of the bikini top.

And the weird phone call.

And the Instagram post.

So far, I've kept up my end of the deal. I haven't told a soul about what I found that day on the boat.

I decide to do the only thing I can do.

I lie.

"I believe you."

I lie because I have to, because maybe the truth is too strange and too sad to make sense of anymore.

TWENTY-TWO

Trevor's calling hours are on Thursday evening. I let Coach know I'd be missing practice, and he just said "Thanks for letting me know." I guess his words in the hallway were just another empty gesture. At least I'm used to it by now.

Mark drives us to the funeral home. Mom said all of her coworkers were going. Or were obligated to go, more or less, given the Crestmont tie to Valley Hospice. I said I'd join her in support. She's still in the dark about me and Robbie.

There's no way Mark told Ainsley he was coming with us. I think she'd actually lose her mind if she knew. Jess was her best friend. But he's going to support Mom, too. Since they do everything together now.

After we park, Mom signs her name in the guest book near the entrance. I'm distracted by how stuffy it is in here, like stale potpourri and discontinued cologne. Everything's made from cherrywood and the glass windows are cloudy instead of clear.

Mom passes the pen to me. My fingers are sweating and it keeps slipping from my grasp.

"Are you okay?" Mom whispers into my ear. "These things are never easy."

I snap my gaze back to her. "Yeah. I'm fine."

"If it's too much, get some fresh air outside. Okay?"

I nod my thanks. All of this is too much.

She reaches for Mark's hand, and then they're making their way into the viewing room. I follow behind them, grateful I'm their third wheel for once. I don't know what the protocols are. I plan on mirroring whatever they do.

Faded wallpaper with a faux Victorian design covers the walls. A giant photo of Trevor is framed in the middle of it all, next to a closed casket with white flowers. I try to avoid staring at it for too long. It's surreal, knowing his body is inside.

I spot Lionel and Stacy, surrounded by people paying their respects. Lionel's tan looks like it faded overnight, and his lips are thin and dry. Stacy keeps one hand on his back, as if she's propping him upright.

Then I see who could only be Robbie's mom. The resemblance is striking. She's petite, wearing sky-high black heels, a tight black dress, and a hat with an old-fashioned, spotted black veil. Her arm is looped through a much younger guy's. The younger boyfriend Robbie mentioned.

My eyes scan the room for Robbie, but he's nowhere in sight. I can't find John, either.

I don't recognize anyone from Valley High. There's barely anyone else my age here. I don't know what I was expecting, exactly, given that Trevor's a pariah.

I swallow the lump in my throat. With the Instagram post, I'm essentially one now, too.

Then the receiving line moves up. I inch forward, lingering behind Mom and Mark. They approach Robbie's mom. Sweat drenches my armpits.

"There are no words," Mark says, reaching for Robbie's mom's hand. "I'm sorry, Janet."

"Thank you, Mark."

Her voice sounds flat, like saying anything at all is an Olympic effort.

"This is my girlfriend, Kat. She just moved here from California," Mark says.

"I'm so sorry, Janet," Mom says. Her chin quivers. "We can't imagine the grief you're carrying."

A curious look comes over Janet's face. At least, the part of her face I can see through the veil.

"You're Lauren's mom, then?" Janet asks.

She knows who I am?

And then, I think, *Fuck*. Because Mom still doesn't know about me and Robbie.

Mom glances behind her and meets my gaze, wide-eyed. Then she turns to Mark and furrows her brow. It's like I'm having heart palpitations. My words come out way too quickly.

"I'm really sorry to meet you under these circumstances," I say, meeting Janet's eyes.

Then she does something I don't expect. She reaches out and wraps her arms around me. "Robbie's told me all about you," she says, clutching on to me so tight, it's like I can feel the weight of her grief. She smells expensive, but also like something decadent and comforting, like a buttercream cake.

When she pulls away, I feel her almond-shaped nails linger on my back. "Thank you for being a friend to my son," she says. "He doesn't have many allies."

I nod quickly, feeling like a fraud. Feeling like I can't stand to see this woman's heart break any more than it already has.

Mark and Mom offer their condolences to Lionel and Stacy, and I step out of the receiving line. I'm not sure I can handle this anymore. Just like I can't handle telling Mom all the ways I'm connected to Robbie.

I'm relieved to find John near the refreshments table. He serves himself a cupful of punch. I wonder if it's spiked, because I can smell the vapor when I get close to him.

When he sees me, he holds his goblet in one hand and gives me a hug.

"This stuff is actually ingestible," he says, but his voice is devoid of his usual energy.

"Where's Robbie?" I ask.

John frowns. "He's been taking a lot of smoke breaks." He shakes his head. "I honestly don't know if he can do this again. Trevor's . . . his body isn't even in the casket."

My mouth falls open. "What do you mean?"

"It's still at the morgue. Lionel's in denial about Trevor's death. They haven't even scheduled his burial," John says.

I fidget with the prayer card in my hands that has Trevor's

picture on the front. There have been three deaths in three years at Valley High and none of them have been straight-forward. Did Trevor discover what I found on the boat, and he couldn't handle it?

I upheld my end of the deal. I kept me finding Vic's bikini top a secret. But someone still died.

I'm doing this my own fucking way now.

"I need to tell you something," I say.

John is the person closest to the Crestmonts. The person who says he has an alibi for the weekend Vic died.

"Okay . . . Like what?" he asks.

I shake my head. "We have to go somewhere a little more private."

He arches away from me. "I'm not sure if I like the sound of that," he says, but he still follows me into an empty viewing room.

I close the door behind us. "I found something at the lake," I say quickly. "I haven't told anyone about it. But now . . . I feel like if I don't . . . I feel like I have to do something dif-ferent."

John peers at me. He sits down on one of the old wooden chairs. "Okay, Ms. Suspenseful," he says. But I hear the nerves in his voice.

My heart races.

John told me he was with his mom the weekend Victoria died, I remind myself. If that's true, then I have to trust him. Or else I keep facing this alone.

"I need you to promise not to tell Robbie, or Lionel, or anyone. Especially not right now. Not yet."

John bites his lip. "I don't know if I can do that. I don't know what you're about to say."

"I'm not fucking around. My life could depend on it."

John's eyes go wide. "What kind of shit are you mixed up in?" he says.

First of all, I never asked to be mixed up in it.

"I need you to promise me first."

"Okay, okay," he says, relenting. "I promise."

I sit down in one of the velour armchairs, the color faded to silvery-gray. I take in a deep breath. "I found Victoria's bikini top on Robbie's boat," I say, the words tumbling out of me. "It had blood on it."

Now it's real. It's out there.

John's voice drops an octave. "You found *what*, exactly?"

"While you two were floating on the lake," I explain. My adrenaline speeds up my words. "I found it by accident, in the compartment under the steering wheel. It was buried really far in the back. There's blood on the underside of it. Lex told me Vic had a cut on her chest when she died. I looked at her Instagram, and she's wearing the same top in her last Instagram post."

I rub my collarbone, trying to steady my hand. "It's hers. Without a doubt."

John doesn't say anything for a while. He's focused on the old paintings decorating the wall, of historic hearses and funeral processions.

It feels eerie, telling him what I found, here, of all places.

When he finally turns his attention back to me, his gaze is heavy. "Did you take a picture of it?" he asks.

My cheeks flush. "No. I put it back where I found it."

John twists his ankh earring with his hand. I feel like he's weighing what to believe. Who to believe. His best friend, or a girl he barely knows, who doesn't even have proof of the evidence.

At least not yet.

"Why would her bikini top still be on the boat?" he asks. "It doesn't make sense."

"That's what I thought. But if you think about it, if . . ."

If Robbie.

I can't say his name aloud. Even if it's implied. It's still too weird. "If the person who killed her wanted to hold on to something of hers, especially when he couldn't keep her necklace . . ."

The way I had kept the frayed, burned piece of shirt Clint had been wearing the night of the fire, the same shirt the EMTs cut off his body.

I wanted to remind myself of what I'd done. Of how close a call it had been.

Then I buried it in the yard outside our apartment complex before I moved.

"If the boat was already searched, no one would think to look there again," I explain. "It's actually a genius hiding place."

John's expression doesn't change, so I continue. "There's

something else, too," I say. I go to my voice mails. Because this is what's going to get John to believe me.

I play it for him. The creepy, synthesized voice fills our ears.

I know you're a good girl, Lauren. Don't tell anyone about what you found on the boat. And I'll keep you safe.

I look up at John and he stares at me with wide eyes. It's like for the first time, everything I've said finally hits home.

His face changes. He believes me.

"Wow. Lauren, I'm sorry."

"I'm just glad they haven't called me again."

"Maybe this ... could help clear Robbie's name," John says. "If what you said you found is actually there."

"What if they ... already moved it?"

My words crush him.

"We have to try," John says. "This could change everything."

TWENTY-THREE

The trees are beginning to turn at Lake Monarch. Shades of red and gold overtake the green leaves as sunlight floods the horizon. If I were here for any other reason, I could appreciate the beauty of it. A real fall. Something I've only seen in movies. But all I could think about during the drive with John is seeing that bloodstain again.

We left at dawn, so I can make it back in time for practice later this afternoon. This might be our only chance to see if the bikini top is still here.

I follow John to the dock. Each step we take is met with a creak louder than the last, like the cool weather has caused the wood to shrink. I look out across the lake. The sandy area where the kids played two weeks ago is desolate. No other boats cruise by; no swimmers in bright caps swim laps. The wind that stings my cheeks has a clear message: Summer is long over.

"Lauren?" John says. "You ready?"

I'm still undecided, but I nod anyways. The boat groans as it rocks from side to side. I pull my coat on tighter to shield myself from the damp wind. John steps on first. He offers me his hand. I take it, steadying my feet as I hit the deck.

My throat tastes like pennies.

I lead John to the front of the boat. I bend down, finding the compartment below the steering wheel. Then I get on my hands and knees. My shorts snag on the planked wood floor as I struggle to pry open the compartment. My hands are ice-cold.

You're not alone this time.

I finally unlatch it and see the old magazines first. I clear them to the side, then reach my hand into the far left corner. Exactly where I left the bikini. Under the ripped floatie.

I must not be reaching far enough.

"Can you shine your phone flashlight in here?" I ask John.

A beam of digital white light illuminates everything. And all the dirt and dust with it.

I turn over the old magazines, the old floatie, another bottle of tanning oil.

That's when I know.

I remove every single thing from the compartment, stacking it on the deck. Then I wipe my filthy hands on my shorts. I sit back on my knees, staring at all the objects. My eyes dart back to the compartment.

"Lauren—"

"They really did it." My voice is fast, all staccato. "They saw me and got rid of it."

I look up at John, at his downturned mouth. His eyes inspect every single object I just unearthed.

I run through all the possibilities of what could have happened that day. Robbie could have seen me when he was floating on the lake. I don't even have to say his name out loud, because John is already shaking his head.

"He couldn't have," John says. "I was with him. We couldn't see what you were doing from where we were, trust me."

"Then it was Trevor," I say, breathless. "It had to be him."

"He wasn't even with us," John says.

"He knew we were out boating and he was watching my every move that weekend. He thought the only reason why I came here was to spy on Robbie."

Then I remember Lionel's love of stargazing and bird-watching. The detail we could see with the telescope alone was incredible.

I glance back at the house. Every shade is closed, even the massive ones with the open view of the lake. "Between Lionel's telescope and binoculars, it wouldn't have been that hard to spy on us. It's not like we were even anchored that far from the house."

I get up from the deck, brushing myself off. "What if Trevor saw me with the bikini top," I say, gaining conviction, "and then he got a look at it for himself, and he knew that it proved Robbie killed Vic. He wanted to protect Robbie, so he got rid of it. Then he called me and threatened me to make sure I wouldn't tell a soul. I haven't gotten any more calls since he died."

Just like there haven't been any more Unhappiest of Valleys posts.

"I'm telling you, Trevor thought Robbie was innocent," John says. "Nothing could have changed his mind."

"But that top changes everything," I say. "It could have . . . completely . . ." I quiet my voice. "That could have pushed him to overdose . . ."

I sit on one of the benches. A small collection of lake water pools at my feet.

"I have to accept that whatever you found is gone," John says. His lips tremble. "I don't know what happened that weekend. I don't think we'll ever know. But I do know what I told you before. My best friend said he didn't kill Victoria. And I believe him. Whether we have Vic's top or not."

TWENTY-FOUR

Robbie is absent from physics Monday morning. I notice that the weird glances normally reserved for him are now directed at me. The room is quiet when I take my seat. A couple of blond girls a few rows ahead of me keep turning around to look my way. I pop my gum loudly and the backs of their heads finally turn around for good.

Even Lex is quieter than usual. We haven't spoken since before the pep rally.

It's better this way. We were starting to . . . to actually be friends.

I'm relieved when the bell rings. I pass by John's locker on my way to second period, but I don't see him. Usually he'd be getting out of AP Spanish. He's probably with Robbie. Making sure he's okay. The steadfast best friend who sticks by Robbie no matter how much of a shitstorm his life becomes.

John texted me late last night, saying just as much.

I never went to Lake Monarch with you, by the way

I got the hint and left him on read.

I know that if John had held that top in his hands, he'd feel differently. He'd have the same doubts I have.

Now he'll never get the chance.

I'm yanking on my practice shorts when I feel someone lean into me.

"Coach wants to see you in his office," Lex whispers.

Great. Never a good sign.

I throw on my jersey, slam my locker closed, and carry my cleats with me into the sports admin hallway. I find Coach in his office. He's leaning over his desk, looking at something I can't see. His head is almost touching the girl sitting next to him. A girl with curly, strawberry-blond hair.

Ainsley.

What is she doing here?

I lean in the doorway. That's when Ainsley rolls up whatever they were just looking at. Like she doesn't want me to see.

"Hey, Lauren," she says easily. "I was just helping out Coach Holliger with a special project."

I lock eyes with her. *Special project?* Why is she being so weird?

Coach clears his throat. "Thanks for stopping by, Ainsley."

"Yeah, no problem," she says.

She brushes past me, like she can't get out of here fast enough. Then I'm left alone with Coach.

"Am I here because of a *special project,* too?" I ask.

He doesn't take the bait.

"Take a seat," he says sternly.

He takes another sip of his energy drink before tossing it in the garbage. On his desk are a couple of extra whiteboards and scattered pieces of paper with some of our old plays on them. Behind him hangs our team photo from this year, along with one from each of the past three years, and a single photo of Victoria. Her memorial photo.

"Your teammates are concerned about you," Coach says. "I am, too."

"Concerned how?" I ask.

Coach sighs. "You switched schools because of an incident involving your ex-boyfriend."

"We both survived a fire," I snap.

Coach frowns. "It's more than that, Lauren. I know you haven't broken it off with Robbie."

"Going to his brother's calling hours makes me a bad person?"

Coach's face reddens. "I never said that."

He didn't have to. I remember the way he interacted with Trevor back at the lake. Like he hated him.

"Victoria was taken from us way too soon," Coach says. For the first time, I notice his eyes are watering. "I don't think it's in the best interest of the team to have someone playing alongside us who . . . has such an *intimate* relationship with the person who hurt our Vic."

My stomach is in knots. His words sink into the parts of me I haven't felt in a long, long time.

"I think it'd be best if you took a break," Coach says, "until you can demonstrate that your loyalty is to your team."

I feel like I walked into a trap.

"A break?" I hear myself saying. "Whose idea was this? Mara's?"

"This was a team decision—"

"Right. That sounds like a super-ethical way to make a decision, going behind my back."

"I know you're upset. I can understand why you might want to support Robbie during the loss of his brother," Coach says. "But I'm responsible for the health of all my players, and some of them barely survived Vic's death. Think of this as a mental health break. A reset. I hope you understand."

A mental health break. Is he joking?

"That's it? It's all decided, then?"

"Lauren, please don't make this any harder than it already is."

"This is so fucked," I say. Somehow my feet are able to carry me out of the chair and out of his office.

Even through everything, soccer's always been my constant. My old coach never benched me. She knew how much I needed to play. She knew it was all I had, even if half the team wanted me to quit.

But I'm an outsider here, no matter what Lex told me before.

Eight more months. Eight more months left of school.

Sooner than later, I'll be at a big-ass university where I'm just a number.

I find an empty stall in the bathroom, slam the toilet lid down, and pull up my Finsta account. I search for the Unhappiest of Valleys, the account that's tried to ruin my life for the second time. I scroll backward, looking at the dates of the other posts. Whoever this person is, they were posting about twice a week. Mostly small things, like hookups and rumors of STIs and pregnancy scares.

I enable push notifications from their profile. When there's a new post, I'll be notified.

But if there isn't, then it tells me everything I suspected: Trevor was the one who aired my dirty laundry.

———————————

"You're home early, babe."

Mom looks over at me from her yoga mat, spread out in the living room. She has chronic back pain from being on her feet most days as a nurse and stretches whenever she gets the chance.

Some part of me wishes she was working a shift right now. The other part of me is glad to know there's at least one human on planet Earth who will love me no matter how much I continue to mess up. I know it breaks her heart when I get myself into these situations.

Part of me wants to protect Mom. Shield her from the

latest bad news I just received. The other part of me just wants to be her daughter right now.

I slump down into a kitchen chair. "I'm off the team," I say.

Mom gets out of her latest contortion and comes into the kitchen.

"What do you mean?" she asks, her voice filled with concern. "Is this because of what happened at the game the other week?"

"Someone leaked info about me and Clint to this gossip account and now everyone knows I'm an arsonist. Including my team, apparently."

I have to tell her the truth. Right now.

"I lied to you. The weekend at Lake Monarch, I was with Robbie. That's why his mom knew who I was. That's also mainly why the team wants me gone."

Mom sits down next to me. "I wondered," she says quietly, "if there was another reason why you were bringing me Starbucks every week."

Now it's my turn to be wide-eyed.

"You knew?"

"Well, I suspected," she says. "You seemed a little happier, too. The best I've seen you since before the fire."

I drum my fingers on the table. Trying not to fixate on what she just said. Did Robbie really make me happier? I drum harder. Whatever. It doesn't matter. That chapter is over now.

"Is that why you called me as soon as you heard about Trevor?" I ask.

She nods. "I was hoping you'd tell me on your own, when you were ready. I'm sorry I couldn't be there for you."

Ugh, her words hit me in the feels.

I look up, seeing her pretty face scrunched with worry.

"Did you try to work things out with the team?" she asks.

"Of course I did," I say. "I'm not trying to sabotage my life."

"Oh, honey, I know you're not."

"I just thought . . ."

I try to keep my voice steady but my vocal cords have other ideas. "This is never going to go away, is it? This is . . . this is something that's going to follow me wherever I go. For the rest of my life."

I don't know if it's the look on Mom's face or replaying that creepy phone call in my head or seeing the image of Vic's bloodied top in my mind, but it's like everything finally catches up to me. Mom reaches for me. "It's okay," she says, stroking my hair. "It's all going to be okay."

I want to believe this lie. I want to believe it so badly.

Mom holds me as I heave with sobs. For the first time since I've moved here, I just let myself be small.

TWENTY-FIVE

The scent of coconut pomade wafts into my nose as I open my locker. I don't even have to look up to know who it is.

Lex.

"I know Coach talked to you yesterday—"

"Yeah, he told me everything I need to know. Thanks," I say. I slam my locker closed.

"I'm sorry—"

I whip around to face her. "You don't have to pretend like you're actually confronting Mara on her shit," I say. "You know, maybe if the team knew she set me up, they wouldn't even care at this point. This is what everyone always wanted. Since day one."

Lex looks at me with deer-in-headlights eyes, and I'm satisfied as I storm off. I let her off the hook, just like Rachel. I've learned it's better to save people from the effort of having to walk on eggshells around me.

Now that I'm off the team, I don't have any other distractions. All I want to focus on is proving everyone wrong. Proving that I do care, that everything I'm doing with Robbie, with the Crestmonts, is because I care, even if it doesn't look that way.

Sooner than later, they're going to find out the truth. And Robbie is the one with the answers.

I pull out my phone and text him.

Hey. You at school today?

I find him at his smoking spot. It's a little alcove with a bench. I can faintly make out the cigarette symbol carved into the concrete, leftover from decades past when you could actually smoke at school. There're even a few ashtrays.

Robbie lights a fresh cigarette next to me. I haven't seen him in person since last week and I notice he has the beginnings of a beard. His normally pink lips are almost colorless, like Trevor's death sucked part of his own life force away.

My knee jostles up and down. Partly due to my forever being addicted to nicotine, I guess, and partly due to the fact that every time I'm around Robbie now, my pulse quickens. And not in an I'm-dying-to-hook-up-with-you way. In a you-could-have-murdered-your-girlfriend way.

I'm tempted to say fuck it and ask him for a cigarette because at the very least, it would calm me down. But I worked too hard to relapse.

I reach into my bag, rummaging around for my pack of peppermint gum. I pop two to keep my mouth busy. In my hands, I fidget with my pen. I need the physical sensation of doing something right now, and it helps curb the intense craving. It helps me focus, too. Because the point of all of this, of me being this close to him, is to find out what he's willing to let slip.

I sigh out a deep breath. I can do this.

"This is torture for you," Robbie says.

"Maybe I like to torture myself," I say, turning from his gaze.

That's kind of what I live for, actually. Ruining every single good thing I have.

"Are we the same person?" Robbie says dryly.

I mean, I can say with certainty I didn't kill my boyfriend.

I turn my pen over in my hands as the smell of the smoke hits me. I close my eyes, breathing it in. I can't help it.

I see Clint's face. His skin. How it looked in the hospital. Covered in gauze and weeping.

I open my eyes as Robbie exhales.

"My brother didn't intentionally overdose," he says. "He wouldn't have given up on Jess. On Vic." His voice takes a dark turn. "On me."

But I know that could be exactly what happened. If Trevor found Vic's top, it would have turned his entire world upside down.

"What do you think happened?" I ask.

"I think someone drugged him and staged it to look like a suicide," he says.

I try to keep my face as neutral as possible.

"The more I thought about it . . . If Trevor was going to kill himself, he wouldn't do it in such a public place. He had a contusion on his temple and one on his forearm, too," Robbie says. "The police chalked it up to him hitting the pavement, but come on, being bruised in two places? His phone was also smashed. They said the ambulance could have run it over, but I don't think it was accidental. My dad hired a private medical examiner to get a second opinion on his autopsy. He also hired a private investigator to see if there are any inconsistencies in the police report."

I remember what John said, about Lionel keeping Trevor's body at the morgue. Now it makes sense.

I look at Robbie and his gaze is penetrating.

"He was incoherent when he called me that night," he says, his voice suddenly unsteady. "The night Jess died. I could barely tell him what to do. I just couldn't believe it. What are the fucking chances it happens to both of us, that both of our girlfriends ended up dead?"

I clench my jaw, twisting my pen even harder.

What *are* the chances?

TWENTY-SIX

The downside to being off the team is that I have fewer excuses to get out of Mark and Mom's "family" dates. But I'll never be the person who turns down dinner at the brand-new Cheesecake Factory in town. Food is basically one of the only bright spots I have in my life right now. I put in an order for nachos as my appetizer and Mom and Mark order salads.

"We have one more coming," Mark says to the waiter. "She loves the avocado eggrolls."

I take a sip of my soda and wonder what Ainsley must think about Trevor's death.

"Lauren, cheers!" Mom says.

I'm pulled back to the present and "cheers" my glass with theirs. Then they kiss. I catch a glimpse of Mom's tongue and want to crawl out of my skin.

"One rule. No make-out sessions allowed," I say, and Mom instantly reddens.

Mark chuckles. "Physical affection is your mother's love language," he says.

I try not to dry heave.

"I know it's a few months away," Mom says, composing herself, "but I think we could all use something to look forward to. I'd love to take Christmas off this year and plan a lunch for the four of us. That way Ainsley can join, too."

Christmas is the furthest thing from my mind right now. Usually Mom works over the holidays, because the pay is double. My tradition is loading myself up with a tub of Toll House cookie dough and plopping down in front of the TV. Sometimes we'd go to my grandparents, if it was a year when they weren't fighting with Mom.

"Sounds good," I say.

Mom smiles. She must be happy she's gotten approval from the resident grinch.

"We can make it really special this year," she says. "We deserve to."

"I appreciate you including me in your holidays," Mark says, nodding in my direction.

I mean, does he think I actually have a choice?

I slide out of the booth. "Hopefully when I'm back the appetizers will be here," I say.

I speed walk to the bathroom, thinking that this is my new normal now that Mom has a steady boyfriend again. He's going to be at everything. Holidays. Birthdays. My graduation. He'll be there every break I'm home from school.

If I come home, that is. I could always do summer school.

I exit the stall and I'm washing my hands in the sink when I hear something shatter on the tile floor.

"Shit," a voice says.

I crane my neck, seeing what looks like a thousand tiny shards from a cracked compact mirror all over the floor. I walk toward it.

"Are you okay?" I ask.

"Yeah, yeah, I'm fine," the girl says. She scrambles to collect the pieces with her bare hands.

"Hey, those are really sharp—"

"Don't worry about it, okay? I got it."

Something about her tone sounds familiar.

"Ainsley?"

She works even faster, picking up the shards. "Lauren?"

"Yeah."

"Oh. Hey," she says. "I'll be right out. I told my dad to order me the eggrolls."

"He did," I say, watching as her pale hands carefully sweep up the pieces.

I can't help but notice that it's not just the cracked mirror spilled all over the floor, but something white and powdery.

I've been at enough parties to know what it is.

Ainsley was just doing coke?

I take a step backward. She told me she didn't do drugs. Because of Jess. That she'd never touch them because of what happened.

She lied.

"I'll see you out there," I tell her, pushing open the doors to the bathroom.

Plenty of people do coke. She's just one of them, I remind myself, as I find my way back to our booth. My nachos have arrived. Mom and Mark are eating and talking but I'm totally tuning them out.

Because the weird thing is, we're not at a party. We're at dinner on a Wednesday night. With our parents. At the Cheesecake Factory, of all places.

When Ainsley finally joins us, she slides in next to me and gives me a hug. Her body's warm. She's more animated than she was at our last dinner together. She engages with Mom, asking her about nursing. She cracks the ice cubes from her water in between her teeth.

I chew my nachos. The sting of the jalapeños stays on my tongue even after chugging my second soda. Ainsley probably did a bump, I realize, back at my house. After dinner. That's why she seemed like a totally different person in my bedroom.

It's a weird coincidence, that Jess died of an overdose, that Trevor died of an overdose, and that Ainsley has a coke habit so bad, she's doing lines before having dinner with her dad.

I wonder if every time the white powder hits her nose, she thinks of Jess.

TWENTY-SEVEN

I drive by the entire junior class working on their homecoming float. They carry paint, papier-mâché, and chicken wire into a huge red barn that houses their precious cargo. The homecoming theme this year is "destinations" and each float is kept top secret. Some part of me aches for the time when I'd kill to have an unforgettable homecoming weekend.

But girls who set fires don't get to enjoy homecoming weekend anymore.

When I get out of my car, the air hits my skin like a sheet of ice. The days are getting shorter, and I can make out a faint half-moon in the sky. I wonder what moon phase we're in. What Victoria would have to say about it. If it's trying to send me some kind of message that I'm obviously clueless to decipher.

The inside of the Creamery, Penn State's historic ice cream shop, isn't much warmer, but the smell makes up for it. I order a double scoop of Alumni Swirl in a cone: vanilla ice cream with mocha chips and blueberry swirl. I pay and take the first lick. The sweet creaminess hits the back of my throat as I carry my cone to one of the outside tables. There's an old copy of the *Centre Daily Times* next to a few sticky rings left behind from old ice cream bowls. I glance over at it. It's from September 12. The day after Trevor died.

PROMINENT LAWYER'S SON DEAD IN APPARENT OVERDOSE

I avert my eyes. I've already read the article. Twice.

It made no mention of Jess or Vic. I wonder if Lionel had to pay big PR money to get them to leave the other shady parts of his family's life out of it.

I reach the waffle cone part of my ice cream, biting down just as the wind picks up the leaves. Then I use my phone to continue my research on Jess Ebenstein.

She preferred oils to watercolors. She was looking at MFA programs in New York City and LA even though she was barely into her sophomore year of high school. And she loved Trevor Crestmont.

This is all according to the long-form profile written in the *Humans of Valley High* Facebook account, after Jess won a local award for one of her oil paintings. It was a portrait of Trevor, of all things. It's amazing how she captured him, with his sharp cheekbones. There's something about him that's radiant, that comes through in the way she painted his eyes.

Something I never saw in Trevor while he was still alive.

I hear footsteps, and look up to find Mara and Lex.

They're hand in hand, their T-shirts flecked with paint and glitter from building the senior class float.

I chose the Creamery because I didn't think any other seniors who have a life would want ice cream at five o'clock on a Friday night homecoming weekend.

Guess I was wrong.

I catch Lex whispering something to Mara, who says something back. She looks annoyed. Then they're headed my way.

This will be a fun little reunion.

"Hey, Lauren, how've you been?" Lex says. She's trying to extend an olive branch. Mara looks at me like I'm an animal in a cage.

"I've never been better," I say, giving her a sarcastic smile.

"Really? Even when your boyfriend's brother died?" Mara says. Her voice drips with even more venom than usual.

"He's not my—"

"His death *screams* guilt," Mara says.

"Let's not start this again," Lex says, tugging her arm, but Mara's eyes don't leave mine.

"Trevor was such a fucking liar, saying he didn't do drugs, that he didn't give her any drugs. Did you know Lionel got him out of getting drug tested the night she died?"

"I wouldn't know, Mara. Just like I didn't know you were setting me up when you gave me Vic's necklace," I say, crossing my arms. My eyes dart over to Lex, but she doesn't take the bait.

I'm not about to blow up her relationship. That's between them.

"I saw you with Robbie the other day, at his smoking spot," Mara says, completely bypassing what I've just said.

Guess she's stalking me now.

"He's the only person at Valley High who doesn't hold a personal tragedy against me," I snap back.

I surprise myself by how true this is.

Maybe that's why I've stuck this out. Maybe because some part of me can't accept that the only person who doesn't judge me for the biggest mistake of my life could have murdered his girlfriend.

I have to know the truth, one way or the other.

Lex frowns. She stuffs her hands into her jean pockets. "You shouldn't have been let go from the team. It was the wrong decision and I told Coach just as much," she says.

I shake my head. "You don't have to stick up for me anymore. I appreciate it, but—"

"She's not sticking up for you. She's just diplomatic. More than I'll ever be," Mara says. "You were a distraction more than anything else. We're serious about states this year. We're winning for Vic. We don't need anything or *anyone* getting in the way of that."

"What you went through with Vic was horrible," I say. I try to keep my voice steady. "I'm not pretending to know what that's like. But I'm not your punching bag."

"No," Mara says. The edges of her mouth curl up just slightly. "But you are an arsonist. Right?"

"I guess you'd better be careful," I tell her as I walk past them. "It's almost been a year since I watched a house go up in flames. I'm getting a little antsy."

The horrified look on Mara's face almost makes up for the shittiness of this entire fall.

Almost.

TWENTY-EIGHT

I'm a little confused by Mom's outfit when she emerges downstairs Saturday night. She's in really tight, borderline I-can-see-her-underwear jeans, and a blue-and-white shirt. Even her eyeshadow is a glittery blue.

"Where are you going?" I ask. I preheat the oven for the pizza I found in the back of the freezer.

"We're headed to the Valley game," she says, flashing me a smile. Her teeth look brighter, like she's whitened them. "Mark says it's the best game of the year."

This town feels so small sometimes. Too small.

"You're going to my high school's football game?" I protest.

"It's a big deal here."

"Right," I say under my breath.

"Are you staying in tonight?" she asks, eyeing my tried-and-true ensemble of my old practice jersey from Winter-green High and sweats.

"I think it's for the best if I never go out again," I tell her, grabbing a can of soda from the fridge.

I crack it open and catch the disappointed look on her face.

"You don't have to keep punishing yourself, Laur," she says.

"I'm not," I lie. "I'm working on college apps."

Which is semi-true. I've at least started the process. Created my own login on the Common App's website.

Mom touches up her lip gloss and throws the tube into her purse.

"All right. Well, if you get bored out of your mind, you can always crash our plans."

Is it sad when your mom keeps inviting you to third-wheel?

"Thanks," I say.

I tear open the cardboard pizza box, inspecting the degree of freezer burn I'm up against. Then I notice today's *Centre Daily Times* on the kitchen island. A key clue Mark was here earlier, since Mom and I always forget to bring in the paper. The above-the-fold headline is hard to miss.

LOCAL ATTORNEY INVESTIGATES SON'S DEATH
Attorney Lionel Crestmont has hired a private investigator to investigate his youngest son's death by overdose, disagreeing with the opinion of medical examiner Dr. Roland Croft, who has twenty-four years of experience in the field, and the findings of the Valley High police department, who ruled the death a suicide.

"My son was not a drug user. I'm going to get justice for him," Lionel Crestmont commented.

Chief of Police Alan McCarthy responded, "It's a tragedy all the way around. Drugs take the lives of our young people every day. It's an epidemic."

Mom peers over my shoulder. "How's Robbie coping?" she asks.

"I think he's trying really hard to make sense of it all," I say, remembering what he said. That he thinks Trevor's death was staged.

"I can't imagine," Mom says quietly, and then her phone rings. For some reason, her ringtone is suddenly grating to my ears. "I hope you have a cozy night in," she says, kissing my cheek.

"Thanks. Have fun."

She runs out the door.

I mean, this *would* be a good night to at least put a dent in some of my college apps. University of Miami and Arizona State are on my list. The bigger the school, the better. The easier it will be for me to fly under the radar.

I pull my laptop onto the counter as my pizza cooks, and log in to the Common App. I glance at the essay questions.

What is something meaningful from your personal experience that has shaped who you are?

Then my phone's vibrating. John's calling me. Which is weird because we haven't exactly said much to each other since our little excursion to Lake Monarch. He asked me to pretend like it never happened.

"Hey," I say.

"You need to get here as fast as those soccer legs can carry you," he says in a panicked voice.

I can barely hear him. People are screaming in the background, and it doesn't sound like the normal kind of football-crazed screams.

"What's going on—"

"Park on South Avenue," he says. "The lot's full. I'll meet you there."

TWENTY-NINE

John frantically waves me over to an empty spot. I haven't parallel parked since I lived in California, and it takes me two tries. Then John's at my door.

His eyes are wide, and he wraps his arms across his chest.

"Are you okay?" I ask, opening my door.

"No," he says. "No, I have never been more not okay in my entire life." He looks at me, his mouth quivering. "This year is getting weirder and weirder, I swear."

He offers his arm, and I take it. Then we're crossing the street, walking into the lot of our high school. Valley Highers walk to their cars, looking shell-shocked. Some are crying.

I try to keep up with John's long legs, wondering what the hell I'm about to walk into. Then we're in the football stadium. To say it's a complete shit show would be an understatement.

It's chaos. People push through the crowds, phones in their hands, working on Instagram posts. I try to glance at one but then I'm being pulled away.

John finds a clearing along the metal fence. I lean against it, taking in the scene.

A state-of-the-art projection screen is set up at the back of the field. Two police officers are next to it, talking to the two football coaches.

"We hadn't even kicked off yet," John says. "We start every game with a hype video. It's tradition. I've done the music composition for the AV club for the last three years. Except at the end of the video, instead of the meatheads hyping one another up in the locker room, it faded out, and I was like, what the hell is happening? Then Carson, the AV club president, made an announcement. He could barely get it together. Said they'd found a note tucked into their booth, instructing them to show it to the entire school. They felt it was important."

John sucks in a breath. He pulls out his phone and holds it out to me.

I zoom in on the picture of what looks like a typed letter.

Valley Highers,

I'm sorry for a lot of things, and it's why I'm writing to you now.

For years, you've accused my older brother, Robbie Crestmont, of being involved with the death of his beloved girlfriend, Victoria Moreno. You've turned him into an outcast. And I've let you.

But Robbie's innocent. He didn't kill Victoria. And I couldn't live anymore with the fact that I was making his life a living hell. You didn't deserve it, Robbie.

That's why I'm coming clean.

I have a confession to make. I killed Victoria Moreno. It wasn't planned. I'm not a psychopath. It was an accident. You see, we'd been involved, me and her, when Robbie and Victoria took a break. I'd always been in love with her. It was easy, falling in love with Victoria. She was beautiful, kind, and so talented.

But when she decided to get back with my brother, I didn't know how to handle it. I couldn't handle it. I'd gone to the lake to plead with her, to make her see that I was the right Crestmont brother for her.

When she refused, I lost it.

I tried to move on, by falling for Jess. I did love her, too, but I didn't kill her. She made a stupid mistake, taking drugs that night.

It's what gave me the idea for how to end my own life.

Robbie, please forgive me. I know it's probably impossible to.

To Victoria's family, I'm sorry. This has been the biggest regret of my life.

And to Valley High, I'm sorry for all the pain I've caused.

If there is any doubt that lingers in your mind, even

after this confession, I've hidden something of hers on the back of the scoreboard.

The world is better off without me in it.

Goodbye,

Trevor Crestmont

I feel my grip loosen from the metal fence. "What did he hide?" I ask.

John swipes to the next photograph. "You were right, Lauren," he says quietly.

I glance down and see a zoomed-in image of a bikini top hanging on the back of the scoreboard. Just like the letter said.

It's the right color. Tie-dyed blue and white.

I can just glimpse the bloodstain peeking out from the other side.

Holy shit.

This is why Trevor was obsessed with keeping tabs on me. It's why he threatened me. Robbie's theory was wrong. Trevor killed himself because his guilt consumed him.

I look at the crowd around us, at the chaos and commotion. The whispers. The shock that their pariah is no longer. Robbie Crestmont, the boy they've shunned for years, is innocent.

THIRTY

I turn on my phone's flashlight and follow John over the damp cemetery grounds. We maneuver through the graves, all dark and moss-covered. I try not to step on any wilting bouquets.

John finds him before I do.

Robbie's sitting on the ground, next to a reserved plot without a headstone. Trevor hasn't been buried yet, since Lionel requested the additional autopsy.

Robbie doesn't look up when we get near him. John sits down on the edges of the plot, and I follow his lead. I turn off my flashlight. My eyes slowly adjust to the soft moonlight.

Robbie runs his fingers along the earth like he's smoothing out a blanket. His hands are filthy. He's probably been here for hours. John told him everything that happened before we drove over. He was met with silence on the other line.

"There's something else we need to tell you," John says. His eyes meet mine.

I take a deep breath, nodding. In the car, John told me we

had to come clean about me finding Victoria's top. He said we couldn't keep it a secret any longer, not after this.

I agreed.

Robbie looks at the two of us. John angles his body toward mine. I pluck at a tuft of wet grass with my left hand.

"I found her bikini top over Labor Day weekend," I say, "on your boat. While you and John were floating in the lake."

Robbie's face doesn't change, doesn't even twitch. His eyes stay locked on mine. "I was looking for sunscreen. I stumbled upon it by accident. I didn't know what to do so I put it back where I found it."

It's hard for me to watch the way Robbie's face changes. Like he's caught in between disbelief and rage.

"She told me at Trevor's calling hours," John says. "I wanted to see it for myself. We went to Lake Monarch." John almost winces. "But it was gone."

"I got a phone call after I'd found it," I say. "The voice mail warned me to not tell anyone what I'd found. I played it for John. That's what convinced him to go back to Lake Monarch with me in the first place."

I take a deep breath. "I haven't gotten any calls since."

The weight of what we've just shared feels oppressive, like someone's sitting on my chest.

"I'm sorry," John says. "Robbie, I—"

"I already knew," Robbie says.

My stomach sinks.

He glances up at me. "My dad got an alert on his phone. From the security camera on the boat."

"Oh, shit," John mumbles.

But then I have an idea. Because this gives me hope—

"I know Trevor didn't do it," Robbie says. He digs his fingers into the plot. Black earth stains his skin. "He didn't write that note."

"He saw me, Robbie," I say gently. "Then he removed the bikini. If we looked at the security cameras we can prove—"

"They only store footage for three days," Robbie says. "Whatever it is you think happened, it doesn't matter. We can't see it."

Robbie wraps his arms around his legs, rocking back and forth. "Trevor didn't believe Jess's death was an accident. That's how I know he didn't write that letter."

He turns to me. "You saw the binder. You know how obsessed he was. Whoever wrote that letter wants to deflect the blame away from themselves. They want everyone to stop asking questions about what really happened to Vic and Jess."

I frown. Because I feel like Robbie doesn't want to face this. Face the truth of what Trevor did.

It's horrific. I don't blame him.

Robbie flicks a pile of dirt away from himself. His shoots me a cutting glance. "You barely knew my brother," he says, as if he could read my mind.

He's right. I didn't.

But I also know what I saw. I know how the pieces add up.

I feel John shift next to me, sitting up straighter. His nose ring glints like a diamond under the moon.

"Okay," John says. "After the incredibly traumatic experience of just trying to process everything we saw tonight, I'm realizing the bikini was just sitting there at the back of the scoreboard . . . since Trevor died? And no one saw it?"

"It was hidden well," I say.

"Homecoming weekend is bigger than the Met Gala here, Lauren," John says. "They clean everything. Make it look pristine. The scouts from Penn State come out to watch the team. Someone would have noticed it if it had been there for more than a day or two."

"Then you're saying someone else planted it?" I ask.

"I have an alibi," Robbie says. "Just in case you don't believe me." He chucks his phone in my direction like it's a torpedo. "I've been here all day. Just look at my location."

Heat rises to my cheeks. If he wants to go there, I will.

"If you were the one who planted it, you wouldn't have risked being seen during the day," I say. "You would have gone last night."

His mouth falls open. "You've kept me as a suspect in the back of your mind this entire time—"

"Can you blame me?" I explode. "I found your dead girlfriend's bloodstained bikini top on your boat, okay? And then some psycho left me that voice mail."

"Damn," John says under his breath.

Robbie wipes his hands on his black jeans.

The three of us are silent as the wind picks up around us. It sends the loose dirt on top of Trevor's future grave into the air.

Robbie looks at me. His eyes are soft for the first time tonight and they shouldn't be.

Why is he looking at me like that?

"I wish you didn't have to be the one who found it," he says.

Part of my heart breaks when he says those words.

Everything made sense earlier this evening. It was all tucked into a nice, neat little bow. Now it's all coming unraveled.

THIRTY-ONE

Monday morning feels like I just walked into a completely different high school. Before I enter physics, I catch Lex farther down the hallway, near one of the labs.

His back is turned, but I know from the way he's standing that Robbie is the guy she's talking to.

I know I've officially entered a different dimension when they hug each other. Robbie looks shaken. Like he doesn't know what to say.

Right now, that letter has given him his own fresh start. Whether Trevor wrote it or not.

I duck into physics. When Robbie enters, a few guys give him nods. That's new. Someone strikes up a conversation with him. He's cordial, but I can tell he'd rather be anywhere but here.

When Lex sits down next to me, I give her a nod. It's kind of been our new normal, ever since I've been off the team. But today I can see out of the corner of my eye that she's angled her body in my direction.

"We were wrong," she says.

I glance her way. Part of me still feels spiteful. The only

stable thing I had going for myself was ripped right out from underneath me. I never got a say in it.

I drop my pen, flexing my fingers. Then I remind myself Lex and the rest of the team don't know what I found. All this time, they thought I just . . . couldn't keep myself away from Robbie. They have no idea I've been trying to make sense of it all.

Which may be impossible at this point.

"It's okay," I tell her.

My eyes drift to Robbie, to his mop of dark hair in the front row. The moonstone and onyx rings that decorate his fingers catch the light of the morning sun coming in through the windows.

I keep waiting for him to glance backward at me. He never does.

———————

I work on the Common App during lunch. I make a dent in the personal essay, trying to milk surviving a fire for all its worth. Make them think I've overcome my trauma. I've learned enough catchphrases in therapy to make it sound convincing. Maybe if my subpar GPA can't win them over, my life story will. At least part of it. I'm leaving out the part where I hook up with a guy whose family is such a mess I can't tell where the lies end and the truth begins. I don't know if Trevor wrote that letter or not. I don't know if his death was something other than what it seems like: an overdose.

I'm realizing that maybe I'm not meant to figure it out.

I thought that if I could, if I could find out what really happened to Vic and Jess, that it could be some sort of karmic makeup for everything I put Clint through. I could finally right my wrong.

But I'm not sure that's true anymore. It's incredible, really, that I even thought it was a possibility.

When the bell rings, I slip my laptop into my bag. I only have one more period to get through before the day is over. I push open the library doors when I see Andrea, twenty feet away. Headed in my direction.

Then, I realize, she's headed straight for me.

"Lex said you might be here," she says.

I take her in, all five feet three of her. Her round brown eyes are identical to her sister's, at least from the photos of Vic I've seen. "I want you to hear it from me first. We want you back on the team."

I'm not expecting this. At all.

I wonder how the news hit her and her family this past weekend. I can't even imagine. I've really never considered it from her perspective. I've been too selfishly consumed in my own shit. But if my sister had died, and my teammate was hooking up with the guy who I thought killed her?

I'd be fucking livid.

"I owe you an apology," I tell her. "I mean I owe you more than that, but I just want you to know that I'm sorry."

"Just so you know, Mara told me about her idea with the

necklace," Andrea says. "I told her to do it. If it ended up saving another girl from the Crestmonts, I thought it was worth it."

"I understand," I tell her.

Andrea clenches her jaw. "The police are testing the blood on the bikini top. I mean, it's going to be Vic's. But seeing it ..." She shakes her head. "It was like finding out she was dead all over again."

I swallow hard.

Do I tell her about finding it? Would that make things worse? I don't even know how I would begin to explain everything.

"I'm sorry," I mumble again.

Her hands fiddle with her backpack zipper. She opens it, revealing a package of something that looks like a glazed breakfast pastry.

"Stickies are a Happy Valley staple." She hands the box to me. "My family fries them up and we eat them with champurrado. It was Vic's favorite comfort meal. That's the only thing getting me through this right now. Focusing on the happy memories."

"Thank you," I tell her.

I'm overcome with emotion. I bite my cheek. My old habit.

"I know we didn't really welcome you to the team," she says. "My sister was always the best at that."

"My past sort of preceded me," I say honestly.

"That account has always been total bullshit, by the way,"

Andrea says, zipping up her backpack. "I know the team reads it but I stopped ever since they posted some nasty shit about Vic."

I clench the box of stickies in my hands. I kind of remember Lex saying something about that, when we were in the basement together.

"That's awful."

"Yeah," Andrea says. "They said she slept with anything that had a pulse. I tried to get them banned from Instagram but that's a joke."

"Do you remember if . . . they ever said similar things about Jess, after she died?" I probe.

I'm wondering if I missed anything.

Andrea shakes her head. "I don't think so. They completely trashed Trevor when Jess died. I guess they pick and choose which victims they want to support."

Weird.

Would Trevor really trash his own reputation in some kind of self-sabotage if he was the one behind the account? There haven't been any new posts since he died. Which is noteworthy.

John is the only other person I can think of who would have had intimate details about my life, about Clint and the fire, seeing how close he is to Robbie. Then I think of the way he's always trying to hide his phone. It's like as soon as he gets a notification, he puts his phone away.

Maybe after he hooked up with Robbie, he was mad at

Victoria. He took it out in the only way he knew how. An anonymous forum.

"I still report every post with the hopes that one day it'll get shut down," Andrea says. "But anyway. Friday is senior night, and we're going to do something special for my sister since this would be her senior year, too." She slings her backpack up on her shoulder. "I hope you'll be there."

"I will," I promise.

She walks away. I'm left clutching the stickies in my hands, trying to make sense of all the info she's just given me.

THIRTY-TWO

"I think the question is, do you want to rejoin?" Mom asks me.

She's at the stove, stirring a pot of homemade sauce. I guess Mark's cooking has really rubbed off on her.

The old me would never. The old me would have clung to my ego, held a grudge until I graduated. Punished myself. But I'm trying to move on from that. I'm trying to be better.

I think about everything Andrea told me today.

"If Andrea wants me to rejoin the team, I will," I tell Mom.

She tears off fresh basil and adds it to the pot. "I'm glad that you'll be able to play out your last season."

"Senior night's on Friday, by the way," I tell Mom.

"It's on my calendar already," she says, smiling. "Mark and I will be there to cheer you on."

I don't know what it is. I've been doing so well, tolerating this relationship, but this time I can't stay silent.

"Why can't it just be you sometimes? Without Mark?"

It's finally out there.

Mom turns off the burner. I watch the way her shoulders sink. She bites her lip, gripping her wooden spoon in one hand. "It has always been just me. For years. Now you have two people in your corner. Three if you count Ainsley—"

I roll my eyes. "He's like your parasitic twin at this point," I snap.

"That's a really nice sentiment," she says, turning from me.

"I'm just saying. Sometimes I like doing things with just us two."

"He's been nothing but nice to you—"

"You're missing my point. He's a nice guy, but I just—"

"He's gracious and generous, Lauren. He cooks meals for you every time he's here."

"I'm not saying he isn't!" I explode. "I'm not the one dating him, Mom! I don't want to spend every waking second of my life with him. He's not my dad."

Mom runs her spoon under the faucet. She shuts the water off with such force it almost makes me jump. "You're right. He isn't," she says darkly. "Your dad really set you up for success, didn't he?"

My heart's pounding. "What is that supposed to mean?"

"We got the chance to move across the country and start over thanks to Mark. Your dad could never hold a candle to that. Now we're here and I'm finally, I don't know, I feel like you can't even let me have this one good thing."

I bite the inside of my cheek. My old comfort. I feel my teeth slip deeper inside the tissue until it finally pierces the surface and the familiar taste tangs in my mouth.

Mom stares at me, her eyes wide. "I feel like you're not

even giving this place a chance. You're not giving Mark a chance—"

"You're right," I say. "I'm trying to fuck up your life just as much as I did back home. In fact, I think I can do even worse."

"Do you know how lucky you are to be able to start over?" Mom's yelling now. "How lucky we are?"

But I'm already gone. I slam the door on my way out.

Because she's wrong. I might be the unluckiest person alive.

I can do one good thing, at least. Let her and Mark eat in peace tonight.

I hit the McDonald's drive-through and sit in the parking lot, cranking my seat back. I told myself I didn't move here to make friends. But it low-key sucks. I don't even have a reliable hookup anymore.

I shovel a few fries into my mouth. If I would have just brought my own bottle of sunscreen on the boat, would Trevor still be alive right now? Would any of this have happened?

I can't go down that rabbit hole of what-ifs.

Stay in the present.

At least I learned one useful thing from all those therapy sessions.

My phone dings with a notification. I glance at it, where it sits in the empty drink console. It's an Instagram notification.

I choke down the last bit of fry, knowing I've only set alerts for one account. The Unhappiest of Valleys.

My heart thuds in my chest.

I wipe my greasy fingers on a paper napkin and pick up my phone. I slide it open.

The new post from the infamous account is a photo of the *Centre Daily Times*. I catch the date in the top corner. September 26. Tomorrow's date. This is tomorrow's newspaper that hasn't even gone out yet.

LOCAL ATTORNEY CALLS OFF SECOND OPINION
IN SON'S DEATH

A shadow of uncertainty has swirled over the Crestmont family for years, but after Trevor Crestmont's untimely death, that uncertainty may be coming to an end. As we reported last week . . .

My eyes dart to the caption below the photo of the article.

Thanks to our inside source, we're sharing the news before it's official tomorrow. And I have to say, good thinking, Lionel. Better to pull out of the second medical examiner's opinion now before it reveals how much of a complete embarrassment you and your family are. Because all that it would reveal is what the first medical examiner said: Trevor killed himself by intentionally overdosing. He killed himself because he couldn't live with what he'd done. Except he didn't have the guts to admit he murdered more than one girl.

Giving someone a speedball who's never even done a line before is premeditated behavior.

And before you all go pity poor emo-heartthrob Robbie, ask yourself: How much did he know? He and his brother were, allegedly, best friends. This can't come as a total shock to him.

Something tells me you aren't as innocent as you pretend to be.

Ketchup burns the back of my throat.

I scroll backward. I keep scrolling until I find a caption that mentions Vic. It's from last October. Right after Jess died.

It's a picture of a small, makeshift memorial in front of Valley High, with cards and photos and flowers.

It's time to show up for Jess Ebenstein. It's funny how some of you are such big fans of Victoria now that she's dead. You're romanticizing her. How quickly you forget.

Remember the sophomore girl who got caught with the freshman boy in the biology lab on top of each other?

Yeah, that was Victoria. With Trevor Crestmont. Our source says she—

I can't read any more. This is stooping low. Really low.

I may not have all the answers. But if I can, at the very least, find out who is really behind this account, that'll mean more to Andrea than just my apology.

THIRTY-THREE

I cleat up for the first time in over a week. A soft drizzle of rain hits the back of my neck as I jog over to our field. I ditch my bag on one of the benches and join our warm-up, working on foot skills.

No one acknowledges I'm back. I wasn't exactly expecting a homecoming, I guess. But neutrality is better than the alternative.

After thirty minutes, we switch to first-touch drills.

"O'Brian!" someone shouts.

Andrea.

She's halfway across the field, at the goal. She takes a ball and punts it. Toward me.

It launches through the air and I run to meet it, catching it with the inside of my cleat. A perfect trap.

I smile. At least I can still do one thing right.

I take a chance, passing the ball over to Gwen. She peppers with me for a bit, practicing different strikes, until Coach blows his whistle. We jog over, huddling up.

"I'd like to welcome Lauren back," Coach says, nodding in my direction.

All eyes are on me. I should be used to it by now but it never fails to make my stomach twist.

"Thank you for handling this situation with grace," Coach says.

"You've been really patient with us as we navigate this," Lex says, ever the diplomat. Then her eyes lock on Mara. She clears her throat.

I feel the heaviness of Mara's exhale from across the huddle.

"I felt like our warnings weren't being taken seriously," Mara says. "I tend to escalate things . . . especially when it comes to Vic."

I think back to what Andrea said.

"It was warranted," I say. I mean it.

Mara gives me a look that tells me she accepts this truce, and it's like for the first time since we've met, I feel like we might actually begin to understand each other.

"Thank you, ladies," Coach says. Then he turns to address the entire team. "Let's transition into some corner kick plays."

The huddle breaks. We jog onto the field and that's when I feel a forceful tug on my practice jersey. I turn around. It's Coach. His eyes peer down at me.

He's clean-shaven today. For the first time, I notice he has freckles. Light ones. Across his nose. Some under his eyes.

"I wanted to apologize, too. For not giving you the benefit of the doubt," he says.

"Thanks," I say. "I appreciate it."

"Now get out there and make me proud," he says, letting me go.

This is the feeling I've missed. The soles of my feet aching; a spot under my left shin guard already ripening with a fresh bruise; my skull sore from my tight ponytail. My mind isn't racing like it normally is. When I'm on the field, I'm at peace.

I haul my stuff toward the outdoor vending machine. I haven't bothered stocking up on Gatorade since I wasn't exactly prepared to finish out the season. I put a couple of dollars in the slot and select A4.

It drops under the metal flap with a satisfying clunk: Glacier Cherry. Ice-cold. I grab it and chug half the bottle, sugar and salt rushing into my veins.

"I know this took a while. But I told you I wouldn't give up."

I turn around, finding Lex. Alone.

"Thank you," I say, hiccuping a deep breath. It's like I'm suddenly getting choked up. I'm relieved to be back. More than I realized.

"Ever since Trevor died . . ." She tugs the prewrap out of her hair and wraps it around her wrist. Snaps it into place. "It's been really hard. For the team. It brings up a lot of old feelings, you know?"

"I think his death has been triggering for a lot of people," I say in agreement.

Lex takes a deep breath, but I still pick up on the way her voice shakes. "The whole thing is really sad," she says. "Is Robbie . . . surviving?"

"To be honest," I say, because Lex has proven herself, and I feel like I can trust her, "he doesn't think Trevor killed Victoria."

Lex stares at me. She blinks twice, fast. "He thinks someone framed Trevor?" she asks.

"Yes."

Lex fiddles with the prewrap on her wrist. "Does he have any idea who?"

"No," I say. "I know you must have spent time around Trevor while Vic was alive, since Mara was her best friend. Do you think he could really be innocent?"

Lex picks up her cleats. "If he is, I hope the truth comes out sooner than later," she says. She gives me one last look before she leaves. I feel like she wants to say something else, but decides against it.

Then I can't help but wonder if she knows something I don't.

THIRTY-FOUR

After practice, I have the house to myself. Mom's out with Mark, I'm guessing. We haven't exactly been talking since our fight last night. I don't know what she expects me to do. If she only knew what I've been through this last month, I know she'd take back what she said.

There's a knock on the door. I take the last bite of my peanut butter sandwich before I answer it.

I find Robbie standing on the front porch, his hair tousled, his muscle tee tucked into his black jeans.

Did I miss a text from him?

"What are you doing here?" I ask.

Peanut butter sticks to the roof of my mouth. I run my tongue over my teeth, hoping I don't have, like, a piece of crust stuck somewhere.

"I was really hoping we could talk," he says. "If you aren't busy. I wasn't trying to catch you off guard, I just . . ."

"It's okay," I tell him. "I'm not busy."

I lead him into the kitchen. My hands find the silverware drawer. I hold on to it, feeling the cool metal handle in between my clammy fingers. My eyes drift to Robbie. I picture him the way I first met him, at Valley Hospice, with his navy volunteer shirt untucked.

I tie my hair into an even tighter ponytail, trying to get a grip. That version of him is gone.

He's standing by the kitchen table, looking up at the photos of me and Mom on the wall. My fifth-grade graduation. Take your kid to work day when I was seven and wearing a three-sizes-too-big set of magenta scrubs. The cringey photo shoot we did at a portrait studio when I was in middle school.

Robbie touches one of the frames gingerly, like it's a photo of his own family instead of mine.

"I always wished my house felt like this growing up," he says. His eyes meet mine. "I can tell your mom loves you a lot."

I slide my fingers over the metal handle of the drawer, releasing my grasp. "I think you're romanticizing my life."

"Yeah," he says. "I could be."

He leaves the table and slides toward the kitchen island. Until he's standing right across from me. "I know things have been different between us. For a while." His eyes burn through me. "I don't know how to act around you. How you want me to act. How I should act. If I just go with my intuition . . . I don't even know what that feels like anymore."

He bites his lip, and I try not to stare at his mouth. "I swear I practiced what I was going to say to you but now I'm rambling."

"I guess it's because . . . I don't know what to believe any-more," I say honestly. Since he's being honest with me, too. "Or, at least, I didn't. For a while. Until now."

I know I don't have concrete proof. I don't have a video playback I can watch of that night at Lake Monarch, of Robbie and Vic. I don't know what really happened to her out there in the water, or how her bloodied top made its way to that compartment and out again. I don't have any way of knowing if Trevor was actually the one behind it.

But what I've realized is that if Robbie had been the one to kill Victoria, he'd make sure to convince me and John that Trevor's death really was from suicide. It would be the only logical thing to do. To protect himself.

He didn't do that.

I hug my arms together. "You called me on my bullshit that night at the cemetery. You were right. I lied to you."

We both know this. But I need to say it out loud. I owe him that. "I want to say it and mean it this time. I don't know who killed Victoria. But I know it wasn't you."

It's like he's waited a lifetime to hear those words.

"Thank you," he says.

He reaches his hand across the kitchen island that sepa-rates us and takes my hand. I try not to get caught up in the way my body feels when we touch.

"I never thought I could have moments like this after everything that's happened," he says.

"Moments like this?" I ask, but my voice cracks.

Saying we're having a moment goes against our original agreement. Robbie was always just a hookup. Just a distraction.

He—we—could never be more than that.

"After Vic died," he says, "I couldn't stand being in Happy Valley anymore. I went to stay with my aunt in Chicago that summer, and that's when I changed my number. I wanted to disappear. I didn't want anyone contacting me." He grimaces. "But being that far away from home . . . I was too far away from Vic. I came back and started volunteering at Valley Hospice. I mean, I know the only reason why they let me is because of my family's massive endowment."

He swallows. "I just wanted to be close to her. Like if I was in all the places she used to occupy, that somehow, I'd keep her closer for longer. I was already starting to forget the way she smelled. The inflections of her voice. I was desperate."

He walks around the island now, to be on the same side as me. "Then you walked in that Saturday, and . . ."

I inhale sharply. "And what?" I ask.

"I met you right after the Fourth of July. The two-year anniversary of her death."

I get chills. He's so close to me I could reach out and touch the waistband of his jeans.

"It felt like . . . ," he says. "Like I was allowed to have hope again. I know that sounds weird—"

"It doesn't. Sound weird."

I felt the same warmth when I first saw him. Something

I hadn't felt since before the fire. Even if I've done everything since to pretend otherwise.

We're leaning into each other, and his mouth meets mine.

For the first time since I've kissed someone else, I'm not thinking about Clint.

THIRTY-FIVE

I ended the kiss first. It felt wrong to keep going. When I'm here and Vic isn't. When we still have so much work to do.

But I'd be lying to myself if I said I didn't think about Robbie for the rest of last night.

Now I'm in John's finished basement, sitting in between John and Robbie on a leather couch. Robbie's leg is two inches away from mine. I scoot closer to John.

Trevor's binder is opened on the coffee table. I notice Robbie's added a new page that says:

TIMELINE—TREVOR
September 11th—Trevor found near dead in Valley
High parking lot. Day of pep rally.
September 23rd—Letter and bikini top found at
homecoming game

"We need fresh theories," John says. "Fresh energy. Fresh everything."

I glance up, trying to think. On the wall in front of me are family portraits from John's childhood. A Black woman with tortoiseshell glasses and a Mickey Mouse T-shirt has her arm around a much younger John in front of the castle at Disney World. She must be his mom. In another photo, his parents are posing at the Nittany Lion Shrine, both wearing scrubs. John sits on the top of the lion statue, holding on to a play stethoscope.

He catches my gaze. "Cut to: No way in hell am I going into healthcare like my parents," he says.

"Same," I agree.

Then I notice his phone is in his palm. John is never not holding his phone. I glance back up at him.

"What about the Instagram post?" I ask. "The latest one about Trevor on the Unhappiest of Valleys account?"

The post I know inside and out, since I've looked at it almost as many times as the one about me.

"Whoever is behind it has it out for him," John says. "The amount of vitriol in their captions is truly something to behold."

"I actually thought it was Trevor behind the account," I admit, "at least I did, before that last post went live."

"He abhorred social media," Robbie says.

"That'd be impossible," John says quickly.

We make eye contact.

"Exactly."

I pull out my phone and find the account.

I scroll past the recent post on Trevor, then the one about

me. The other recent ones are about a pregnancy test some- one got caught using. Someone giving someone else a blow job at the football stadium. A teacher who got caught buying alcohol for a student. But beyond that, most of the content is about the infamy surrounding the Crestmonts. Mainly Jess and Trevor. Some Robbie and Vic ones are sprinkled in, too, including the gross post about Vic I read the other day.

I look up and catch John typing very, very quickly on his phone before pocketing it.

"What?" he asks.

But then I don't say it fast enough. "Oh, come on. You can't seriously be thinking I'm the imbecile behind this account," John says.

"I didn't say that."

"Just because I don't want the world knowing that I'm talking to a first year at Penn State doesn't mean I'm guilty of anything," he says.

I know my face is scarlet right now.

"With the amount of gossip in this town, I've wanted to keep my romantic life a little more private," John says.

"I didn't actually think it was you," I try to explain meekly.

"Now that *that's* out of the way," John says, scrolling on his own Instagram. "The Unhappiest of Valleys has only been around for the past year or so. People only started talking about it after Jess died."

He pulls up an early post and we look at it.

It's a photo of Jess from a Valley High art showcase.

Jess Ebenstein should be alive right now. But someone got in the way of that. Someone whose name sounds like Shemver Lestmont. Because let's be honest: Jess was an artist, someone who preferred quality over quantity when it came to who she spent her time with. She wasn't a partier. Wasn't the type to do a speedball just for shits and gigs.

But Shemver Lestmont? C'mon. He has to cope somehow, after the shitstorm of last year and everything that happened between his brother and Victoria Moreno, whose death was also anything but straightforward. A wound on her chest and drowning? That doesn't scream accident to me.

This time is going to be different. This time, the Lestmonts will be held accountable.

"Whoever is behind this was close to Jess," I'm realizing out loud.

She never came to mind at first. I didn't think she'd have that kind of access to my own past. But she does. Through her dad.

"Ainsley Anderson," I say, darkening my phone screen.

"Jess's best friend," John says.

"My mom's also dating her dad," I say. "She could have learned about my past from him, or at least parts of it, and then filled in the rest of the blanks. And she obviously has a thing against the Crestmonts. When she found out I was . . .

involved with Robbie, she'd have a reason to try and annihilate my reputation, too. That gives her motive."

I think back to the Cheesecake Factory. "She made such a big deal of the fact that she and Jess never did drugs and she'd never touch them, but we went to dinner with our parents and I caught her doing coke in the bathroom."

"That's one wild family dinner," John says.

"Yeah. Like I get there's shame involved with drugs but it was over the top, how she swore on Jess's grave she'd never do them. Like she was trying to convince me of something she couldn't even convince herself of."

"Jess could have taken drugs with Ainsley the night she died," Robbie says. "That could be why Ainsley lied. She feels guilty about Jess's death."

"But it wasn't like she intentionally killed her," I say.

"But if she gave her best friend the thing that led to her death? That's heavy," John says. "If she was in denial, then she needed someone else to blame."

"Is it completely insane to wonder if she could have killed Trevor?" I ask.

John's eyes widen. I look at Robbie, who's hunched over on the couch. It's so silent that I have to keep talking to fill the void. "She'd have the right motive," I say quietly. "And she has access to drugs. She could have drugged him."

"But how would she even do that? What would make her do it now, after all this time?" John asks.

Robbie plays with one of the rings on his finger. He takes

it off, then pushes it down past his knuckle. "We need to prove she runs the account first," he says finally, "and we need to ask her what she knows to find out whether she's connected to his death or if she's just a shitty person."

"I can ask my mom to have Mark and Ainsley over for dinner. I can try to get access to her phone to get proof," I say.

As soon as I say it, I wonder how the hell I'm going to pull it off.

I just know I have to. Because right now, it's the best plan we have.

THIRTY-SIX

Mom works a double shift, which means I don't see her in person at all on Friday. I text her to remind her to be there an hour before our game starts because it's senior night. Then I ask if we can do a dinner, the four of us, this weekend. She'll be ecstatic. Maybe she'll think it's my way of apologizing for our fight. But work must be unusually busy for her, because all she sends is a text that says *running late.*

She's probably getting a quick nap in before she drives over. A thirty-minute snooze and a chai latte, and she'll have as much energy as someone who just slept for eight hours.

I tighten the laces of my cleats, pull my hair up into a ponytail, and refill my water bottle. The locker room's quieter than normal. All the underclassmen are already out on the field, setting up for tonight. I always imagined what it would finally feel like to be a senior on the team, and have Tori Higgins, the sophomore I was closest to back at Wintergreen High, present me.

Now senior night is just another night. A blip on the radar of my high school career.

I push open the door that leads outside and a cold burst

of air greets me. The sun is quickly disappearing, leaving a rose-gold haze on the horizon. Happy Valley is headed toward winter faster than I'd like, and I'm a little bit terrified. The only time I've been in the snow was for a few days of snowboarding in Tahoe. And a few days was more than enough.

I hustle over to our field. Parents and families already fill the bleachers. Mara's mom sets up a refreshment table with more snacks than I could ever hope to have at a game: oranges, apples, peanut butter, Gatorade, and even sliced stickies. Lining the side of the field, I spot dozens of bouquets, filled with roses, marigolds, and lilies, hanging out in buckets of water. One of the sophomores sets up a microphone in the middle of the field, and a couple of juniors position the speakers.

Mara and Andrea set up a huge easel and place a large oil painting of Victoria on it. She's in her uniform, a soccer ball gripped underneath her arm, the background swirled in a kaleidoscope of color. Then Andrea adorns it with flowers. Mara gives Andrea a huge hug before jogging over to the rest of the seniors.

I can't help but notice the signature in the lower right corner of the canvas. *Ainsley Anderson.*

That's what she must have been in Coach's office for.

I drop off my bag on our team bench.

"Lauren," Coach says.

I whip around. He takes a sip of his energy drink and squeezes my shoulder. "I just wanted to say that you deserve to feel celebrated tonight."

"Thanks, Coach."

He releases me from his grip and I jog over to the other seniors. We line up beside the makeshift stage area with the microphone.

"We're all wearing them tonight," Mara says, materializing in front of me, her hand held out. "I promise."

I look down, finding a gold pendant of the number sixteen in a long, elegant scrawl. Vic's number. When I look even closer, I notice the numbers connect together so that they form what looks like a *V*.

I look up at Mara. True to her word, she's wearing one, too, beside the crescent moon necklace.

"My mom had them custom made for us in India when she went to visit my family a couple months ago," she says. "I wanted them to be perfect."

"They're beautiful," I tell her.

"I know," she says, grinning. She beelines for Gwen.

I go to fasten it around my neck but struggle with the clasp.

"Allow me," Lex says.

She gets it on the first try.

"Thank you," I tell her, taking a breath as the spotlights surrounding the field automatically turn on.

"Robbie aside," Lex says, leaning into me, "I think Vic would have liked you."

It's something I've tried not to think about. What Vic would think of me. What she thinks of me, if she's out there in the ether somewhere, somehow.

I look up at the sky. The moon is pearl white. Every time I look at it now, I can't help but think of Vic. I may have never met her, but I can feel her. I can feel the love everyone has for her here. They'd do anything for her. They'd do anything to have her back.

I can't believe I've held a piece of her clothing in my hands. The clothing she was wearing when she died.

My chest tightens.

Lex rubs my shoulder, like she can sense what emotional wavelength I'm on. I can only nod as a thanks. But it's not just me. When I look up, I see Mara at the mic. The whispers in the stands suddenly hush as she begins to speak.

"Thank you all for coming tonight," she begins. Her voice nearly trembles. "We're here to celebrate our seniors, a class that I'm so proud and honored to be a part of. We've waited years for this moment, this special rite of passage in every Valley Higher's life. And I'll admit, usually it's preceded by a roast of the senior class, paper plate–award style. I know it's not Coach's favorite thing, but he's come to accept it with grace."

Coach looks on from the sidelines. I can't help but notice his eyes are watering, too.

Mara briefly smiles. She grips the mic harder, steadying herself. "But tonight calls for something different. Because Victoria is supposed to be here with us, and she's not."

Mara's gaze drifts to the painting of Vic, to her smiling face. "Victoria Moreno was my best friend. She was a teammate to everyone. She would have been captain this year if she was still with us."

Mara's cheeks are already wet with tears, but she keeps going. "She was the best striker I've ever played with, and I looked up to her, as center midfielder."

A pang of shock hits me. Mara was center mid? She seems like such a natural forward. "After she passed, I wanted to make her proud. I took up her position, writing her number, number sixteen, in Sharpie on the inside of my wrist before every single game. It became my ritual. This year, I finally got it tattooed for real."

She glances over near the food table. "Sorry, Mom."

Mara turns back to the mic and smiles. "Vic's heart was unmatched. Somehow she found time to not only be an incredible athlete but a dean's scholar, too. She volunteered on the weekends and helped everyone without asking for anything in return. Her death broke so many of us, because it was surreal. It isn't fair. It makes no sense to me why she had to die the way she did."

She pauses, taking a sip of water. "I always thought, somehow, if I knew who did it, if I knew what happened in her last moments, that it would make the hurt less. It doesn't. If anything, it just makes me miss her even more."

Lex leans her head on my shoulder. I hold her, as tightly as I can, as her body shakes with sobs.

"Today we carry Vic's memory with us," Mara says. "She's with us every time we take the field, and it makes our wins that much sweeter. She deserves this senior night as much as the rest of us. Now I'd like to welcome Andrea Moreno and Mrs. Moreno to commemorate Vic's senior status."

Mara leaves the mic and picks up the largest bouquet out of the water buckets. Andrea takes a deep breath and then she walks toward her, and Mara hands her the flowers. Then they embrace. Like they need each other more than anything else in the world. Mara says something to Andrea, and she releases her from their hug.

A petite woman dressed in slacks comes onto the field from the stands. Mrs. Moreno. Vic looks just like her. She embraces Mara and then Andrea, holding her daughter tight.

Mara returns to the mic. She pats her eyes with a tissue, then turns to Andrea as she speaks.

"Vic would be so beyond proud of you, Andrea. You've become our secret weapon, a formidable player all in your own right. She knew you'd make varsity when you became a freshman and she was incredibly stoked to be on the same team as you. It was all she could talk about. So much so that she owed me a scoop from the Creamery each time she mentioned how excited she was, because I literally never heard the end of it."

Lex sniffles, letting out a laugh. Andrea laughs, too, and wipes her eyes.

"But in all seriousness, you're carrying on her legacy. I'm giving you my captain's band to wear tonight, in honor of Vic, and to prepare for next year, when you'll be a team captain. I know the team will be in amazing hands with you at the helm. I love you."

Mara takes her captain's band and puts it around Andrea's arm, and then she throws her hands up, gesturing to the crowd. We yell and applaud her, the intense emotion turning into a tour de force of celebration. Mara, Mrs. Moreno, and Andrea all embrace again, and then Sophia's coming up to the mic to introduce the next senior.

Then before I know it, it's my turn. I'm sure the speech I get will be the shortest out of all my teammates, which I'm prepared for. They still barely know me.

To my shock, it's Mara who comes back up to the mic.

Her gaze meets mine, and she smiles. "I promise I'm not here to humiliate you," she says, addressing me. I laugh nervously, glad I have this bouquet to partially hide behind.

"Lauren O'Brian is a newcomer to the team and to Valley High, and let's just say we put her through the ringer to really make sure she fit in with us," Mara says. "I'm happy to say she passed. Even though I can hear Vic in my ear, telling me that sometimes, maybe, I take it a bit too far because I'm extra. The thing is, I knew Lauren was one of us from her first day of tryouts."

She turns toward me, speaking into the mic. "The way you cross the ball, how you do that little leap thing when you land that you probably don't even realize you do? Vic did the same thing. I think that's why I took a while to warm up to you, to be honest. Because it scared me. Because it made me miss her and I'm careful now with who I get close to. It's like the fewer people I let in, the fewer people I'd ever have to miss."

Chills run down my spine. I could have said those same words myself. The fewer people I'm close to, the fewer people I'm likely to hurt.

"I'm looking forward to the rest of our season together," she says, "and I mean it when I say you're one of our most talented players."

The crowd erupts in applause, like they do for all the seniors. I can't even compute what Mara's said to me. About me. Because I don't know if anyone's said anything that nice to me before. Then Mara's giving me a hug, and it feels like a release. Like we're both letting go of everything that's happened.

For the first time, I feel like I'm finally part of this team.

"You've always done everything for the team," I tell her. "I would have done the same thing if I was you."

"Lex never wanted you to take a break," Mara says. "She spoke out when all the captains met, and even after Coach addressed everyone. She always had your back. She's truly my better half."

I squeeze her one more time, and then she steps back into line. I'm left standing alone, waiting for Mom to make her way through so we can take the iconic parent-senior-night photo. But after the clapping has died down, and Mom still hasn't materialized, I realize, for the first time tonight, that maybe she's not even here.

I scan the bleachers, trying to glimpse her face, or even Mark's face, but they're nowhere to be found.

I don't want to hold up the entire night. I take my picture solo, then find my place back in line before the red-hot flush of embarrassment colors my cheeks.

Is Mom still holding a grudge after our little tiff? Or did she sleep through her alarms and is still in bed, completely unaware she's missing this?

During the rest of the senior introductions, I keep glancing up at the stands, seeing if she'll show up late. But then the introductions are ending, and there's still no sign of her. Then I have no choice but to put her out of my mind because our opponents arrive. If there was ever pressure on for us to win a game, it's tonight.

THIRTY-SEVEN

We crush Jamberry Township 4–0. I give Mara two assists, and feel the pressure to prove myself ease up. Postgame, I'm spent. I down two Gatorades and peel off my shin guards, letting the cold fall air hit my legs. I ride the high from our win until I watch as each one of my teammates is embraced by their parents. Some with grandparents, aunts and uncles, cousins, the whole extended family.

My one relative didn't even bother showing up.

I half expected Mom to run up to me as soon as our postgame debrief with Coach was over and profusely apologize for oversleeping, for working longer than she anticipated, for having a flat tire. Some kind of excuse.

But I haven't even gotten a text from her. I darken my phone and chuck it into my bag. As I'm leaving, I notice someone familiar in the stands, talking to Mrs. Moreno.

Robbie.

I wonder if he's been here the entire time.

He's nodding, and then she reaches out to him and hugs him. He hugs her back and they stay like that for a long time.

I avert my eyes, giving them their moment. I wonder if this is the first time they've spoken since Vic died.

As I walk to my car, I see someone speed walking toward me in a flurry, her red hair like wildfire in the chilly night wind.

Mom.

A little fucking late.

Panic sets in her face when she sees me. "Shit, Lauren, I'm so sorry."

I cross my arms, the heat blanket of my own sweat quickly evaporating. I give her a once-over. She's not in her scrubs. She's in one of her nicest dresses, which tells me everything I need to know.

"We were planning on being here but we were seated late—" Mom says.

I'm suddenly getting emotional and I don't know why. I bite it back, channeling my anger instead.

"Your date night couldn't have waited two more hours? You literally just missed the only positive moment of my entire high school career."

Mom clutches on to her purse even tighter. "Mark planned a little surprise—"

"What did he plan, a candlelit dinner? No straight man has ever come up with something so original," I snap.

Mom sighs out a deep breath. "I wanted this to be a happy moment when I told you, but that's my own fault." Then she holds her hand out, and I notice something glittering on her left ring finger. "I'm engaged," she says softly as my blood turns to sludge. "After Andrew . . ."

I stand there, speechless.

"You have every right to be pissed out of your mind at me," she says, "but maybe in some time you can be happy for me after I've made it up to you."

It would be easy to ruin this moment for her. To stamp out her happiness with my disappointment.

But now, I realize, I'll be closer to Ainsley, and she could have answers to what really happened to Jess that night at the party. To what really happened to Trevor.

I've always been a good liar.

It's how I managed to convince Mom and Andrew that I'd only smoked a single cigarette one time, the night of the fire, when I'd been smoking almost a pack a day for a year. I had to explain why I had a lighter on me.

It's how I managed to keep everything with Donovan a secret when Clint was finally released from the hospital.

"I am happy for you," I say, trying to sound as convincing as possible. "I get it. This is a once-in-a-lifetime moment. How about we plan a celebration dinner? All four of us, Ainsley included," I say.

Mom's entire face lights up, but then her smile falls. "Really? You're not bullshitting me?"

Is it sad that my own mom thinks I'd do exactly what I'm doing?

"Of course not."

She pulls me into a hug. The smell of her honey-scented hair fills my nose. "I'm going to make this up to you," she says. "I promise."

THIRTY-EIGHT

John and Robbie set up for their band's gig at a café in downtown Happy Valley while I sit on one of the pleather chairs and scroll through Ainsley's Instagram account. Playing music together is one of the only things keeping them sane right now. The same way soccer is for me. Especially given that Mom is completely checked out of my life. An entire week has gone by since she told me she's engaged and I don't know how to process it. We've already uprooted our lives once this year. I don't want to think about having to change houses again or deal with moving in with Mark. Or God forbid Ainsley.

John tightens one of his drums. "What's your plan for tonight?" he asks. "Going to steal her phone while she does a line of coke in your guest bathroom?"

I glance up from a post of Ainsley at her art showcase earlier this month. She's wearing the same dress she wore the first night I met her, and Mark's arm is around her. I'd bet money that she was high when the photo was taken.

"I was thinking I'll ask to save my contact into her phone," I say. "You know. Now that we're going to be sisters and all."

Robbie tests his mic. "I think the only perks of having my parents date who they date is that they don't have kids. It's just me and Trevor." He sets the mic into place. "Or I guess it's just me now. Fuck."

The mic gets jammed and Robbie yanks it back out. "God, it sucks. I didn't think I'd ever have to deal with it by myself."

"You don't," I say, maybe a little too quickly. "You have us."

"You're going to sleep over every night and listen to sex sounds coming from the master bedroom?" Robbie quips, and the mood instantly lightens.

"Ew," I say. "You can *hear* them?"

"I mean, I have earplugs. But sometimes they're loud."

I shudder, thinking of having to listen in on Mom's sex life. I'd rather die.

Then the little bell to the café rings. I turn around, catching Lionel as he walks through the door with Stacy.

Robbie looks up at his dad. Surprise flashes across his face. "You're staying for the show?" he asks. Almost like he's in disbelief.

Lionel shakes his head. His face looks hollower than the last time I saw him.

"I can't. We have to get a few things in order for the burial," he says.

Robbie's face falls at the mention of Trevor's burial. He moves on from his mic to tuning his guitar.

"But we wanted to tell you to break a leg," Lionel says as

Stacy picks up their mobile order. Then he sees me. "It meant a lot to us, seeing you at Trevor's calling hours, Lauren."

"Oh. Of course," I say quietly.

"Take care, you three," he says.

Then he's opening the door for Stacy, and they're gone. A few goth-adjacent girls and guys come in after him. Band groupies. I'm absolutely the odd one out in my practice clothes. Which is basically my own personal uniform at this point.

"Good luck tonight, Lauren," Robbie says from onstage as the lights come on. I try not to think about how hot he looks, holding his guitar.

———————

Mark and Mom serve a dinner of roasted butternut squash risotto and an arugula salad with apples and blue cheese. I take a bite of risotto and mentally rehearse what I'm going to say to Ainsley so that I can get my hands on her phone.

"Pass the Parmesan, please?" Mom asks.

I pass the cheese to Mom.

Maybe I can take a selfie on Ainsley's phone and set it as my contact photo. That would buy me more time.

"We're thinking of a spring wedding. Maybe in April," Mom says. She takes a sip of her chardonnay. "The weather is supposed to start clearing up by then but it's still not part of prime wedding season. That way we won't have to pay top dollar for everything."

"I think May is safer. Weather-wise," Ainsley says. Her

eyes are two big saucers. She's talking a mile a minute. It's honestly sort of mesmerizing the way she has no qualms about being high at our "family" dinner. "If you're doing an outdoor wedding there's less chance of rain, which I'm sure would be ideal given that you're going to be wearing a beautiful dress."

"That's a good point," Mom says, turning to Mark. "Lake Monarch could be pretty." She looks at me. "You had a great time up there."

A small piece of apple gets stuck in my throat. I chug water, trying to loosen it. "I mean, I didn't think rustic lake town was necessarily your vibe," I tell Mom. "There's also the fact that everyone associates Lake Monarch with Victoria's death."

"Your mom isn't the one involved with the Crestmonts," Ainsley says.

I peer at her, more amused than upset by her comment.

"Ainsley," Mark says. His tone is serious.

But Ainsley's eyes are dead set on mine.

"You mean Robbie? Who's innocent?" I say.

"Yeah. Right," Ainsley says, rolling her eyes.

"Enough, Ainsley," Mark says. "We're having an enjoyable night celebrating our engagement."

"Why am I here again?" Ainsley says. She gets up from the table and tosses her napkin on the chair.

Mom grips the stem of her wineglass. "Great," I hear her mutter.

"I think it's best you head to your mom's tonight," Mark tells Ainsley.

"Already planning on it," Ainsley says. Then she turns to my mom. "I hope this whole thing works out for you and doesn't become just another one of your failed relationships."

It's one thing for her to be a bitch, but to be a bitch to my mom, who's been nothing but nice to her?

"You are so fucking out of line," I say hotly.

"Ainsley, you need to apologize," Mark says at the same time.

But Ainsley's gone. The front door slams.

I suffered through this entire dinner for nothing. I'm not even going to get access to her phone tonight.

I look over at Mom, who stares out across the table like she's momentarily left her body. "Maybe this is all too soon," she says.

"Ainsley feels things deeply," Mark says, grabbing her hand, "but she'll come around."

It's like my heart twinges just then. I know I haven't exactly been super accepting of their relationship, either. I've been a killjoy, at best.

"That was a great dinner," I say, trying to lessen the somber mood. I grab some of the plates and bring them to the counter.

"Oh, it was one for the books," Mom says.

"Thanks for setting such a good example," Mark says,

looking at me. I stare at him, waiting for a punch line, but then I realize he's being genuine. It's probably the first time in my life someone has told me that I'm the one setting the good example. "Ainsley's mood is all over the place sometimes."

Probably because she does so much coke, Mark.

I run the water and soap up the sponge, telling them I'll take care of the dishes. As soon as I'm done, I text Robbie and John.

> **Unsuccessful. Ainsley left in the middle of dinner. It was kind of a shit show.**
>
> **She was already high.**

John is the first to reply.

> **There's a party tonight at Kevin McKinsey's house**
> **I bet she's going**

And then Robbie chimes in.

> **We should go in case**

I sigh out a deep breath. The last party I went to was Lex's, and that was sort of the beginning of . . . everything bad. But this is less for distraction and more to get access to Ainsley's phone. And I do not want to get stuck watching a John Wayne movie with Mom and Mark tonight.

Give me like ten minutes to get ready

I make a promise to myself: I'm not going to drink. I'm not falling into my old habits. Robbie replies.

Cool. We'll pick you up.

THIRTY-NINE

"Pulling out all the stops tonight," John says, meeting my gaze from the passenger's seat.

"Gotta fit the part," I say.

I catch Robbie eyeing me in the rearview and butterflies flood my stomach.

I'm wearing a low-cut black dress, tight in all the right places. My old go-to for nights out. Putting it on tonight felt like slipping into an old skin. It still smells like my old gardenia perfume, one I stopped wearing after the fire. I even did my hair tonight, curling it into waves. My normally plain lips are glossed, and I threw on some mascara and bronzer for good measure. For the finishing touch, I untied the necklace Mom gave me from my key ring and threaded it around my neck.

I can't believe I used to do this every weekend. It's way too much effort.

I look out the window as Robbie drives us in the direction of school, near where Kevin's house is. I have no idea who he is, just that he's a junior with a huge basement and his parents are the type that think if you're going to party, do it at our house.

Robbie parks up the street, far enough away from the epicenter of the chaos we're about to walk into. I can hear the bass vibrating through the sidewalk as we make our way up to a large brick house on a half acre of land. Valley Highers pile through the front door, descending down into the synth-y beat echoing from downstairs.

I trail behind Robbie and John, taking in the full scene. People are spilling drinks and making out on the suede couches. A group of varsity soccer guys play beer pong and watch Arsenal highlights on TV. The glass doors that lead outside open to a hot tub that's overflowing because too many barely clothed people are trying to fit inside.

John finds a handle of vodka and holds it up. "I'm indulging," he says.

"Go for it. I'm driving," Robbie says. He grabs a few red Solo cups off a stack and gives each of us one. Robbie fills his with soda, and I do the same. John mixes up some kind of concoction, then offers the handle to me.

I shake my head. "I have to be clearheaded tonight," I tell him.

"Right. You're our star tonight," he says, taking a sip of his drink. "Mm. Nothing like warm alcohol," he says.

"You're too bougie for this," Robbie jokes.

"I am, but this is complimentary so I can't complain," John says, sipping it. "It's not *terrible*."

I spin around the room, scanning for any sign of Ainsley.

"She's most likely in the bathroom if she's doing lines," Robbie says.

"Right," I say, trying to get in the headspace of someone who frequently does coke.

I spot a line of girls leaned up against a wall that turns the corner. Bingo.

"I'd give it a little time," John says, following my gaze. "You know, let the party warm up. The alcohol seep in. Especially if she was in a bad mood."

He's right. I don't want to come in too hot, either.

I take a sip of my drink. Part of me wishes it were alcoholic, to dull the nerves I'm feeling as more and more bodies surround me. More arms reach for handles. More fingers grasp for cups and chasers.

The other part of me is a little impressed that I've stuck to my plan of staying sober.

I sip my soda and follow John and Robbie through the thickening crowd when I bump into Lex and Mara.

"Hiiii!" Mara says, giving me a hug. This is still new for me, that she doesn't hate my guts. I tense up at first, out of habit, then relax into her embrace.

"Hey," I say, giving Lex a hug next.

Mara's eyes dart to John, then Robbie. There's an awkward

pause and I feel like I'm infringing on this . . . reunion. Vic was the connecting thread between them all.

Mara makes the first move. She gives John a hug, then Robbie. "It's been a while," Mara says.

Robbie squeezes her tightly. "It feels like yesterday that we were at Vic's birthday," he says. There's a warmth to his voice that I've never heard before.

"I still can't look at Mike's Hard Lemonade the same way," John says, and Mara laughs.

"Can you imagine if she could see us right now? She'd be proud of us," Mara says.

"She was always proud of you," Robbie says. "Your speech at senior night was really beautiful."

"Okay, stop. I am *not* crying tonight," Mara says, fanning her face. "I've already cried enough this week."

Robbie smiles. It's a real, genuine smile. He takes a step closer to me and I can't help but smile, too. This must be healing for him, in some way. For all of them.

Even if there is still the elephant in the room: Trevor.

"You two look cute together," Lex says, glancing at me, then Robbie, and Mara elbows her. Robbie chuckles. I'm way too sober for this.

Lex looks at me and smiles. Her face is flushed. "I already did two shots."

"We gotta pace ourselves," Mara says jokingly.

I laugh. It's nice to see Lex let loose for once.

Then some senior is shouting at the top of his lungs.

"WE ARE THE SENIORS!" he yells, and the basement erupts in cheers. Someone almost crashes into me, and another senior's drink trickles down my back. Then I'm separated from Lex and Mara, who are pulled in one direction. I feel a hand graze my back.

Robbie.

"This way," he's saying, pulling me out of the hurricane's path as the music blares into my skull. We find a pocket of relief near the stairs. I can finally hear my own thoughts again.

"I didn't necessarily disagree with what Lex said," he says.

He looks up at me, trying to read me.

I suck in a breath. Definitely too sober for this.

This is the part where I tell him I can't do this anymore, that our hookup is long over, that me pretending to still be into him served its purpose when I realized he's innocent.

But another part of me longs to stay. My legs find their place, perfectly in between his. I lean into the feeling, but then his hand grazes my hip and it's almost too much. I can't let myself go there right now.

"I should find Ainsley," I say.

He squeezes my hand, nodding. "Yeah," he says quietly.

I leave him by the stairs and make my way toward the bathroom. The line of girls becomes a trickle. One emerges, and I push in after her, finding a huge, sprawling bathroom filled with girls; some touch up their makeup at the mirror with two sinks; one pees; one yanks a towel off the shower door to soak up the alcohol on her skirt; another opens the door that leads outdoors.

I take a peek and see a gleam of pale skin under the moonlight, the huge tattoo on her leg almost iridescent. Ainsley. Laughing with a few other juniors I don't know near the hot tub. I watch her as more girls brush past me, giggling as the alcohol courses through their bloodstream. Everything seems way danker, being sober. I'm glad I'll wake up tomorrow morning without a raging hangover.

I decide not to approach Ainsley. Not yet. Not in front of her friends. Instead I perch myself atop the bathroom counter, where she's in my perfect view, and text Robbie and John that I've got eyes on her. Her friends are bound to get refills, and she's bound to want to do another line.

It takes a few more minutes before my prediction comes true. Her friend gestures toward inside, and Ainsley says something back before she heads for the bathroom.

I prepare by mussing up my hair, smearing my eye makeup just a little bit, and channeling my best inner drunk Lauren. When Ainsley walks into the bathroom, I swivel my head toward hers.

"Ainsley!"

I slur a little bit for effect, hopping down off the counter. Her face is confused at first, but after I give her a hug, I feel her defenses come down. I pull away, touching her shoulder. Drunk Lauren is always touchy-feely.

"Heyyyy," she says, her eyes bright, the inner corners

speckled with glitter. She's wearing a crop top and the tiniest of minidresses.

"I love the look," I tell her, touching her skirt. "Where is this from?"

"My mom," she says, smiling. "It's vintage."

"Amazing," I tell her. "I guess we're going to be, like, sisters?"

Ainsley laughs. "I guess. I'm sorry for dinner, I was just—"

"Oh my God," I interject. "Don't be sorry! It's, like, a lot, you know? I don't even know," I say, adding more slurring, squeezing her arm. This comes so naturally to me that it's scary.

Her arm relaxes against mine.

"Thank you. You're . . . really cool. I know I've been kind of all over the place."

"It's sooo understandable," I tell her.

She keeps shifting her weight, and I can tell she's antsy.

"I'm gonna go get a refill," she lies.

No, you're trying to find someplace where I won't see you do your next line.

I have to get access to her phone. Like right now.

"I know you're straight edge but do you have anyone who, you know . . . ," I say, whispering, trying to be coy. "Has any coke? I've been looking all night."

It's like she comes to life.

"My friend gave me some," she says, and I know she must

be in deep. She's not even trying to hide it right now. "I only did one line tonight. I know I told you—"

"You don't even have to explain," I say.

"I just didn't want you to think I was using, you know, with Jess . . ."

"This is a judgment-free zone," I tell her. I squeeze her arm again. I'm trying to put her at ease.

Her shoulders relax. Then she glances up and motions for me to follow her as she steps into the shower. I do, and then she slides the clouded glass door closed once we're inside. Then she reaches into her purse for a little baggie filled with white powder and what must be a new compact mirror. She holds it out to me.

With Trevor gone, maybe she doesn't have to hide who she is, or what she's doing. Because he was the one asking questions.

"Have as much as you want," she says, "this is like wayyy more than I'd ever know what to do with."

A lie. But that's okay. I'm lying, too.

"You first," I tell her. "Please do the honors."

She doesn't fight me on it, because I know she's been dying for a line ever since she walked into this bathroom. She sets her ID on top of the flat shower ledge, and pours some coke on top of it. Then she uses a credit card to ready her line and snorts it. It's like her eyes roll back in her head.

"Mmmmm," she says, sighing. "Your turn."

"We have to take a sister picture first," I say, hiding my

phone in the side of my bra. "Oh my God, I don't even know where my phone is! Can we use yours?"

"Later," she says. Her pupils are fully dilated. She grabs my wrist. "Mind if I do another?"

"Go right ahead."

Coke is the only thing she's focused on.

Think faster, Lauren.

"Let me at least put my number in your phone, then, so we can take one later," I say as she readies her next line.

Then she's unlocking her phone and handing it to me. The first thing I notice is her wallpaper. It's a photo of her and Jess, arms wrapped around each other, paint splattered all over their clothes and faces.

"I think I'll try one more," she says. "Only one."

"Go for it," I tell her.

With her head bent over, I work quickly, pulling up her Instagram. It's her main account. I hit the login button, seeing if any other account will pop up.

Then I see it. What I've been hoping to find all night.

The Unhappiest of Valleys account.

For a second, all I can do is stare. I knew it was her, but now the proof is staring me right in the face. She's the one who posted everything about Trevor and my past. And I can't forget the disgusting way she treated Vic.

Now Ainsley's going to be legally connected to me for the rest of my life.

"I'm almost done," I tell her, my fingers sweating all over

her phone. She snorts her line, relishing in the drugs hitting her bloodstream. I quickly take a screenshot of the Instagram login page with her personal account next to the Unhappiest of Valleys and send it to myself.

And then my phone dings. Right in my bra. Shit.

Ainsley looks up.

"I think I heard a phone," she says, confused.

"Oh my God, you did? Where?" I ask. I delete the text I just sent, and the photo. Then I type in my contact as fast as humanly possible.

"Call yourself on my phone," she says.

My heart races like I just did a line.

I hand her phone back, and then I force myself to give her a hug. "I think I left it near a handle in the kitchen," I tell her, sliding open the shower door.

I can't find Robbie and John fast enough.

FORTY

The three of us take a back booth next to a window at the Waffle Shop, which apparently has the best breakfast in all of Happy Valley. Since it's eight thirty on a Saturday morning we're the youngest people in here by at least forty years. I fidget with my key ring, retying the necklace Mom gave me back onto it. Maybe I tried a little bit *too* hard last night to look the part.

"She is *messed up* for posting that stuff," John says across from me. He knocks two Advil back and washes them down with coffee. "I mean, she really didn't hold back."

Once Andrea finds out it's Ainsley behind the account, I don't see Ainsley ever being able to recover her reputation.

I glance over at Robbie, who's sitting next to John, but he's staring out the window. Even after the waiter brings our waffles, which smell like heaven, Robbie's unusually quiet.

I pass the syrup around.

"How should we do this?" I ask. "Should we threaten to post the screenshot to Snap and Instagram?"

"There's different strategies for this," John says. "We might want to use that as our last resort."

Robbie takes the syrup and the glass bottle lands with a sharp thud on the table. It startles me almost as much as the anger shining through his eyes.

"I thought about this all night. I want nothing more than to expose her, but we have to wait to do anything until after Trevor's burial," he says. He takes a sip of coffee and sets the mug down with as much force as he did the syrup. "His body has been sitting in a fridge for weeks because my dad can't bring himself to bury him, even after he called off the second postmortem opinion. We've already had to reschedule the burial once and I just can't . . . have anything ruining this one moment of peace for Trevor. It's the fucking least he deserves."

John and I are shocked into silence. We nod in agreement. Ainsley can wait.

———————

She sends me a text later that afternoon.

Last night was fun <3

Ainsley must have sociopathic tendencies if she can act this way to my face after everything she said about me online.

I can keep up a charade, too. I text her back.

Loved seeing you!

Then I darken my phone and head downstairs. I find Mom, alone for once, her laptop open to Pinterest. A fake candle glows in the middle of the table.

It's something she's done for me, ever since the fire. She used to love burning real candles, especially the seasonal ones from Bath & Body Works.

But it's okay, because in less than a year I'll be gone. Soon she can burn all the scented wax her heart desires.

"What do you think of this?" she asks, turning the computer screen toward me. I glimpse a picture of a woman in a tight, silky white dress. It clings to every part of her body.

"It's hot," I say. "You'd really wear something like that?"

Mom shrugs. "Maybe."

"I like it," I tell her.

"But you don't love it."

I sit down next to her. "It's not your usual style. I'd have to see it on you," I say.

"Would you want to go wedding dress shopping with me?" she asks. "Maybe we could grab coffee before, just the two of us? Like old times?"

This is Mom's first time getting married, I remind myself. Even if trying on dresses for four hours is the last thing I want to do right now.

"Sure," I say, smiling.

Mom beams. "How about next Saturday?" she asks.

"Trevor's burial is next Saturday," I say, my voice taking a turn. "October fourteenth. I guess Lionel's changed the date a few times."

She looks up at me. "That's right," she says. She shuts her laptop screen and pushes it to the side. "You know, Mark was apprehensive about going to his calling hours. Because of Ainsley."

"And you convinced him?"

"Of course. I had my hunch that you were close with Robbie. I wanted to support him. I wanted to support you. I know I haven't done a great job of that lately."

She reaches for her mug of homemade chai. The smell wafts toward me and it's like drinking in a cup of fall. "I was thinking, maybe over winter break, the two of us could get away for a couple days and go to, I don't know, New York City or something? A girls' trip. Something fun?"

I'm not good at hiding my surprise. "Really? Without Mark?"

"Since I couldn't be there for senior night, I thought we could celebrate in a big way."

Warmth spreads through my chest.

"I'd like that."

"It'll be good for Mark to get some one-on-one time with Ainsley, too," Mom says. "He said she ran into you yesterday? She said she had fun. Maybe she is really warming up to the idea of us becoming a sort of family."

Right. Family. The four of us.

I'm sure Mark thinks we're basically sisters now.

"Yeah, we were at the same party. She apologized for everything at dinner."

"I don't hold it against her," Mom says. "I know it's not easy, seeing your parent with someone else."

How do you think I feel?

FORTY-ONE

I work my ass off in practice all week, since my starting spot is no longer guaranteed with the "break" I was forced into. Sometimes Coach starts Taylor instead of me. I want that to change. I need it to.

I also need to work myself past the point of exhaustion because all I can think about is this weekend. Trevor will finally be buried, but we still aren't any closer to figuring out what really happened or didn't happen to him. It's like history is repeating itself. Secrets died with Vic and Jess, and they'll die with Trevor, too.

Unless we do something about it.

On Friday, Coach has us run through our corner kick drills. I flawlessly cross each one, each time. Mara meets the ball like she's a magnet for it, and Andrea only manages to block one of her shots.

I look up at Coach after Mara heads the ball into the left corner of the net. He's nodding. Excitement swells in my belly. Coach's nod is like a good omen, something he does whenever he sees something he likes.

Remember this when you're creating the lineup for this week's game.

Then he blows his whistle, and practice is officially over. I jog over to my bag, noticing the low-hanging moon. It's barely a sliver of a crescent. Then I sense someone standing next to me.

"Do you need a ride tomorrow?"

I look to my left, finding Mara. She wipes the sweat off her forehead with her shirt, exposing her neon sports bra underneath. Lex comes up behind her and tugs her shorts, then gives her a peck on the cheek.

"I thought we had practice off tomorrow," I say.

"To the burial," she says more quietly.

"Wait, you're going?" I ask.

"We thought you could use the extra support," Lex says. "We can pick you up."

I must not do a good job of hiding the shock on my face, because then Lex says, "Whatever Trevor did or didn't do, Robbie was wrongly accused."

Whatever Trevor did or didn't do.

I search Lex's face. "You don't think Trevor killed Vic, either," I say.

Lex's eyes dart to Mara and then back to me, and whatever she just communicated in that glance I've missed entirely.

"I never said that," she says quickly.

"Lex—"

"Pretend I never said anything, okay?" she whispers. She grabs her monster-sized water bottle and looks at Mara expectantly. Mara quickly slides off her cleats, tosses them into her bag, and puts on her slides.

"Just so you know," I say, lowering my voice, "I—"

"We'll see you tomorrow," Mara says, cutting me off. "Meet us outside your house at three."

I text Lex later that night to ask her what the hell that was all about, but she says it's better if we talk in person. By 2:50 P.M. on Saturday, I'm desperate for information. I throw on the same black dress I wore to Trevor's calling hours, and then I'm climbing into the back seat of Lex's car.

She locks the doors. Mara pops a piece of gum into her mouth.

Lex's eyes dart outside her window, and Mara's eyes dart outside hers. Neither has said a word to me yet.

I'm sweating even though it's 55 degrees outside.

"You have to tell me what's going on. Please."

Mara lets out a deep sigh. She squeezes Lex's hand. "It's time," she says.

I close my eyes for a brief second. I should be used to this by now. Bracing myself.

Lex drops her hands from the steering wheel. "The night of Vic's death," she says, "Trevor was with me."

I stare at the back of the driver's seat. I give myself a moment to digest what she just said.

"Trevor and I first got close because we were in the same

253

group therapy," Lex says. She takes the prewrap off her wrist and stretches it between her two hands. "Both of us struggle with . . . or struggled with, I guess . . . disordered eating. I didn't want anyone knowing where I went every Sunday afternoon. I told him I wouldn't acknowledge him at Valley High. I know that's very unlike me, but it's what I needed to do for my own survival. Even though we were spilling our guts to each other for two years in group session.

"That night he asked me if he could come over. Said he didn't know who else he could trust. I gave Mara some lame excuse because we were supposed to go on a date, but the frantic way Trevor was texting me told me it was serious," she says. "He'd been looking for his favorite pair of boxers because he was, as he put it, about to take things to the 'next level' with Jess. He couldn't find them and they weren't in Robbie's room, and he thought they might have gotten mixed up in the laundry. Then he looked in his dad's dresser drawers. Instead of finding his boxers, he found a pair of Victoria's underwear. He'd seen her wear them before, when they all went late-night swimming at the lake."

I'm trying not to hyperventilate.

"He even brought them to my house and showed them to me," Lex says. "He didn't know what to do. He didn't know if his dad stole them or if Vic had somehow given them to him. He wanted to see what I knew, since she was best friends with Mara, but I didn't know anything. I never got the chance to ask Vic. Neither did he."

Lex stretches the prewrap so far it breaks. She flicks it onto her lap.

"After she died, Trevor asked me if I'd be willing to hold on to the underwear. He didn't want his dad finding it. I told him I would. It's been in a pencil case in the back of my closet for the past two years."

Lionel. Fucking. Crestmont. Had Victoria's underwear in his dresser.

My legs are shaking.

"Trevor said he had to build a bulletproof case before we could come out and say anything," Lex says. "I knew Lionel had the money and the legal expertise to get away with it. One of his good friends is also a deputy with the Lake Monarch police. Who knows what kind of favors he's asked for. So, I pretended in public that I believed Robbie was responsible for Vic's death. It got easier, after a while. Especially because Mara thought he did it and I was obsessed with impressing her."

Mara squeezes Lex's hand.

"I just didn't fucking know," she says.

"Because I made sure of it. I had to," Lex says darkly. Her eyes flash up to the rearview mirror. "Then Trevor died, and I knew Lionel was completely unhinged. He'd do anything to protect himself. Even if that meant killing his own son." Tears splash onto her cheeks. "Trevor must have been close to exposing everything."

Mara blots Lex's face with a tissue. She holds her face. Kisses her forehead.

I lean back into my seat. I'm stunned. I can't imagine how painful this has been for her.

How painful it was for Trevor.

"Did he think Lionel killed Jess, too?" I ask quietly.

"He thought his dad was obsessed with whoever they dated. I mean, that's the common thread," Lex says. "Trevor didn't have any evidence linking Lionel to Jess's death yet, other than the fact that Lionel used to be a member at the Centre Hills Country Club. Pax, the kid who threw the homecoming party Jess died at, lives right off the golf course."

Lex takes another tissue and blows her nose. "Trevor's initial investigation took a big pause after Jess died. He wasn't doing well. His eating disorder got really bad again. A few months ago, he started recovering. He said he was going to revisit everything. Then you entered the picture.

"The night of the kickback," Lex says, "after I found out you were hooking up with Robbie, I told Trevor to keep an eye on you. To look out for you. He promised me he would. We didn't want to put anyone else at risk."

That's why Trevor dug up my past. He wanted to drive me away to protect me.

I hang my head.

Even though no one was protecting him.

"Does Robbie know?" I ask.

Lex nods. "I just told him. I couldn't . . . keep doing this," she says. "Trevor deserved so much better."

FORTY-TWO

Lex and Mara drop me off at the cemetery gates. They had never planned on going to the burial, in case Lionel was suspicious of their newfound support.

A million thoughts run through my head as I trudge through the graves.

I think about all the times Lionel flashed his neon grin my way. The times he manhandled Stacy in front of us. The way he let us get drunk with him. The way he loves to "stargaze" with his telescope and "bird-watch" with his binoculars.

Trevor stayed behind that day at the lake to make sure I wasn't alone with Lionel, I realize.

I can't believe I was reading into the signs all wrong.

I wonder what else I've been wrong about.

By the time I reach Trevor's gravesite, my teeth are chattering uncontrollably. It's the shock of all the news. The adrenaline. I clamp down, trying to get it under control.

I spot Lionel near the string quartet. I have to look away as he blots his face with a handkerchief or I might actually scream.

Robbie's on the opposite side, with his mom. Now I know that it's for a reason. He probably wants to strangle his dad.

I take a seat in the last row of white chairs, next to John. He gives me a tight hug, and then I'm wondering if he knows the truth now, too. But I can't ask him that right now. We're maybe ten feet or so behind Lionel. I can't take any chances.

Then I hear someone whisper my name and it startles me.

"Didn't mean to scare you, honey," Mom says.

I turn to find Mom and Mark. Mom's diamond ring glitters in the soft fall sunlight.

"Thanks for coming," I tell them.

"We'll be right across from you," Mom says. They take their seats as the music fades and a deacon comes to the front.

"We're gathered here today to celebrate the life of Trevor Crestmont," the deacon says into his wearable microphone.

"Ow," John whispers.

I realize I have his hand in a death grip because suddenly the thought of sitting through this entire burial ceremony seems unbearable. But I'm here. I can't leave now.

"Sorry," I whisper.

"It's okay," John says as I release my grip. "I had to take a shot before this just to be able to sit through it."

I wish I'd done the same. The deacon reads a Bible passage about forgiveness and it's almost too much.

We know you're innocent. We're going to prove it.

Then I feel a nudge. John leans over toward me and I sense his panic.

"Is that who I think it is?" he asks.

I crane my neck, finally seeing what he sees.

A figure in bright red. They weave through the graves so fast they're almost running. A huge poster board is in their hands. Even from this far away, I can clearly make out what it says.

NO JUSTICE FOR JESS AND VIC, NO PEACE FOR TREVOR!

Ainsley.

About to fuck shit up. Real fast, unless we do something about it.

Or I do something about it. John deserves to mourn Trevor, too. He knew him like a brother.

"I'll take care of her," I promise.

"Then you'd better leave right now," John says.

I slide out of my seat as everyone's eyes are glued to the deacon. Even though my run is awkward in flats, I'm faster than Ainsley. I intercept her before she reaches the top of the hill.

This close, I can see she's painted her hands red, too. Photos of Jess and Vic take up residence on each corner of the poster.

"You don't want to do this," I tell Ainsley.

"Stay out of this, Lauren, okay?" she says harshly.

She tries to push past me but I'm in front of her again. I may not be the most skilled defender ever but as right mid, I've had to do my fair share of getting the ball back from the other team. I widen my stance, taking up more space as her eyes burn into mine.

"Jess's family can't be here and that's why I'm here in their stead," she says hotly. "Trevor stole Jess's life and I'm going to remind everyone here feeling sorry for him that I hope he's rotting in hell, if that even exists."

"Do that, and I'll let everyone at Valley High know that you're the one behind the Unhappiest of Valleys account."

Ainsley's jaw drops. Her voice is halted, high-pitched. "What are you talking about?"

"You know exactly what I'm talking about," I tell her as she tries to go around me, but I block her again. "I took a screenshot on your phone. There's no doubting it's you once I release it."

The look of confusion on her face morphs into one of recognition.

"You did it at the party," she says.

"I do a convincing drunk bitch, don't I?" I tell her. "How could you post those things about Victoria?"

Before either of us can say another word, Mark's booming voice is behind me.

"Turn around, Ainsley," he says.

"Dad—"

"Sweetie, we talked about this. This is not the time nor place," he says.

"How can you sit there and support a MURDERER!" Ainsley says, not caring how loud she's getting.

Then Mark steps in, putting his arm around her, leading her away. "This is not how you win people over," he says, his voice gentler. Ainsley sobs, leaning on his shoulder. He holds her like that as they walk through the graves, together.

"He was afraid she might do something like this," Mom says, coming up beside me. "I can't even imagine her grief. But Trevor's family is allowed to grieve, too."

Maybe some more than others, I want to say.

"Gosh, that could have easily been a disaster," Mom says. "It'll be good for her to be around you more. She needs someone to look up to."

Of course that's the only thing Mom's thinking about right now. How marrying Mark is going to give her a perfect little nuclear family.

She has no idea how much of a mess her future stepdaughter is.

Just like she has no idea how close I am to the epicenter of all the murders in Happy Valley.

FORTY-THREE

"What she did was wrong."

Mark's sitting across from me the morning after Trevor's burial. There's a platter of pumpkin pancakes in between us, and a cauldron-sized amount of homemade whipped cream. Mom is next to him, scooping a fluffy white cloud onto her short stack.

"But the death of her best friend is something she has never forgotten, and she hasn't had many outlets to voice her anger," he continues, a solemn look on his face. Wrinkles crease underneath his eyes. "That's why I'm hoping you won't go public with her tie to the Unhappiest of Valleys account."

I guess Ainsley is having her dad fight her battles for her. It's not like I don't have any sympathy for her. I do.

"I know you have every right to," Mark says, "after what she's posted. But she's especially fragile right now. I think processing Trevor's death and all the unanswered questions about Jess is going to take some time."

I set the maple syrup down. Maybe too hard, because it clangs against the table.

I think of what Andrea said. She wants the account gone.

"I won't go public with it," I say, "if Ainsley agrees to delete the account."

Mark sits with this for a second. Then he dishes out another pancake for himself. "I think that's fair," he says.

Mom nods in agreement. "That's very mature of you, Laur. I know the post about you and Clint was really hurtful."

"That was my mistake," Mark says, gesturing to himself. "I told her something that was not my story to tell. I'd just hoped it would bring the two of you closer."

"There's still time for that," Mom says, donning a smile.

I wipe my mouth with my napkin and take my plate to the sink. I scrub it, hard, trying to drown out the rest of Mark and Mom's conversation about their wedding day. It annoys me that it seems to be the most important thing on Mom's mind.

But I know that's only because she doesn't know the truth. No one does. And they won't, unless we can find proof that is so incriminating, Lionel can't worm his way out of it.

We've been at Karen's Bridal Boutique for three hours. My iced vanilla coffee is long gone. Mom can't decide between two dresses that look identical to the photo she'd shown me on Pinterest. One has a pearl trim on the bottom and the other doesn't. My vote is for pearls but she still can't decide.

I glance down at my phone and see a text come through from Robbie.

Come to Beaver Stadium! We have a special tailgate. Spot 43. Wouldn't want you to miss it! ♥

I glance at the text, and then I read through it again, and it seems . . . weird. Especially the heart emoji. It's not really Robbie's texting style. I text John and ask him about the tailgate, and he says it's legit. He also tells me I should get there as soon as I can.

I guess that explains why the boutique has been deader than dead. Everyone's at the Penn State game today.

Mom decides to put the two dresses on hold.

"I'll sleep on it," she tells the boutique attendant, her cheeks flushed from three glasses of rosé champagne. Hence why I drove.

I push open the door to outside and barely take one step toward the car when I see Mark holding a gigantic bouquet of red roses. I hear Mom gasp beside me.

"You're not supposed to be here!" she says, embracing him.

"Just wanted to make today a little extra special," he says, kissing her. Since he's here, now I don't have to drop Mom off at home.

Then he turns to me, opening his arms for a hug, and I oblige. Mark smells like shaving cream and orange juice, since he drinks almost a carton of it on the daily.

"I thought we could all get lunch at the Corner Room?" Mark says, releasing me from the hug.

"I love their chicken parm," Mom says.

"I'm going to meet up with Robbie and John at their tailgate," I say.

"I'm glad Robbie's doing something fun this weekend. He needs it," Mom says. She looks at Mark. "It'd be fun to tailgate sometime."

"You just say the word," Mark says. "I've got the whole setup. Portable grill, chairs, and a freezer full of hot dogs."

"Next home game," Mom says, then she looks at me. "Maybe we can host your friends, too, Laur."

"It's a date," I say without an ounce of enthusiasm, already walking away.

"If you need a designated driver, we can always come pick you up," Mark says. "We'll be right down the street."

"Thanks," I call back.

But something tells me this isn't going to be much of a social tailgate.

———————

Parking is a nightmare. I eventually find a spot on the outer corner of the lot. Then I'm weaving in between tailgates, passing charcoal grills packed with hamburgers and hot dogs and spicy onions. There are beer pong tournaments and I take in the doughy smell of cold beer. I'd be lost if John hadn't dropped his pin with their location.

I find the two of them sitting in lawn chairs. John eats straight from a bag of pretzels. It's probably the most pathetic tailgate I've ever seen. Robbie's wearing a Penn State hat, which looks out of place on his head. John wears a WE ARE shirt that he's made into a crop top.

"Since when are we football fans?" I ask.

Robbie reaches for a third folded-up chair. He props it open.

"As you say, we had to look the part," John says.

"Who are you trying to convince?" I ask.

"My dad," Robbie says in a throaty voice. "He thinks we're getting fucked up, playing beer pong. You know. Because of yesterday. That's what I want him to believe."

His eyes meet mine.

"I know Lex told you about Trevor," Robbie says. "I thought it was better that way. To hear it from her."

Part of me bristles. She left that part out.

"I wish I was more perceptive," John says. "I truly didn't think Lionel—"

"None of us did," Robbie says. His grip on his folding chair is so tight, his rings push in against the flesh of his fingers. "Which is why we're going to clear Trevor's name and nail him." Robbie looks at me. "I have to be careful what I say over text. And you should be careful, too, about what you text me. I wouldn't put it past him to pull my phone logs."

"That's why you sounded weird today," I say.

He reaches into his pocket and withdraws a piece of paper. "I finally unlocked Trevor's laptop. His password was the same one as our old Xbox gaming account. I know he did that for me."

Screams erupt all around us. Another touchdown.

"His texts were synced. Which is how I found out he was

going to meet up with someone the day he died," Robbie says. "Someone who was either my dad, or who worked for my dad."

Robbie holds out the paper to me, a printed-out text exchange from a few weeks ago, between Trevor and an unknown number.

I have info on Vic's death. Actual evidence.

Who is this?

I can't say yet. Not over text.

Right. Let's pretend I'm entertaining you. What kind of evidence do you have?

I'll show you in person.

Yeah, let me just meet a total stranger who could be bullshitting me. Right.

I have Vic's bikini top. The one she was wearing when she died. There's blood on it.

Send me a photo.

I can't.

Then you're lying.

Then there's the photo. Of Vic's actual bikini top.

Not lying.

How did you get this?

I can't tell you any more than that over text.

I get it. Okay. Where and when?

How about the old barn on Sycamore Road? Monday?

Yep. Just so you know, I never come empty-handed.

I get it. I always carry pepper spray. It just has to be this way.

I'm fully aware of that.

Then the texts stop.

I look up at Robbie. At John.

"We wanted to leave together," Robbie says. "With you. I don't think it's safe for any of us to drive there alone."

As we pack up our chairs, I realize we're the only three people in all of Happy Valley who'd dare to leave Beaver Stadium before the end of the game.

FORTY-FOUR

The barn on Sycamore seems like it could sink into the ground at any moment, with its sagging wood, faded crimson paint, and overgrown weeds. As we trudge closer to it, I look back toward the country road. I can barely see it. Only one other car has driven by in the twenty minutes we've been here. It's way more secluded than it first seems because of the overgrowth.

We're not sure what we're looking for, exactly. We split up to cover more ground. John searches at the front of the barn, and Robbie disappears behind it. I take another look at the outskirts of the barn, stepping into the weeds. I hope my jeans are thick enough to stop a tick from burrowing into my skin.

I glance back at the main road again. Trevor would have parked where we did, just off the shoulder of the road. Then he would have walked in the direction of the barn.

I work backward, trying to retrace his steps. There's nothing but tall grasses and a couple of decaying bales of hay. It's not until I'm past them that I notice something that doesn't exactly blend into the scenery.

A little white square.

I turn around, retracing my steps. The white square comes into focus. It's a folded-up piece of notebook paper, tucked under one of the ties keeping the hay together. I coax it out of place and unfold it.

September 11.

Chills overtake my body. That was the day Trevor was found dead in the Valley High parking lot.

To whoever finds this, please get it to my brother,
Robbie Crestmont.

"I found something!" I yell. But it sounds more like a curdling scream.

The two of them race toward me. I hold out the note and we read it in silence.

I'm meeting someone at the Sycamore barn at 8:15 a.m.
I came here because this person said they had answers
as to what happened to Vic. They sent me a photo of
her bloodied bikini top, the same thing she was wearing
the day she died. I'm pretty sure they don't even sell
that bathing suit anymore, so I'm taking a chance and
believing that it's the real thing.
*   I didn't tell anyone to protect you, Robbie.*
Because if Dad killed Vic, and if he had something to

do with Jess's death, too, I know he'll do whatever it takes to cover this up. Even if that means hurting me. Hurting you.

If I'm not here anymore, talk to Alexis. I know it sounds crazy, but she can explain everything.

I had to come here. I was always going to see this through. This is my life's work.

I know that if things go badly, I might get blamed for the murders. Because what's even better than a living Crestmont boy to blame? A dead one.

I just wanted you to know that I did everything I could to try to get justice for them.

Love,
Trev

It's surreal, reading this after the fact. It's like Trevor had a sixth sense. He knew exactly how everything would play out.

But he had to take a chance. He had to see if he could uncover the truth.

I don't know if I could ever be that brave.

I gently give the letter over to Robbie. His eyes dart back to the top of the page. He reads it again. "How could he be so fucking careless?"

His anger shocks me. Robbie crumples up the note and tosses it to the ground. He storms off. John and I don't chase after him. He needs time to process.

I pick up the crumpled note and smooth it out. I refold it.

Because I know Robbie will want to hold on to it. Along with the texts, this helps prove Trevor's innocence. Helps prove that his death wasn't an accidental overdose.

Someone lured him out here. Someone who saw me with the bikini.

The sound of a car driving by is enough to make me gasp out loud.

I've known that this whole time, I've had a target on my back. It started with that phone call, a threat I thought was over when Trevor died. But now, if Lionel's responsible for this? It feels like he's just getting ready for the right moment to strike.

FORTY-FIVE

"**I have to confront my dad.** In public."

Robbie's lying on my bed, his head in my lap. Not that we meant to fall together this way, but he'd asked if he could come over after my game tonight. The note from Trevor rests on top of his wallet, next to his pack of cigarettes. He's kept it close ever since we went to the barn three days ago.

"How?" I ask.

His eyes are like two amber suns in the glow of my nightstand lamp.

"He was going to call off his annual silent auction dinner, but Stacy gave him the idea to start a fund for families that can't afford to bury their loved ones," Robbie says. "It's basically an opportunity for him to look like a saint. With all those guests at our house, there will be too many witnesses. It's not like he can have every single person there killed."

My hand drifts away from his thick hair, and I hug my arms to myself.

I feel Robbie shift. Then he's sitting up, face-to-face with me. "You don't think I should."

"What if he denies everything?" I counter. "It's Trevor's word against his."

Robbie bites down on his lip, grimacing. "He might. But we have evidence on our side."

"When's the dinner?" I ask.

"A week from Friday. October 27." He looks at me. Pleads with me. "Trevor's dead. We have to try. For him."

––––––––––––

I spot at least ten people with fake vampire fangs in their mouths between second and fourth period the next day at school, even though it's only October 19. With the heaviness of the past few weeks, I think everyone is ready for something fun to look forward to again. Or, at least, an excuse to party their faces off.

The old me would be right there with them. Except I'm more focused on the fact that we're planning on confronting the murder suspect who could be responsible for three deaths at Valley High.

It's a familiar feeling. The thrill of anticipation mixed with dread. The same way I felt the week Donovan cornered me about going to another one of his parties.

I'd better see you there, he'd said.

I wanted to jam my fingers into his eyes until he screamed.

Instead I smiled. I said, *Don't worry*.

The idea was forming.

Our game gets canceled due to lightning, and I take it as

sign. I ask Mara and Lex if they'll go costume shopping with me instead. It's a requirement for Lionel's dinner, given the time of year.

The other requirement is that I need to recruit Lex and Mara to help us. Because we're going to need all the help we can get.

Spirit Halloween is chaotic on a good day. Every day that's closer to Halloween, it's an actual shit show. The three of us grab handfuls of costumes off the racks and haul them to a dressing room. We share one so that we don't have to wait in the long-ass line.

I pull on my costume, stepping into the tight, all-black onesie. I wish I could just be in my pajamas right now.

"I'm going full-on slut," Mara says. She shimmies herself into a latex nurse costume with a hemline that just barely skims past her crotch. She unbuttons the top three buttons. "I'm ready to forget about all the shit going on at Valley High for once. What do we think?" she asks.

"Hot," I say.

"It's a lot, but you look amazing as usual," Lex says.

"What? You're not into sexy nurses?" Mara says.

"I'm not into sexualizing legitimate professions," Lex says, and Mara rolls her eyes.

"She's no fun sometimes," she says, and I laugh for what feels like the first time in weeks. I plop a pair of cat ears on my head and call it good.

"Classic," Mara says.

Lex nods her approval. She surveys her own outfit in the mirror: a furry vest with wolf ears and hairy gloves to match.

"I think werewolf is the winner," she says, glancing over her shoulder.

"Should I be a veterinarian instead?" Mara asks, sliding off her costume. She grabs a mint-green minidress from her pile. "That way we'll match. You can be my patient."

She gives Lex a quick peck and changes into the veterinarian outfit. The cool green looks nice against her skin.

"I'm into it," Lex says.

"Perfect," Mara says. She turns to me. "We all kind of match with our animal theme! We have to get a picture at Sam's party next weekend."

I haven't exactly told them I'm not going yet. Robbie's been insistent that we don't talk about anything to do with Lionel over text.

Hence why I had to get them alone in person.

"About that," I say, unzipping my onesie.

"Oh no," Mara says, her face falling. "You're not going. I totally get it. Are you going to stay in instead?"

"Actually, I'm going to be at Robbie's house. For Lionel's fundraising dinner."

I tell them the details, asking what they think of our majorly public confrontation.

"Do you really think that's the safest thing to do?" Lex says. Her face screams worry.

"I mean, he's a lawyer and I think he can bullshit his way

out of anything, but I think it's our only shot. Robbie's going to present all the evidence we have in a room full of witnesses. We have the shock factor on our side. Which is why we need the pair of Vic's underwear Trevor gave to you."

Lex quickly turns to Mara and back to me. She stares at me for a second longer, like she's taking a second to process everything I just told her.

"What are you going to do if Lionel freaks out?"

"What do you mean?" I ask.

Lex shudders. "He could call the cops on you, or follow you after the dinner . . . or . . . I don't know what he's willing to do."

I guess we haven't exactly thought of every possible scenario.

Lex rubs her jaw. "Mara and I will wait outside in my car," she decides. "We'll be the escape plan."

I sigh out a breath I didn't realize I was holding in.

With five of us going against Lionel, I have a little more faith that Robbie's plan might actually work out.

FORTY-SIX

Lex waited to give Robbie the pair of underwear until this morning, because I don't think she completely trusts anyone with it other than herself. Which is understandable. She kept it safe for two years.

For two years, Lionel's been living a lie. And as of tonight, everyone's going to know the truth.

After changing into my costume, I find Mom to tell her I'm leaving. She's in the kitchen with Mark, and they're wearing matching costumes, because of course they are. She's Dorothy and he's the Tin Man. Even though it's slightly cringey, it's still kind of cute.

"You look adorable," Mom says, and I wince. Adorable is not exactly the vibe I'm ever trying to channel.

Mom pours a huge bag of Hershey's candies into a pumpkin bowl that takes up half the kitchen island. This is the first year we've lived in a house, and tonight our neighborhood is hosting a "safe" trick-or-treating event for kids in elementary school and younger, since actual Halloween is on a school night this year.

Mark's at the stove, stirring a pot of homemade cider. I can almost taste the spices on my tongue, the air is so thick with them. I do have to admit that we've been eating like queens ever since they started dating.

"Want some before you head out?" he asks.

"Yeah, sure," I say, and he ladles me a goblet. I take a sip. Cinnamon and cloves and nutmeg hits the back of my throat. It settles my nervous stomach. "It's great. Thanks."

Mark beams. "It's a family recipe. Ainsley's never had much interest in cooking, but perhaps you might?"

Mom's gaze flits to mine, and I shrug.

"It would be nice to be able to make more than microwave meals," I say.

I catch Mom's smile. She empties another huge bag of candy into the bowl.

My phone buzzes. Lex. Which means they're here.

"Have fun with the trick-or-treaters," I tell Mom.

"Be careful tonight," Mom says. "I know there are a lot of parties going on this weekend."

"I'm just having dinner at Robbie's."

"That's a smarter choice," Mark says, nodding.

Is it? Guess I'm about to find out.

Lex parks out of view of the Crestmont house. I take a deep breath, and Mara reaches out her hand from the passenger's seat. I squeeze it.

"We can do this," she says.

"I'll look out for the code word," Lex says.

We decided on *vet*. Mara's costume. Three letters. Quick to type or say. Just in case the shit hits the fan.

I nod, hoping I won't have to use it.

Then before I can talk myself out of it, I'm fixing my cat ears, opening the door, and making my way up to Robbie's house.

If I thought Mom went all out with Halloween decor, then the Crestmonts are like the patron saints of Halloween. Cobwebs drape across each window, glowing fake spiders scuttling across them. Pumpkins of every hue line the winding walkway up to the front door, all carved and glowing with real tea-light candles. I tell myself to walk quickly and try not to think of the dozens of little fire hazards just inches away from my feet.

On the front porch, a massive, realistic-looking zombie figure greets me. It sits in a rocking chair, and I avert my eyes as I reach for the gargoyle knocker that has been newly fastened to the door. But the door swings open before I have a chance to knock.

Revealing Robbie. Dressed as a pirate, in tight pants, an open white shirt, and jeweled rings on every finger.

Maybe I stare for a second too long, because he smiles. It's a smile I've seldom seen since his brother died. For a second, it's just us. For a second, it's like we're back in the Valley Hospice storage room and nothing's falling apart around us.

"You look great," he says quietly.

I loop my arm through his as he leads me inside. My arm's shaking, and I pull him closer to my body to steady myself. Echoes of conversations travel down the foyer, and classical music crescendos in my ear. Above us, the normal chandelier has been replaced by one with dark jewels. I pass by a shattered mirror and a portrait of a woman who seems to age in real time. They've gone full Haunted Mansion.

"Are you ready?" Robbie whispers.

My breath catches in my throat. I nod.

I don't think I'll ever be ready for what we're about to do.

Robbie leads me to the dining room. Dark pillar candles flicker atop tarnished candelabras. A black lace tablecloth is draped over the long table, fine crystal at every place setting. The coffin-shaped donation box sitting in the center of everything feels a little jarring. But I guess it fits the vibe. A fundraiser hosted by a murderer.

A few warlocks, Beetlejuice and Lydia Deetz, and a corpse bride and groom weave in between us. A server dressed as a zombie butler stops to offer me and Robbie something that looks like cheese on little toasts. I pop one into my mouth, grateful to have something to do with my nervous hands.

The witch next to me sips from a goblet of wine, chatting with someone dressed as a scarecrow. I can't hear much of their conversation, but as I swallow the last bite of my appetizer, I catch the words *tragic* and *Lionel must be a mess*. I almost feel bad that they're going to be in for such a rude awakening.

Someone comes up to us, and it takes me a second before

I realize it's John. Half his face is behind a mask: He's the Phantom of the Opera, statuesque in his perfectly tailored uniform of black, a red rose in his hand.

"Your costume's incredible," I tell John, giving him a hug.

"I wanted to at least look unforgettable for the occasion," he says.

Robbie leans into the two of us. "My dad usually makes a toast. I'll let him say his piece, and then I'll chime in. I'll start with Trevor's letter. Okay?"

I nod.

"I'll start recording as soon as he starts talking," John says. He turns to me. "And you'll be ready with the text."

"Lex is waiting down the street," I say.

Robbie squeezes both our arms. "We can do this."

Then a different server comes up to me, this time with salmon canapés on his platter. I tell him no thanks. I don't think I could stomach fish right now. But someone dressed as a skeleton takes him up on the offer. He pops one under his mask, into his mouth.

Then all our heads turn, because the host and hostess make their grand entrance, in costumes that, I'd venture to guess, are probably bespoke. Lionel wears a long velour cape and realistic fangs as white as the rest of his teeth. He looks at Stacy, and his eyes are watering. I wonder if he's trying to make himself cry. Stacy's his damsel in distress in a gauzy tulle nightgown and contacts that make her eyes look cloudy. Her neck is punctured by two fake teeth marks. Stacy does a subtle nod, and then Lionel grabs her by the waist, dips her, and pretends to bite her neck. It's like the somber mood eases for a second. The dinner guests clap and a few even cheer. Then Lionel brings Stacy up for air. She playfully touches his mouth with one of her long pearlescent nails.

A server brings Lionel a martini in a skeleton-hand glass. He drinks half of it in seconds. My knees are locked and I remind myself to bend them. Passing out is the last thing I need to do right now.

John reaches for my hand. "We're seriously incredible for doing this," he whispers to me. "Don't forget it."

I try to take his words to heart.

"Stacy and I are so thankful you could join us for our autumnal dinner," Lionel says. His voice is hoarser than normal. I notice the lines in his forehead are more prominent. Like his Botox wore off overnight.

"As you know, the death of my youngest son, Trevor, has been the most difficult thing I've ever experienced in my life," he says. "The events surrounding his death . . ."

Lionel gets choked up. He gulps down more of his martini, his hand shaking. I look around the room. A few guests dab their eyes with tissues. Lionel is one hell of an actor, and they're completely buying it.

"I pray that none of you have to experience this kind of grief. Ever," he says, and Stacy places her manicured hand on Lionel's back for support. "There have been too many deaths of too many young people in this town."

Robbie bristles next to me.

"I wanted to cancel the dinner this year," Lionel continues, "but Stacy encouraged me to host it. To use it for good. You are all making that possible."

"You're such a narcissist," Robbie says under his breath.

"I hope you'll join me in donating to the Crestmont fund at Valley Funeral Home. No family should ever have to face the burden of not being able to bury their loved one."

Of course, he had to make sure it was called the Crestmont fund. That way everyone will know about his good deed.

Then Lionel raises up his nearly empty martini glass. But before he can say another word, Robbie steps forward.

My heart pounds in my chest.

John checks his phone, making sure the recording is still going.

"I'd like to say something as well," Robbie says.

There's no turning back now.

Lionel gestures for him to take the floor. "Of course, Robbie. Go ahead."

I ready my own phone in my grip, ready to text Lex our code word at a moment's notice.

Robbie unfolds the note he's been holding in his hands.

"I'd like to read a little something from my late brother. He left this note for me."

I watch Lionel's eyes widen, his mouth open in shock. He turns to Stacy, and I can just make out the words. "He left a note?"

"'I'm meeting someone at the Sycamore barn at 8:15 A.M.,'" Robbie begins. "'I came here because this person said they had answers as to what happened to Vic. They sent me a photo of her bloodied bikini top, the same thing she was wearing the day she died. I'm pretty sure they don't even sell that bathing suit anymore, so I'm taking a chance and believing that it's the real thing.'"

Stacy puts her hand over her mouth. A few gasps escape from the dinner guests.

"'I didn't tell anyone to protect you, Robbie,'" he continues. His voice is a knife blade. He commands the entire room. "'Because if Dad killed Vic, and if he had something to do with Jess's death, too, I know he'll do whatever it takes to cover this up. Even if that means hurting me. Hurting you.'"

"What?" Lionel says, his face awash in confusion. He takes a step toward his only living son, but Robbie continues with the letter.

"'If I'm not here anymore, talk to Alexis. I know it sounds crazy, but she can explain everything. I had to come here. I was always going to see this through. This is my life's work. I know that if things go badly, I might get blamed for the murders. Because what's even better than a living Crestmont boy to blame?'" Robbie locks eyes with Lionel. "'A dead one.'"

"Robbie," Lionel says, his voice as weak as I've ever heard it. "Can I see the letter?"

Robbie thrusts the letter toward Lionel. "I've made copies."

All I can hear is my own pulse as Lionel looks over the

letter, his eyes darting from word to word, sentence to sentence. He looks like he might have a heart attack.

"He thought I killed Victoria? Robbie, you have no idea all the work Ben and I have been doing—"

"We both do," Robbie interrupts, and that's when the whispers start. Stacy comes forward but Lionel motions for her to stay back.

"I loved her like a daughter," Lionel says.

"You sure loved her all right," Robbie says. "That's why Trevor found a pair of her underwear in your dresser drawer."

The entire room goes silent. Robbie reaches into his pocket. My pulse beats like a drum in my ears.

The plastic bag rustles as he pulls it out. Soon everyone is going to see the underwear that Lex has held on to for the past two years.

My phone's buzzing as Robbie shows the underwear to the entire room. It buzzes again. I finally glance at it to see a dozen frenzied texts from Lex just now.

THE HOUSE IS ON FIRE!
GET OUT!

It's like there's a millisecond of time before everything becomes real, before the plumes of smoke rush into the dining room like an avalanche.

A familiar shrill echoes in my ears.

This can't be happening again.

There's a stampede of dinner guests and then John's telling me we have to go and then there's Clint, on the ground, writhing in pain.

I choke down smoke. My lungs heave with every breath I try to take.

Then I'm moving. Pulled by some unseen force. Robbie. He leads me out of the room and through the back sliding door.

By the time we're outside, half the Crestmont house is engulfed in flames.

FORTY-SEVEN

I'm too fucked up to remember to call 911. Donovan shoves past me. He's shouting into his phone. I stumble toward Clint. The side of his face is red as lava, honeycombed with white. There's no skin left.

"Lauren."

Lex is in front of me, holding both my hands. "Everyone's okay."

I hiccup, trying to bring myself back to reality.

The five of us stand huddled together on a neighbor's lawn, watching the firefighters hose down flames. Smoke hovers in the air like a thick, awful fog. The front of Robbie's house is charred beyond recognition. The stench of melted Halloween decorations fills my nose.

My phone rings. I glance at it. Mom. Probably a mess. I answer it. "I'm okay," I tell her.

She's near hysterics. "Oh my God. Thank God."

I watch as Robbie walks up to one of the firefighters. The firefighter points to the walkway, and the area that used to be the lawn. "I'll be home soon," I tell her.

Lionel and Stacy talk to another firefighter. I notice when Lionel tries to put his arm around Stacy, she shrugs him off.

"I love you," Mom says in my ear.

"Love you, too," I say.

Then Robbie's walking back toward us. His makeup is smeared, and his white shirt sticks to his skin. It's semi-see-through now from his sweat.

"Probably someone kicking over the pumpkins. Not that hard to fathom given what everyone thinks my brother did," he says.

My temples pulse.

"Did you see anything?" John asks, turning to Mara and Lex.

Mara shakes her head. "We were too far away. But when we saw smoke we drove closer, and by that time it was raging. Then we called 911."

"I'm sure the Crestmonts have a security system. Don't you?" Lex asks, turning to Robbie.

"Yeah," he says. "We have an app."

Robbie pulls it up on his phone. "What time did you notice the smoke?" he asks Lex.

She checks her phone.

"I texted Lauren at nine twenty. I'd guess we first noticed it a minute before, by the time we saw it, drove over, and saw the fire."

Robbie swipes open a video.

We all peer at the footage from just before the fire started, watching as someone in reflective gear passes by the front of the house, walking their dog. Probably a neighbor.

"Maybe it was an accident," John says. "The dog could have sniffed a pumpkin or something and it tipped over."

But then they're out of frame, and someone else appears. This time on the porch. We can't see their face, and they're dressed in all black.

They flick something onto the grass with their right hand and some kind of liquid rains down on the lawn.

"What is *that*?" John asks.

Robbie rewinds. We watch the footage again. I can just barely make out the liquid being shaken from a white container.

Lighter fluid.

The person kicks over three pumpkins in succession, the ones closest to the house. The grass lights up like wildfire.

Then the person hurries away, but not before glancing backward one last time.

I recognize them. They're from the dinner party.

The skeleton.

"He was one of the guests," I say.

Robbie pauses on the skeleton's face. Two black gaping holes stare at us where eyes should be. We all peer at it, hoping for some sort of clue, but that's the thing about costumes: Anyone could be anyone.

"Did your dad have a guest list?" I ask.

"Yes. People are allowed plus-ones, too," Robbie says.

"We could go through the list and do process of elimination. We can also see if anyone came with the skeleton," I suggest.

Robbie darkens his phone screen. "Honestly," he says, "I should thank them."

My body goes rigid.

"The fire completely interrupted your plan," I say. "We're lucky no one got hurt."

"Exactly. No one got hurt," Robbie says, and I feel my fists tense at the blasé way he's treating this.

"Because we were lucky," I repeat. "Because we had people looking out for us and smoke alarms that did their job."

"I know you have your own trauma around fires but you're overreacting. I'm not wasting my time on someone who became just as disgusted by Lionel Crestmont as I am. I don't blame them. I wish I'd started it. Just burn the whole house to the ground."

He walks away. John makes an *Oh boy* face but follows him.

I'm left standing beside Mara and Lex, who tell me it's time to go home.

FORTY-EIGHT

I'm standing on the Crestmonts' front porch, a bowl of melting candy in my hands. The plastic bowl is melting, too. Melting into me. It's like I'm helpless. All I can do is stare as my skin boils.

Then I feel something else. Something sharp.

I look down. A hand grabs hold of my ankle.

I glance behind me, following the arm to the body. I see his hair first. Dark blond. Then he lifts his head up and smiles.

But he's not Clint anymore. He's a skeleton. His teeth gnash together. A piece of burned flesh falls out of his jaw, and it takes me a second before I realize it's my own. A deep, oily hole gapes open at the back of my calf.

I wake up to completely soaked sheets. I pull my covers off and reach for the water on my nightstand.

I check my phone. It's 4 A.M. Guess I'm up for the day.

After sweating my guts out, now I'm freezing. I throw on my hoodie before heading downstairs. The smell of something warm and sweet hits my nose. It smells like comfort.

And I need that right now. I find Mark at the kitchen table, reading today's paper.

"You're up early," he says.

"Couldn't sleep."

The dinner last night was nothing short of a nightmare, to say the least.

"Your mom just left for her shift," he says. "Coffee?"

"Sure. Thanks."

He gets up from the table and pours me a mug. I take a sip. Then another. I'm not going back to sleep, no matter how exhausted I am from the events of last night.

"Did you guys give out a lot of candy?" I ask.

"Believe it or not, I had to make a run to the store for more," Mark says.

"I bet Mom was stoked."

"She loved every minute of it."

Then the timer on our oven goes off. "My second batch of cinnamon rolls is done," he says.

"I don't think Mom could bake a sheet of Pillsbury rolls to save her life," I say.

He chuckles, pulling the pan out of the oven. "We all have our strengths."

Then he plates two fluffy rolls, frosts them, and sets one in front of me.

I sink my teeth into it. "This is probably the best thing I've ever eaten."

Mark smiles. "They're Ainsley's favorite, too," he says,

taking a bite of his. "Although she won't be enjoying these anytime soon. She's grounded right now."

I polish off the rest of my roll and fight the temptation to lick the extra frosting from my fingers.

"Can I get you another?" he offers.

"Please."

"Lauren?"

"Yeah," I say, plugging my phone in to charge.

Mark opens my bedroom door.

"Robbie's here," he says. "Should I send him up?"

I must hesitate a second too long, because then he says, "You weren't expecting him. I can send him away?"

I unclench my jaw.

"No," I say. "It's okay. You can tell him to come up."

"Just holler if you need anything, okay?"

"Thanks," I tell him.

Soon I see Robbie leaning in my doorframe. He opens his mouth like he's going to say something, and closes it again.

"What, can't find the right words?" I say. "Used them all up last night?"

He sighs, hanging his head. "I came here to apologize—"

"Good. I deserve one."

He lingers in my doorway before he takes a step forward.

"I didn't say you could come in."

"Lauren—"

I unfurl my fists. "Tell me again how I was overreacting."

He grimaces, twisting the rings on his fingers. "I was feeling a million things—"

"How can you be okay with someone trying to light us all on fire? That's pretty nihilistic. Even for you." I stand up from my chair. "You should be pissed. Whoever that skeleton was, he ruined your moment. Your big reveal. You know that, right?"

Robbie's whole body curls forward. "I honestly don't think it would have mattered," he says.

"What are you talking about?"

"Stacy asked to meet me at the Waffle Shop this morning. She asked to see the underwear. I showed it to her." He looks up at me. "It's hers."

I stare at him, and then it's like I can't help it; I let out a laugh. "Oh, come on," I say. "You can't buy that."

"I believe her, Lauren."

"Why?"

"Because she lent them to Vic after Vic got her period one time at the lake, and she'd run out of clean pairs. She was wearing them when we all jumped into the lake that one night. Stacy had a few pairs of her underwear in that drawer but Trevor only found one of them. He had tunnel vision, because it was the pair he'd seen Vic wear. Of course he thought they were hers."

"You're just taking Stacy at her word. She's dating your dad. Don't you think she'd lie for him?"

"She broke up with him," Robbie says.

Now it's my turn to be shocked. But I remember the way Lionel tried to put his arm around her after the fire and she'd shrugged him off.

"When? Last night?"

"No. She waited until after Trevor's burial to tell him she accepted a job offer in Boston. She wants kids and my dad doesn't want any more, and the job gave her an out. She hosted the dinner with him given the circumstances."

I bite my lip, processing this. It's logical. It makes sense. Even though I don't want it to, because that means Lionel's entire motive for killing Vic, for killing Trevor, and for possibly killing Jess, has fallen apart completely. The underwear was our major clue that Lionel was obsessed with Vic. It was going to lead us to answers. Now it's completely meaningless.

Robbie takes a step toward me, and I don't protest it this time. "Whoever Trevor met up with at the barn thought that he was getting too close to finding answers," Robbie says. "They felt threatened enough to reveal they had the bikini. I don't think Trev even knew how close he was to the truth, because he was laser-focused on my dad." He fixates on a piece of lint on his black jeans and picks at it. "That's my theory, anyway."

"We still have Trevor's binder," I tell him. "We can go through it, beginning to end. Look at every single thing he found."

It's two years' worth of notes, tokens, and mementos. We've only scratched the surface.

Robbie squeezes his eyes shut and opens them again. For the first time since he's entered my room, I realize how exhausted he is.

"His binder . . . got drenched when the firefighters were putting out the fire."

Fuck.

I look up at my ceiling. I'm so angry I could cry. Or explode. Or both.

"What if that was the whole point?" I say finally. "That's why the skeleton started the fire." I shiver, glancing at Robbie. "If that's the case, then he could be the killer."

The skeleton hoped the fire would solve all his problems.

Just like I did when I set mine.

FORTY-NINE

At Wintergreen High, I had a reputation. Even before I was with Clint. It's why his mom never liked me. I'd only hooked up with a few guys by then but it didn't matter; once the story of me and Zac Lee hooking up under the football stadium bleachers got out, everyone at my high school thought I was easy. And reputations stick, whether they're true or not.

Soon I became known as the girl you could count on to give you a blow job in the bathroom during second period if we were hooking up, or sleep with you in my car after a game. Part of me thought that's all Clint wanted. My body. That's all anyone ever wanted. Thankfully I was wrong. He'd crushed on me just as long as I'd pined over him.

No one took our relationship seriously at first, including Donovan, Clint's best friend. Who I'd hooked up with before.

"You're not the monogamous type," he'd told me at a party when Clint was out of town. He said it like it was a dare, his dark eyes moving over my body.

"I am," I told him.

"That's too boring for you," he said, leaning into me. A lock of his long hair touched my cheek.

"I love Clint," I said.

"I didn't say you didn't," he said, his other hand finding my neck.

I didn't tell him to stop. Clint was in Denver, meeting with a college scout. He'd gone to a college party and I'd seen his Snaps, his Instagram stories. I'd seen the way girls were already draped all over him. Because Clint is not only hot, he's kind. Basically, a unicorn. I couldn't blame them. I couldn't blame him, either, for soaking up all the attention. But I saw what my future would look like.

I was feeling insecure. I was tipsy. When Donovan said he had a pack of cigarettes for me in his guesthouse, I followed him.

He wasn't lying. He handed me the Newports and we took a handle pull from the fifth of Green Apple Smirnoff sitting on the dresser.

Then he pulled out a Polaroid camera. I froze.

"What are you doing?" I asked.

"Sit on the bed."

"Donovan—"

"I can tell Clint you followed me in here tonight. You knew we'd be alone." He moved closer to me. "You wanted to be alone."

My hands shook as the pack of cigarettes crinkled in my palm. Clint loved Donovan like a brother. They'd been best friends since fourth grade. I didn't know who Clint would choose if it was Donovan's word against mine. I wanted him to choose me.

But I wasn't confident enough to take that chance.

"Take off your shirt," Donovan said.

I thought he was right. I'd already allowed myself to go this far with him. I felt like I couldn't back out. I took another swig from the fifth of Smirnoff. I wanted to be so drunk I could no longer feel anything in my body. It helped me convince myself it wasn't a big deal. The pictures wouldn't even be on his phone. Donovan was vying to be a Division I athlete, too, and a photo scandal would ruin his chances.

My body numbed with alcohol, I obliged. I arched for the flash of his camera, and then for him.

Then it was over. The sun rose. I tiptoed over the used condom on the floor.

After that night, he had complete control. Anytime Clint wasn't looking, his hand landed on my collarbone. Or his lips grazed my cheek.

I'd turn away, and he'd whisper, "Don't forget, Laur."

It was humiliating. I wondered how many girls he had Polaroids of. The worst thing was I couldn't tell the one person who I told everything to. I knew Clint would never forgive me.

Each time I imagined those snapshots, my face burned with shame.

I wanted them gone. Forever.

Even if that meant destroying everything I loved in the process.

FIFTY

The man sitting next to Lionel Crestmont jots down notes on pen and paper. His name is Ben. A former lawyer turned private investigator who Lionel's retained ever since Trevor was found dead.

I feel awkward, sitting across from Lionel. His grief is real. It's why he couldn't bear to bury his son. Not because he was guilty, but because it's the worst truth he's ever had to accept.

Ben has the footage from two days ago pulled up on his iPad. He scrubs back to the beginning, when guests were just beginning to arrive to the dinner. I lean over, peering at the tablet. I spot John in his *Phantom* outfit arriving just ahead of Beetlejuice and Lydia Deetz. A few other guests trickle in. Then I see myself walk up the path. It's another minute before we see him enter the frame.

"Stop," Lionel says. "Right there."

Ben pauses on the skeleton man. No other skeleton woman or man dangles off his arm; no grim reaper friend accompanies him. He's completely alone.

"Did any of you speak with him that night?" Ben asks.

"No," I answer. "I saw him take something from one of the appetizer trays, but that was it."

Ben jots it down.

"No," Robbie says. "Barely noticed him."

Lionel finishes the rest of his double espresso.

"You were focused on preparing your speech," Lionel says. He makes eye contact with Robbie.

I wonder what conversations they've had since the fire. If Robbie apologized. If Lionel forgave him.

Robbie doesn't exactly give me any hints.

"Stacy spoke with him briefly," Robbie says, and I notice the subtle way Lionel seems to flinch. Their breakup must still be pretty raw. "She talked to him for a couple minutes. Said he knew her name, was friendly. She felt bad because she couldn't recognize him. She just pretended to go along with knowing him, too."

Ben adds this to his report.

"John didn't talk to him," Robbie says, "but thought he was a little under six feet tall. They were standing next to each other at some point."

Ben jots this down, then returns to the footage and presses PLAY.

We watch as the skeleton man makes it to the porch. Before he enters through the front door, he glances back behind him. Then he quickly off-loads something from his shoulder. A bag. He stuffs it behind the Halloween decor before walking inside.

"That must be the lighter fluid," I mutter.

"It was naive of me not to hire security," Lionel says. He crosses his arms.

"Have you had any dinner crashers in the past?" I ask him.

"Never." Lionel sighs. "I didn't want people to think we were worried about retaliation. I thought maybe everything could go back to normal."

Robbie grits his teeth. "It will never go back to normal," he says.

Lionel runs his hands through his hair in the exact same way Robbie does. Some of their mannerisms are almost identical.

"My default coping mechanism is escapism," Lionel says, turning his gaze toward me. "I'm working on it in therapy."

I nod. I mean, it makes sense. If I had the money Lionel did and experienced the tragedies their family has faced, I'd spend it on whatever I could that helped me forget.

Lionel turns to Ben. "What's our strategy? I don't exactly want my dinner guests knowing this was arson. I already have my work cut out for me trying to convince them I'm innocent."

"I told you I'd help you," Robbie says gruffly.

"Pretend you're trying to send out thank-you-for-attending favors, and you didn't catch his name," Ben says. "You wanted to see if anyone talked to him. I think they'll be more receptive to that, if you want the investigation to remain private."

"He probably gave out a fake name anyway," Robbie says.

Ben folds the cover over his iPad. "Any details he might have revealed could help lead us to the right person. Even a fake name."

"I'll work my way through the Rolodex," Lionel says.

"Good," Ben says. He slides his iPad into his briefcase.

"Look into the Lakeforest Firm, too," Lionel says. "We had a couple cases dealing with their attorneys and it didn't go very well for them. Maybe one of the lawyers got a little vindictive."

I glance over at Robbie, but he doesn't look convinced. Neither am I.

"I feel like if it was a professional thing, wouldn't they target your office or something?" I ask.

"The house is an easier target," Lionel says. "Our office is right in the middle of downtown."

I mean, it's not a huge *downtown*. Not like the downtown of a major city.

I guess there is the remote chance that the fire could have nothing to do with Lionel's family and everything to do with his professional life. But it seems unlikely.

Then I think of Valley High's security system. Because they must have one. Every high school does, with all the school shooter threats we get.

"Did you ever look into the security system at Valley High?" I ask Ben. "To see if there was footage from the day Trevor was found?"

Ben defaults to Lionel.

"It's okay," Lionel says, "you can tell them."

"I don't think it's a good idea—"

"I deserve to know," Robbie says.

Ben sighs. "This has to stay confidential," he says.

Both of us nod.

"Valley High had a very rudimentary security system," Ben says. "The camera that had been at the parking lot entrance had been out of commission as part of the school-wide upgrade. There's no footage from the day Trevor died."

I turn to Robbie, and it's like we're both on the same wavelength.

"That can't be a coincidence," Robbie says.

"That's what we're trying to figure out," Ben says.

Either it was someone's incredibly lucky day, or the killer knew exactly what they were doing.

A large part of me thinks it has to be the latter.

FIFTY-ONE

"O'Brian, you're starting," Coach says as I jog toward our bench. "Make me proud."

I take a swig of my water, getting into game mode. My mind's been racing all day with skeleton man theories. Each time I text Robbie for an update, he says Ben doesn't have any. Or, at least, none that he's willing to share. Yet. But it's already been three days since we met up with him and my impatience is making me bite my nails off.

I look up into the bleachers out of habit. I'm not expecting to see Mom's face, since she texted me earlier.

Good luck tonight honey! We're at our rescheduled cake tasting. I think the winner so far is chocolate with a caramel ganache

I felt too spiteful to respond.

Then Lex is next to me, reaching for her water bottle. "Some guy named Ben called me?" she says. Her voice sounds unsteady, which is so unlike her. "Said he's a private investigator and he got my number from you. Is he legit?"

"Yeah, don't worry," I say. "He is."

"Wasn't sure if it was a scam or something," she says, glancing over her shoulder. "I got a weird phone call."

Heat rises in my throat.

"What kind of call?" I ask.

"A voice mail of someone breathing," she says. "Mara got one, too."

My stomach sinks. Then the ref is blowing his whistle.

I feel like we're not putting the pieces together fast enough.

———————

"How was the game?" Mom asks when I walk in the door.

"We won," I say flatly.

"That puts you in a great position for states!"

"Yeah," I say.

She gestures to a pink box on the kitchen island. "I saved you a sample. We both ended up loving the vanilla with strawberry buttercream."

She sips her wine and smiles at Mark. He's plopped on the couch with his own glass of wine.

"I think it's more seasonally appropriate than caramel and chocolate. You have to try it," Mom says, grabbing a fork from the silverware drawer.

She's just so out of touch with my life right now. I'm

thinking about a thousand things and her wedding cake isn't one of them.

"After I eat," I say. I slide the pizza slices that I didn't have time to eat before my game into the microwave.

"Just one bite as an appetizer," she says. That's when all the patience I've been trying so hard to channel completely disappears.

"How about you come to one of my games, and then I'll try a piece of your stupid cake."

Mom instantly deflates. "It was the only time they could reschedule us—"

"A quick trip to New York can't fix you missing almost my entire season," I spit out.

"I know nothing will truly make up for—"

I slam the microwave door shut. "Honestly, if watching me play in my last season ever is that much of a headache for you, I'm glad you've missed nearly every single game."

"I've really tried to rearrange my work schedule. But I'm the newest nurse there and they're already letting me take Christmas off. I don't have much wiggle room—"

"Right. Christmas. The four of us can be together. You're obsessed with forcing us to be a family. Clearly Ainsley doesn't want any part of it—"

"It's my fault," Mark says. "I could have planned our engagement timing better—"

"Respectfully, Mark," I tell him, "this is between me and Mom."

"I'm just trying to explain," he says.

"Do you not understand?" I tell him. "I'm having a conversation with my mom."

"Please, Lauren. Let's keep this between me and you, like you said. Mark doesn't deserve to be treated this way."

"He's a big boy. I'm sure he can handle it," I tell Mom, crossing my arms. "Why don't you just move in with him for the rest of the year, and I can live here until I go to college? Since you spend every waking hour at his apartment anyway. That way you won't even have to be reminded that you have a daughter."

Mom throws her hands up, her green eyes suddenly wild. "We've been seeing a fertility doctor, okay?"

The blood drains from my head.

She takes the fork she was holding, the one she took out for me, and shoves it back in the silverware drawer. "That's why I've missed so many of your games. We've been trying to speed things along. We're both committed to doing everything we can and I'll admit that I haven't been giving you the attention you deserve. It's been a stressful process."

Mark comes up to her and puts his hand on the small of her back.

"My ovarian reserve isn't great," she says. Her voice breaks. "We're going to try IVF. I really want it to work out."

Black specks dance across my vision.

This is why it's been weird between us. She knows I'm leaving soon. It's the perfect time for her to start her life over.

With Mark. She can have the perfect family she's always dreamed about.

They look at me expectantly, like I might say, *Congratulations*, or *Oh my God I've always wanted a sibling*, or *I can't wait to babysit when I'm home on college break.*

Maybe if I wasn't so jaded, I would say those things. Maybe if Mom pretended to acknowledge my existence, I'd be a little happier for them. But right now, all I'm feeling is rage.

"I get it," I say, watching the way Mom's face softens, the way Mark's eyes crinkle.

"Thank you for being understanding—" he starts saying, but I'm not finished, and I cut him off.

"It's pretty easy to see now, actually. You had the practice kid, the one without a dad, who fucked up so badly we had to move states, and now you know what *not* to do. The next kid will be perfect. Your perfect nuclear family. It's finally becoming a reality now. I'm really happy for you."

"That is not true," Mom says, but her voice is quiet and faraway.

"Your mother loves you very much," Mark says. The sound of his voice, how patronizing it sounds, nauseates me.

"You're not my father, Mark! Stop trying to fill a gap I don't want filled, okay?"

"I'm sorry, Lauren," he says, but it's not enough to stop me. I know I'm going too far and I want to. I want to burn this bridge. That's what I'm good at. What I excel at.

"Maybe you should actually focus on the daughter you

currently have who does lines of coke on the daily. Maybe you should look into her addiction a little bit," I say.

I feel sick when the last word is out of my mouth. But it's too late now.

Mark's eyes glaze over, and Mom's jaw drops. I turn to her. "I mean, couldn't you tell Ainsley was high as a kite at the Cheesecake Factory? If you couldn't, then maybe you should work on those parenting skills before you bring another kid into the world."

I know I've just ruined their happy news. But they had it coming. They've been living on cloud nine when my world's literally been on fire.

FIFTY-TWO

I can't imagine Mom's belly swelling up. Growing a child. She's never hinted at wanting another kid.

Maybe she thought about it with Andrew. Then I took that dream away from her.

It's 2 A.M. and I'm ravenous. It's been almost impossible for me to sleep through the night ever since the Crestmont fire.

I sneak down into the kitchen, using my phone to light the way. I open the fridge, pulling out a Tupperware of leftover beef stroganoff Mark made the other night. Then it hits me that I'm basically freeloading off his generous cooking after I was a total bitch. I feel ashamed for outing Ainsley's addiction the way I did. I did it to shock them. To have leverage. It feels gross.

I'm putting the leftovers into the microwave when my phone lights up. Someone's calling me. Right now. At 2:09 A.M.

I look at it. The caller ID says UNKNOWN.

A chill runs down my back.

The microwave beeps that it's done. It beeps again. I answer my phone.

I pause, listening. I'm met with silence.

"I was wondering if you'd ever call me again," I say.

Then I hear it. What Lex mentioned. Heavy breathing.

"Hello?" I say. Their breathing grows more rapid, and rhythmic. My stomach lurches with every breath they take.

"We're going to find out who you are," I tell them.

I hang up because I'm too terrified to hear their reply.

"The first call was after I found Vic's bikini top," I tell Lex and Mara later that morning.

I'm sitting with them in the cafeteria, drinking my second bottled Frappuccino of the day. "I thought it could have been Trevor, until that theory fell apart. But when they called me again this morning, it was exactly like you said. They didn't say a single thing. Their breathing got heavier and . . . I told them we'd find out who they are."

Lex holds up a french fry like she's examining it. Then she quickly dunks it in ketchup and puts it in her mouth. "You threatened them?" she asks.

"No," I say quickly. "I mean. I guess I did."

"I think that's what they wanted," Lex says, lowering her voice. "Like they get off on it. Hearing us sound desperate."

"What a fucking creep," Mara says.

I bite the inside of my cheek. The only thing giving me any comfort right now is knowing I'm not utterly alone in facing this.

"I know you didn't see the skeleton by the time you pulled up to the Crestmont house," I say. "But maybe he saw all three of us. In your car together. Before he went inside. That's why we've all gotten the calls this time."

Mara ties her hair up in a ponytail with more force than usual, making sure every single strand of hair is off her face. "I bet he feels powerful. Making anonymous calls to teenage girls. That's incel-level pathetic."

Lex and I nod.

She takes a sip of her water and looks down at her food.

"I'm going to be honest," she says, looking up again. "I'm struggling a little bit with eating right now. The most I have in a long, long time."

Mara rubs Lex's shoulder. "Thanks for telling us," she says.

"Ever since Trevor died . . . and now I keep replaying that phone call in my head."

"Me too," I say quietly. "That makes sense."

Lex grabs another fry and puts it into her mouth. "I'm trying not to let it win." She chews. "Besides. We need our energy for states. We're going this year. It's not an option."

After lunch, I meet Robbie in the library. Trevor's damaged binder is in his lap and I almost wince at the sight of it. I slump into the beanbag next to him and he reaches out, touching my knee.

"I think we need to be more careful," he says. "Since his calls are ramping up, I feel like . . . it's a sign that something's going to happen."

I feel the same way. Like we're sitting ducks.

Robbie runs his hand through his hair. It's longer now. In a month or two, it'll touch his shoulders. "I don't think you should go anywhere alone right now."

"I'm a girl, okay? I've been hypervigilant since birth." But even as I say it, I know it's not enough.

"I took a guess on your order," John says, coming up to our beanbags.

I look up. He's holding a tray of coffee drinks. He places a venti in front of me. I take a sip, welcoming the distraction.

"Pumpkin spice latte," I say. "It's good. Thanks."

"I thought you might like a basic white girl autumn drink," he says, winking, taking a sip of his own.

"I'll never turn down a PSL."

He sits in the beanbag next to me. "You wanted to show us something?" John asks, turning to Robbie.

"Yeah," he says, gesturing to the binder. "I did my best to dry this thing out. Most of it is unsalvageable, but I found this, stuck in between two pages."

Robbie opens the binder and the cover almost rips off because the binding has basically disintegrated. He smooths out a crumpled piece of notepaper on top. "Jess was helping Trevor look into what happened with Vic."

John and I lean in to get a closer look. I get a whiff of his new cologne, the one he's testing out for winter. It's all cherries and citrus.

Neat cursive writing starts at the top left corner of the page. Jess's writing.

Playing devil's advocate here. S and L were at a Fourth of July party on the other side of the lake that night. He had an alibi.

L must be Lionel.
Trevor's notes are beneath hers.

Everyone was wasted that night. L could have slipped out unnoticed.

And Jess's notes below his.

Robbie said Vic left in the middle of the night once before that same summer, the weekend of June 17, when Robbie and her got into a fight. She took a midnight swim. Someone could have seen her do this, and maybe they were hoping she'd do it again next time she was there. Was your dad at the lake on June 17?

Yes, Trevor writes.

The notes underneath his are completely smeared. The ink bled and the words are impossible to make out.

Robbie tenses next to me. I lean a little closer toward him, resting my head against his shoulder. I feel his muscles relax.

He flips the page over, and the text is a little bit more readable.

Her unexplained cut, Jess writes, *could be from debris in the lake, or what if . . . it was from fishing pliers? I'm thinking the latter, because if it was debris, wouldn't she have had more cuts or scratches? Most boats keep a pair of pliers on board to take hooks out of fish. It would be a convenient weapon.*

Trevor's notes, below it.

The police did take our pliers from the boat. To my knowledge, her blood wasn't found on them.

It's like they passed this piece of paper back and forth, writing down their theories in between classes. Maybe they thought it was safer that way. No digital trail.

That's why I'm saying it could have been anyone on the lake. I guess your dad could have cleaned them well enough, too. But it's hard to truly remove all traces of blood. If he bought a new pair, there would be evidence of the recent purchase. Wouldn't there?

It's like I've been holding my breath this entire time and I finally exhale. Jess was smart. Her theories were well supported by the evidence she had access to.

"She was steering this investigation just as much as Trevor," I say quietly.

I remember what Lex said. Trevor had only returned to investigating recently, a few months before he died. And he had to do it without Jess. His sounding board. "Someone must have found out that Jess was digging into this. If her death really is linked to Vic's."

"Okay . . . but then why would they wait to kill Trevor?" Robbie asks.

"She could have done some investigating without him," I wonder aloud. "Maybe she got in too deep."

"You think she had a big realization the night she died?" John asks.

"I don't know. The timing would be tight."

"That means someone would have had to come to the party and drug her and leave without being seen," John says, "or it was someone at the party."

I bite my lip, thinking. "Can you go to those texts between Trevor and Jess the night of the party?" I ask.

Robbie reaches for a dry green bookmark sticking out of the binder, toward the back, one he must have added after the fire. The page with Jess's timeline is rippled, but it's readable. I glance over it, refreshing my memory.

TIMELINE—JESS

11:03 P.M. Trev, I'm in the kitchen!

11:08 P.M. Thanks be there in five babe

11:12 P.M. Where are you? I'm in the kitchen.

11:20 P.M. Jess?

11:25 P.M. Jess where tf are you

"He hadn't seen her since at least 11:03 P.M., probably before," I point out, "and then by 11:25 she's still unaccounted for. That's twenty-two minutes at the least and could be thirty or more minutes at the most."

"He called me at 11:45 that night," Robbie says. "He found her right before that."

"Then it's not unreasonable that something could have happened to her during that time frame," John says. "Twenty or thirty minutes is plenty of time to kill a person." He shoots me a cutting glance. "Not that I would know, Lauren."

I don't think I'll ever be able to recover from the fact that I thought, for a second, John could possibly be the person behind the Unhappiest of Valleys account.

"I wonder if Ainsley saw her at all then," I say.

"Ainsley refused to talk to Trevor afterward," Robbie says. "She hadn't talked to him since Jess died."

"Maybe she'll talk to me," I say.

After all, we're going to share a sibling soon.

FIFTY-THREE

Ainsley hasn't answered any of the texts I send her by the end of the day. I'm not exactly shocked. The last time we saw each other was on pretty terrible terms. My only option is to surprise her.

I show up at her locker once the last bell rings. She can't avoid me forever. In fact, it's going to be pretty impossible to given the fact that our parents are getting married and trying to conceive a child together.

"Ainsley."

She sees me and grimaces. She's carrying a gigantic portfolio stuffed with artwork.

"I deleted the account, okay?" she says, opening her locker.

I've been so preoccupied by everything going on, I almost forgot.

"Oh. Right. Thanks for upholding our deal."

With her free hand, she grabs two books on art theory and shoves them into her bag. "Need a locker shelf? Pens? Magnets? Paper?"

"No. I'm good."

Her expression darkens. "Then I'm just going to leave them here. The school can clean it out."

I stare at her, feeling like I'm missing something. She glares at me. "Oh, didn't you hear? Someone told my dad about my habit. Now I'm being shipped off to rehab."

Shit. My shoulders instantly hunch.

"I didn't plan on outing you," I say.

"Yeah," she says, "right."

She slams her locker closed and walks away from me. I hustle, keeping up with her.

"They told me about the baby thing and I said a lot of things I regret, okay?" I explain. "I'm sorry."

She laughs. "Guess they're getting rid of both of us, then, huh? With you going to college. Me all the way in California. They can have their new kid all to themselves."

She pushes open the doors to the parking lot. I can't help but fixate on what she just said.

I run after her.

"They're sending you to California?" I ask.

"Apparently your mom knew of some 'state-of-the-art' places through her nursing friends and Dad will do anything she says."

"I could say the same thing about my mom," I counter.

Ainsley reaches into her tote bag for her keys. She unlocks her beat-up car. She opens the trunk and thrusts all the stuff she's been carrying inside, laying her portfolio on top.

"Honestly, maybe it's a blessing in disguise," she says. "I'll stay out there and never come back."

"What about your mom?"

Ainsley scowls. "She agrees with my dad on this one. Said she's disappointed in me. You know. The whole thing."

Ainsley closes her trunk. Before she can make her way to the driver's side, I intercept her.

"Did you know Jess was helping Trevor in his investigation of Vic's death?"

"Don't start that bullshit with me," she says.

I knew she'd be defensive.

I pull out my phone. I show her the photo I snapped of Jess's theories that we found in Trevor's binder.

"She was all in," I tell Ainsley. "That's her handwriting."

Ainsley's piercing blue eyes dart over the photo. Then she takes my phone in her hands, zooming in. Making sure it's the real thing.

She glances up at me, handing my phone back.

"I'm late," she says.

"For what?"

"For work. Have to make it look like I make money legitimately."

"I'm coming with you," I tell her.

"Lauren—"

"You're about to be on the other side of the country and we're getting close to figuring out who the hell killed Vic and probably Jess and Trevor."

Now I'm in full-on pleading mode. "You knew Jess the best out of anyone, and I know you'd do anything for her. I know that's why you said that nasty shit about Vic on the Unhappiest of Valleys account. Because you knew it hurt Jess that Trevor and Vic had hooked up right around the time Trevor and Jess were getting together."

Ainsley looks at me. "I know it was messed up." Her lip trembles. "To say that about someone who was dead . . . I couldn't even function at the time. I was using a lot. I did a lot of things I regret."

"You can make up for it," I tell her.

Her mouth puckers. Then she nods, like she's resigned to the fact that I'm not going to give up.

And she's right. Because I'm not.

"Get in," she says.

I wait for Ainsley's shift break in the alleyway of the Creamery. The sundae I just inhaled gurgles in my stomach. The door finally opens and out comes Ainsley, bringing a cloud of whipped cream and hot fudge with her.

She reaches into her pocket, fishing for something. Her vape.

"Gotta get it in while I still can," she says, inhaling. She sits on the milk crate next to me. "What do you want to know?"

"Start with Jess. Did you and her ever talk about Robbie and Vic? Did she ever share her theories of what she thought happened?"

"Jess told me she wasn't sure Robbie was guilty," Ainsley says. "I mean, she'd gotten to know him through Trevor, I guess. I was undecided at that point. Vic's death seemed sketch, but they also never arrested Robbie, so I don't know. I know it sounds bad but I didn't really think about either of them until Jess died. I was kind of in my own plane of reality."

She exhales in the opposite direction, then turns to me. Splotches of hot fudge stain the edges of her uniform. "Jess never told me she was helping Trevor. I didn't even know they were doing an investigation or whatever," Ainsley says, her voice softer.

I can imagine how Ainsley felt left out. This was her best friend. Jess kept this all a secret from her.

"I know she did it to protect you," I say.

"Whatever," Ainsley mutters.

"There was about a thirty-minute time frame when Trevor couldn't find Jess at the party the night she died," I tell her. "He'd been texting Jess but she didn't respond."

I show Ainsley the photo of the texts Trevor printed out. She leans in. This close, the berry smell of her vape is intoxicating. I hold my breath, telling myself that's the old me. Being around it always feels like a test. "Did you see her at all around that time?" I ask.

Ainsley shakes her head. "No. I was a little busy that night."

"You were hooking up with someone, right?"

She sighs, exhaling a huge plume of smoke. I pop a piece of gum into my mouth.

Ainsley wipes her fingers on her apron, brushing off the rainbow sprinkles stuck to the fabric.

She finally looks up at me.

"I'm not just a user," she tells me.

"Of course not—"

"I deal," she says.

"Oh."

"That's why I'm at like every single party. And yeah, I know you're not supposed to use your own shit, but I do. Guess I'm the worst drug dealer ever."

She shifts her weight and takes another hit from her vape. "I never wanted Jess to start using like I did. I kept that shit away from her. It almost fucking killed me when I found out she OD'd."

Ainsley's eyes burn through me. "I didn't lie about that part. I know Jess had never done drugs before. I would know, okay? She didn't. And when word got out of what she had? I knew it was from my stash."

"You're saying—"

"The drugs in her system were the ones I deal. Or used to deal. I don't deal heroin anymore."

Holy shit. Heroin? "But when you mix heroin and coke together you get a speedball and it can cause a massive heart attack and that's what she died of," Ainsley says. "I was the only dealer at the party that night."

She closes her eyes. "Someone from the party told the police they thought I dealt drugs. They brought me in for questioning."

She opens her eyes and her gaze is faraway, like she's looking past me. "That's another reason why I started the Unhappiest of Valleys account. To make sure the focus stayed on Trevor."

"Did they arrest you?" I ask.

"No. My dad asked me if anyone had taken pictures of me with drugs that night. If anyone had actual proof. I said no. I'm not that much of a mess. I only do deals behind closed doors. Without my confession, the police had basically nothing. They let me go."

She shakes her head. "I couldn't admit to that. I couldn't do that to Jess's family. I was her best friend."

It takes me a minute to process everything she just said.

"Your dad knew, then? About you doing drugs?"

"Yeah. He made me promise to ditch the drugs, and to never tell my mom about the entire ordeal. I swore I would." She rolls her eyes. "Obviously that turned out well."

The door opens, and Ainsley's manager sticks her head out.

"Hey, Ains, rush has started," she says, before disappearing back inside.

"Okay, be right in," Ainsley says.

"Did Trevor buy drugs from you?" I ask quickly.

She scoffs. "No."

"But you think he killed her—"

"He stole them," she says. "Some of my stash was missing when I went over it the next day. I couldn't account for it with any of my sales. And before you ask, I know how much I use. It wasn't like I accidentally took more than my usual share."

Ainsley puts her vape back into her pocket. "He was also the only person I could think of that Jess would be with on the golf course that night."

I think back to what Lex said when we thought Lionel was the murderer.

"Centre Hills Country Club," I say.

"Yeah. There were like some trees and shit in Pax's back-yard, but beyond that is the golf course. When Jess was found by the pool, she had leaves and stuff stuck to her. Like she had come from back there. It would make no sense why she'd be out there by herself."

Ainsley stands up from the crate. I stand up to meet her. "Have you ever thought about the fact that Trevor could have just texted Jess that night, asking where she was, to make it look like he was concerned about her?" she says. "He was covering his tracks."

I hadn't thought of it that way before.

"I think it ate him up inside," Ainsley says. "He even called me the week he died. Begging me to believe him."

I reach out to steady myself against the brick wall of the alleyway. This is news to me.

"What did he say?"

"He left me a voice mail saying he wanted to retrace Jess's last night, starting from when me and her got ready together before the party. That he was close to building an exact timeline and he needed my help filling in the gaps. He wanted to meet in person."

"Did you?"

"Hell no. I told my dad I wanted to change my number so he could never call me again. That didn't stop him from showing up to my art showcase though. I told him to fuck off."

Then she's pushing open the door, heading back inside the Creamery. But before she's gone, I have to ask her one last thing.

"How did you get access to that newspaper before anyone else? On the Unhappiest of Valleys post?"

"Oh," she says. "Easy. My mom writes for the paper."

FIFTY-FOUR

"**Anyone at that party could have** stolen drugs from her," I explain to John and Robbie after leaving the Creamery. "It could have even been someone who *bought* drugs from her."

"We could get a list from her. Of everyone who bought off her that night," John says, cupping his face with his hands as he lies on the hotel bed.

Robbie stares up at the ceiling. He's been staying here while they repair the damages to his house, because his mom's condo doesn't have an extra bedroom.

"If she even remembers every single person," Robbie says. "I doubt she has a detailed log."

"It's worth a try," John says.

I lean over, getting a better look at the updated master timeline.

TIMELINE—TREVOR
Two years ago
July 3rd—Trevor finds underwear he thinks is Vic's; shows Lex

July 3rd/4th—Vic drowns

One year ago

September 21st—Jess dies at homecoming party

September 22nd—Ainsley realizes some of her drugs were stolen

This year

September 11th—Trevor goes to meet mystery person; found near dead in Valley High parking lot. Day of pep rally.

September 23rd—Letter and bikini top found at homecoming game

October 27th—Confront Lionel; skeleton man sets Crestmont house on fire. About 6' tall.

My eyes dart over all the key dates, focusing in on September 11. The day Trevor died.

The same day as the pep rally.

The pep rally. The day the security camera was offline, according to Ben. The day where everyone in the entire school except me and Trevor Crestmont were inside the gym.

Except, I remember, that's not entirely true.

"Coach Holliger," I say, "was late to the pep rally. I saw him in the hallway because I skipped. I was on my way to the parking lot. Literally no one else was around. When I got outside . . ."

I've never told either of them this. "I saw the ambulance."

Robbie puts his hand on my leg. He leans his weight into me. His eyes are huge. "You saw my brother?"

I can't bring myself to look at him. My ears are ringing. I feel like I've betrayed him in some way.

"I couldn't even . . . I didn't know how to tell you," I say.

"What did he look like?" Robbie asks.

"I don't know—"

His voice shakes. "You have to tell me, Lauren. Tell me what you saw."

I swallow. "I saw his face. He didn't look like himself. But he didn't look like he was in pain, either."

I glance up at Robbie as he blinks. Like he's imagining what I saw.

"Before I got out there," I say quietly, "Coach was coming from that direction. That puts him in direct proximity to Trevor. Then there's Ainsley," I explain, trying to get the words out fast enough. "I saw her in Coach's office the day he kicked me off the team. She was showing him what I'm guessing was the painting she did of Vic . . . and let's just say they looked close."

"Jess used to paint the banners for soccer banquet nights," John says. Maybe Ainsley took over that tradition. "Jess's older sister was a senior on varsity when Jess was a freshman. She was teammates with Vic."

"That would have given Coach close access to both Jess and Ainsley," I say.

I text Ainsley and ask her if she's ever sold drugs to Coach or if she remembers seeing him at the party that night.

I look up at Robbie and John after I send it. Robbie rubs

his mouth with his hands like it's the only thing keeping him from falling apart.

"Coach was at Lake Monarch during Labor Day weekend, too," I say quickly. "I ran into him at the general store that his family owns. He was talking to Gwen. They looked . . ."

"Like your coach has a thing for younger girls?" John says.

I grimace. "Yes. He could have been partying on one of those boats that day. He could have seen me with Vic's top."

All of us are silent for a moment. The pieces are piling up, fast.

Robbie looks up at me. His cheeks are drawn in, like he's bracing himself.

"Vic was close to him," Robbie says. "She trained with him alone sometimes, to work on her foot skills."

Coach would have known the ins and outs of her relationship with Robbie. He could have easily figured out when she was going to be with him that Fourth of July weekend.

Now my heart's racing.

"I never thought . . . ," Robbie says, "I mean, he wasn't even a possibility to me . . ."

"You were just focused on surviving her death," John says, "not playing detective."

"He has access to the school after hours," I say. "He would have known when to place the bikini and the note without anyone seeing him."

Coach left the bikini behind, a key piece of evidence, because he was so confident that no one would ever trace it back to him.

"He could have known about the security updates at Valley High, too. I'm sure the staff did. He knew he wouldn't be caught on camera with Trevor." I swallow the lump in my throat, knowing Coach is perfectly strong enough to subdue someone like Trevor. He could have been the reason why Trevor had those bruises. "There's also the fact that he's just the right build to be the skeleton man."

Robbie pulls out his phone and presses Ben's contact. He puts him on speakerphone.

"We have a new theory for you."

We made your favorite! Be home late tonight.
Xoxo Mom

Her note is stuck to the top of a perfect, golden-brown pumpkin pie. She's trying hard to make up for the other night. For everything. As my teeth sink into a gooey slice, I know I was too hard on her. She's excited to have a life again after the shit show of last year. She deserves to.

I shovel a huge bite of crust into my mouth and text Mara and Lex.

Just eating real quick then I'll be over

I'm crashing their sleepover to talk about Coach. Except they don't know that yet. I only told them we have a new working theory, and that I'd share the details in person. Because I know that it's going to come as a shock. They've known Coach for years. They might even be a little defensive at first, but we have to gather as much potential evidence as we can. In the meantime, Ben is going to run a background check and try to establish whether or not Coach had any alibis.

I'm so in my own head that it takes me a second to realize I hear the sound of footsteps upstairs.

My heart beats faster. I'm the only one who's supposed to be home right now.

"Hello?" I call out.

"It's just me," Mark says.

My panic subsides.

I head upstairs to grab my phone charger. When I reach the landing, a box of Halloween decor greets me. Half the garland from the stairs hangs on the edges as Mark undrapes the rest. Mom must have started taking everything down since it's already November 2.

"I didn't see your car," I say.

"Your mom's check engine light is on so I told her to take my car in today. I worked remotely."

"Oh, right."

I brush past him, almost knocking into the wall. I grab ahold of it, feeling weirdly unsteady, like my legs might give out at any moment.

Mark unwinds the rest of the garland from the staircase to

put into the storage bin and my phone vibrates in my pocket. I struggle to pull it out.

"You feeling okay, Lauren?" he says, but it's weird, because his voice sounds further and further away.

"Yeah," I say, lying. I glance down at my phone. Ainsley texted me back.

Coach Holliger? Yeah right. He's never come to a party

I try to reply but it's like my fingers aren't working right. Like I'm drunk or something.

I notice Mark is watching me.

I look up at him. At the Halloween bin at his feet. And then it's like my eyes are drawn to something in the bin, something familiar and unexpected. It's tucked in between my mom's Dorothy costume and Mark's Tin Man costume.

A skeleton costume.

Fuck. It can't be.

My eyes meet Mark's, and I watch as the edges of his mouth curl up into a twisted smile.

"No," I hear myself saying. I'm trying to press the side button on my phone five times, because it'll send a call to 911, but then I'm struggling to even keep myself upright.

I grab ahold of the doorframe, but it's too late. My knees buckle. Everything turns to black.

FIFTY-FIVE

Mark allows himself a moment to stand over the body in the doorway. He watches the way the chest rises up and down. Up and down, steady.

He watches, and the thing in the pit of him, the thing that is always ravenous and never satiated, uncurls itself like a centipede emerging from its cool, dark corner to surprise a larva.

His phone rings, shattering the still quiet. Mark answers. He speaks to his fiancée, Kat, who is at work. She tells him she misses him. He tells her he misses her, too, as he looks down at her daughter. Her body is motionless, ready to be moved at will. When the call ends, his fingertips burn.

He reaches into the bottom of the decorations bin and retrieves the pieces of rope. It is thrilling, to finally touch them. Goose bumps travel down his arms.

Mark lays out the pieces, then bends down beside Lauren. He places a hand on her forehead. Her skin is milky white and so, so soft. He steadies his breath. He must keep working.

He turns her onto her side. He places a hand on her chest and feels her heartbeat. *Thump. Thump. Thump.*

Her hands are limp as he brings them together behind her back. A few nails have chipped dark polish. Mark runs his fingers over the cracked edges of the polish and imagines the nail beds underneath. He wishes there was no polish left. He wishes her nails were perfectly clean.

When he tries to pick the polish off, one of her hands accidentally drops from his grasp and falls onto the carpet.

"Sorry," Mark says.

There is no response.

"Let's try that again," he says.

He brings Lauren's hands together once more. He ties them in a handcuff knot and does it swiftly. When he is finished, he runs his hands over the knot. He closes his eyes. Another detail he savors.

He ties her ankles next. They are bony and bruised from years of soccer. He makes sure this knot is very tight, because her legs are the strongest part of her body.

Mark rubs his lips together.

"When I came across your mom's dating profile, I remember she had a photo of the two of you. It was after one of your games in California. You were wearing green shorts."

Mark closes his eyes. "I knew, then, immediately: You were my next one."

He opens his eyes. He stares at the motionless girl before

him. "Then we matched. A very happy moment for me, indeed. Your mom is a nice woman. It was easy to connect with her—so easy, in fact, that I was going to apply for a job to transfer to the California office permanently. But then she told me the awful year you had. I suggested the two of you move."

Mark smiles to himself. "It was meant to be."

He reaches into his pocket for the piece of silk. He has saved it for last.

He fastens it over Lauren's mouth. He ties it around her head and tightens it against her light brown hair. His fingers brush up against the strands and he grabs a handful, marveling at how lush her hair is. He was hoping it would be freshly washed, but one day old is a close second.

Then he picks her up by the shoulders and drags her down the hall.

FIFTY-SIX

Mark takes a sip from his coffee thermos, freshly brewed from Kat's coffeepot.

"You know, this time around, the entire operation is much smoother already," he tells Lauren. Her head rests on the kitchen floor, near Mark's feet. "With Victoria, I thought the element of surprise would be enough."

He takes another sip of his coffee. It is thick with creamer from the bottle he keeps in Kat's fridge. "But it was my first time, and I made mistakes. I learned again with Jess. She sensed something about me. The way she'd look at me when she was hanging out with Ainsley . . . Her wheels were turning. Smart girl."

Mark looks outside. Across Kat's yard, through the smattering of trees, the neighbor's kid swings on his swing set. It makes a loud, grating sound every time he pumps his feet. The set needs to be oiled. Mark grimaces.

"Jess began taking an interest in me. Asking me about my work. The couple of dates I went on with Mrs. Moreno. When she was getting ready with Ainsley in my master bathroom for homecoming, I caught her looking through my drawers. I knew she suspected me. I did not choose her, but I was forced to act."

The neighbor kid jumps off the swing midair. He lands and rolls, and then his face twists in pain. He cries out for his mom. The screen door slides open and she comes running outside.

I told you not to jump like that!

Mark closes the blinds on the kitchen window. Then the ones on the sliding glass door. He dumps the rest of the pumpkin pie in the garbage. It was a perfect pie. Kat mixed the dry ingredients before she left for work. Kat says she enjoys doing activities together. She says it makes her feel closer to him. She says she has never felt the way she feels about Mark about anyone else, ever. It is nice, to hear these things. But that is all it is. Nice.

Mark places the pie pan in the sink. He fills it with soap and water until the bubbles spill over the sides.

"Well," he tells Lauren as he dries his hands with the Penn State dish towel Kat gave him, "we should get going."

There is nothing in the trunk of Kat's car except for a Horizon Networks ball cap and her daughter.

A red pickup truck cuts in front of Mark. He white-knuckles the steering wheel. Then he sighs, chuckling to himself.

"It's not worth it. There are too many hotheads out here," he says.

His eyes flash to the rearview mirror. He glances at the trunk. "Jess was a good girl. I knew she always called her mom a half hour before her curfew, at 11:30 P.M. When she stepped outside that party to make the call, I surprised her. I told her I was planning an intervention for Ainsley. I told her I needed her help."

A police car cruises by in the fast lane. Mark is silent until it is past him. He is good with police, but a stop might make things more difficult.

"Jess believed me," Mark says quietly. "She followed me just a little farther, into the wooded area. I think she felt safe, because the party was only thirty feet away. But no one could hear us. The music was too loud."

He grimaces. "I didn't inject her with the right dosage. She made it to the backyard. It was too close."

He exits the highway, taking a country back road. A road shrouded in foliage, a road much less traveled this time of year. "I didn't make the same mistake with Trevor."

Mark puts on his turn signal and makes a right turn.

"He was getting desperate. I had to protect Ainsley."

The sun begins to dip into the sky as the lake comes into view. Mark glances out at the setting sun, feeling a familiar rush of adrenaline.

"Trevor was a liability. I thought of all the work he must

have done when I set that fire. I wanted it gone, the same as him."

Mark pulls the car onto a gravel driveway of the cottage he's been coming to since he was a boy, the one owned by his uncle, who leaves for Florida every year after the first frost.

He parks. He takes the key out of the ignition.

It's finally dark.

"We could have had more time together, but you just had to reveal Ainsley's little habit. Didn't you?"

Mark grabs the skeleton mask off the floor of the passenger seat. He unlocks the car.

FIFTY-SEVEN

Lauren's head lolls to the side as Mark drags her around his uncle's garden. There is no one to witness him other than a doe. She rifles through the decaying vegetables.

If Mark had his gun, he would shoot it. Deer always ruin what his uncle plants. Lake Monarch is overrun with them.

"Get," Mark hisses, gritting his teeth. The doe stares at him with her pupilless eyes.

They pass by a small bench. Underneath it is a metal compartment where Mark keeps his pair of binoculars. He has used the same pair for years. They have always picked up the smallest details, like the tie-dyed print of Victoria's bathing suit as she dove into the water.

He drags Lauren onto the dock. It is a dock his uncle built by hand, obscured by trees that have rooted in the lake itself. He tips her into the rowboat. Then he lowers himself inside and unties the rope from the dock.

They float out onto the calm, still waters of Lake Monarch.

Mark looks out over the water and imagines Victoria. She is swimming. She has never stopped swimming, in his mind. He sees her tanned, golden-brown skin. Her long dark hair, pulled into a ponytail. Her athletic body.

There was nothing soft about her. She was perfect.

"She could have been on the varsity swim team if she wanted," Mark says, picking up the two oars.

The mask muffles his voice. "You know, I'm not a violent person. She's the one who grabbed the pliers."

Mark reaches for the pair that he keeps underneath his seat. He holds them out, in front of Lauren's face, as if she might see them for herself. "This little doodad caused me a bit of a mess. But I'm sure you knew that, since you found her top."

He sighs, dropping the pliers over the side of the boat, into the water. He strokes Lauren's cheek as the pliers sink. "Their boat was the safest place for it, after they'd torn it apart. I could pay it a visit any time I wanted. All I had to do was schedule a security update and Lionel would be locked out of his camera view. And if anyone did find it . . . Well. Then the Crestmonts would have been to blame."

He touches the soft, meaty part of Lauren's earlobe. Oh, *yes*. She is perfect, too.

"You lied to me that weekend. The Okadas vacation in Hawai'i. They've never had a cottage at Lake Monarch."

He brings Lauren's hand to his nose and smells it. Pleasure rushes through him.

"I was preparing the barbecue for your mom the moment you found it. I watched you on the back end, from my iPad. From the camera on their boat."

He smiles.

"Now the two of us are finally here. Together. The only way we can be."

FIFTY-EIGHT

Dampness underneath my cheek. There's a bad smell, like rotting fish.

Something is tight over my mouth. I try to flex my fingers but I can barely feel them. I can barely feel anything.

I'm not alone.

"Shhh," he says.

I wince. His breath is sour and awful. "I remember that early morning we spent together."

My chin is in his hands. I smell the nutmeg underneath his nails. "The way you devoured my cinnamon rolls . . ."

Fuck you, I want to say. All I can manage is a whimper.

Then he's lifting me up. My head drops to the side. I have no neck control. Splinters bury themselves into my skin.

Suddenly, I'm in midair.

The water is a shock.

Then I'm sinking. He must have tied weights to me. The pressure in my chest is unbelievable, like I'm being ripped open and crushed at the same time.

I think of Mom. I try to remember the last thing I said to her.

I inhale, and my world goes dark. I am alone and I am terrified and I wish my brain would black out. I don't know how long I'm there. In the darkness. Filling up with water until that's all I am.

Until something tugs at me. Pulling me upward.

By some miracle, I'm no longer underwater. I can smell the woods. I'm coughing and the water keeps sputtering out of me.

I hear the crackling of radios and so many voices.

One breaks through.

Oh my God, you're okay.

Robbie.

I strain to open my eyes. I can just make out his skin, ghostly pale. There's someone next to him. Huddled over him. John.

I see something white. A medical mask above me. Something is going over my face.

My eyes fall closed. I swear I can smell the pomade in Lex's hair. Mara's floral perfume.

You're safe now, Lex says.

FIFTY-NINE

I groan as I try to turn over in bed. Pain radiates down my forearm.

"Let me help you."

Mom.

She moves my IV lines to the side and helps me turn over. "How are you feeling?" she asks.

"Like shit," I rasp.

Damn, my throat hurts.

"Here."

She's bringing something to my lips. Tangy and ice-cold. Cranberry juice. I gulp it down, and for a moment it soothes my sore throat. Then a nurse is next to me, putting something on top of my finger and a blood pressure cuff around my arm.

"How's your pain on a scale from zero to ten?" she asks.

"Six," I say. It hurts to talk.

"I'll put in an order for more Tylenol for you," she says.

"I think she needs something stronger," Mom says in her own nurse voice.

"I'll ask the doctor to come in," my nurse says. Then she's gone.

My eyes refocus. I see a whiteboard with today's date. November 4.

The last day I remember being awake was November 2.

I taste pumpkin pie again and feel sick. I don't know what it is, but suddenly my legs are shaking underneath the hospital blanket.

"Where is he?" I ask. It comes out like a cough.

"He's being held without bail," Mom says quietly.

Something just shy of relief floods my body.

Mom shakes her head. Pieces of her vibrant hair fall across her face. Her eyes are red-rimmed and wet. "I'm so sorry, Lauren."

"It's not your fault," I say, but then I'm coughing, and Mom is rubbing my back.

"Shh," she says. "Don't exert yourself. I just want you to know," she says, choking on her words, "if I could take it all back, if I could have never matched with him, I would."

Part of me wishes she could.

"You didn't know," I remind her. And myself. "You were finally going to have the life you dreamed of."

"No. He was pulling me away from my dream life," she says. "I have you."

Her hand comes to her own throat. She rubs her skin, back and forth, like she's massaging a bruise. I notice her engagement ring is gone.

Then she looks up, past me. Whatever she sees makes the sadness etched into her face disappear for a second.

"Are you up for visitors?" she asks. "Since they saved your life and all."

I follow her gaze. Four familiar faces stand in the doorway.

"I'll run down to the cafeteria," Mom says, leaving my side. She gives every single one of them a bone-clenching hug before she goes.

"You look amazing for someone who nearly drowned," Mara says.

The surrealness of it all, of what she just said, makes me laugh in spite of everything. Then I'm coughing again, and Lex is handing me my juice.

"Oh my God, sorry," Mara says, and I try not to laugh harder.

John sets a jar of something on my bedside table. "My mom swears by this salve," he says. "She always saves extra for her patients since Penn State's PT department tends to run low. It's like Icy Hot but better."

"Thank you, John."

I can feel Robbie's gaze. He sits in the chair closest to me, and takes my hand in his. He looks like he wants to say something but can't bring himself to say it.

The room goes silent. It makes me anxious. I have so many questions I don't even know where to begin.

"How did you find me?" I ask. "I didn't imagine that, right?"

"No," Lex says, and it's like she shudders. "When you didn't answer any of my texts and calls after we were supposed to meet up, I called Robbie. He was still with John, and they said you had gone home."

"They told us the Coach theory," Mara says. She tightens her hold on Lex's arm. "It literally made me sick. Thinking it could be him after all this time."

"I thought we should go to your house," John says. "See if you were there. Or if your mom had seen you, at least. Your car was there, but the house was dark. Which felt ominous. The signs were not pointing in a good direction." He glances over at Robbie. "Robbie noticed it first. He's the only one of us that had been inside your house before."

"Noticed what?" I ask.

"We went around to the back," Robbie says, "and all the blinds in your kitchen were closed. They were open when I'd been there before at night. Every single one. I noticed it because my dad hates when we forget to close ours."

He's right. I don't remember Mom shutting the blinds. Since moving to Pennsylvania, it's the first time we haven't been right on top of our neighbors.

"I told them we had to break in," Robbie says. "Even if I turned out to be wrong . . . it was better than the alternative."

"We were on board," Lex says, glancing around the room. "We yanked the sliding glass door over and over again to loosen the lock, and it finally clicked off."

"We flicked on the light and called out for you, but it was

dead quiet. I saw a plate with crumbs on it at the table," Mara says. "Like someone had just been there."

My stomach twists. My plate of pumpkin pie.

"The coffeepot was still on, too," Mara says. "I went over to it, and noticed the mugs next to it. One was a Valley Hospice mug. The other was a Horizon Networks mug. I kind of remembered that name ringing a bell. Then it finally clicked, where I had seen it before. Vic's house."

Horizon Networks. Where Mark works.

"The Morenos have a Horizon Networks sticker on one of their front windows," Mara says. "It was their new home security system that they got right before Vic died."

I vaguely remember Mom saying Horizon did something with IT and security. Maybe if I was actually invested in her relationship, I would have asked her more about it. Maybe I could have suspected Mark before he drugged me.

"I remembered that Vic's mom went on a couple dates with someone who worked at Horizon Networks," Mara says. "It was Mark."

"They *dated*?" I ask.

"They only went out a couple times. They kept it on the down-low because Mrs. Moreno had told Vic and Andrea she'd never remarry after their dad died. Vic only mentioned it once. It didn't work out between her and Mark so I never gave him a second thought. But standing in your kitchen, it was all I could think about."

Lex wraps her arm around Mara's waist.

"I thought, what are the chances he dates Mrs. Moreno, and something happened to Vic," Mara says, "and now he's dating your mom, and none of us can get ahold of you when you're supposed to be with us?"

Mara briefly shuts her eyes. "I started spiraling."

"Meanwhile," John says, "I wasn't being precious with your privacy. I thought we'd better look in more rooms than the kitchen for clues, so I went upstairs. That's where I found the box of Halloween decorations on the landing. I saw something familiar after sifting through it. The only thing missing was the mask."

"I was doubled over at that point," Mara says. "I knew it was him. I knew what he did to Victoria. I knew we had to find you before it was too late."

"I called Ben," Robbie says. "I told him the skeleton was Mark, and that you were with him. He told me our boat security cameras sent an alert for motion minutes before I called. It was a rowboat, twenty feet away. Helmed by a man in a mask. The Lake Monarch police were already on their way."

"We hightailed it to the lake," Lex says.

"I made her drive like twenty miles over the speed limit," Mara says.

"They found you just north of our boat, in the middle of the lake," Robbie says. He strokes my hand. "One of the ropes he tied you up with got caught on a tree root and it was visible from the surface. That's what saved you."

I was going to be the second girl to drown in Lake Monarch.

I know how close it was. My body remembers. Every time I move, I relive it. Pain stretches from my throat down into my chest. Like something reached deep inside my lungs and clawed its way back out.

I close my eyes. I remember thinking about Mom. Thinking I'd never see her again. I wasn't ready to die.

Why couldn't someone save Victoria? Why did Jess and Trevor have to die, too?

Robbie wraps his arms around me as my tears fall. He's lost so much. The girl he loved. His only brother. He's barely eighteen years old.

I don't understand how any of this is fair.

I hold on to him tighter. I wonder why bad things are allowed to happen to good people. As Robbie lays his head against my chest, I wonder what category I'd fall into.

Because I'm thinking of the person who I almost burned to death.

SIXTY

"Lionel called," Mom says.

She grabs her Diet Coke from the console.

It's November 7, and we're in a rental car, driving back to Happy Valley from the hospital in Hershey. Mom's car still hasn't been released since it was taken in for evidence. I'm grateful I don't have to ride in it. Even if I don't remember being driven to the lake against my will.

I twist the hospital bracelet that's still on my wrist.

"What'd he say?" I ask.

I take another bite of my McChicken sandwich. Swallowing is barely tolerable.

Mom sets her cup back in the drink console. Her hand shakes.

"They're offering Mark a plea deal. If he takes it, then there won't have to be a trial."

Nothing registers except my anger.

"He's a coward," I say.

Mom tightens her grip on the wheel.

"I think everyone wants to just . . . forget he ever existed."

I look out the window.

My memories from that night are incomplete. I don't know that I'll ever remember everything, but some things have come back to me in blips.

Like when I went over the side of the boat. I took his words with me as I sank into the lake. The last words I heard before I woke up.

We're implanting our embryos tomorrow.

I close my eyes, beyond grateful they never got the chance.

"It's here," John says.

He sets a copy of the *Centre Daily Times* in front of me and Robbie. We're at a library table, trying to finish the last section of the Common App so we don't have to work on it over Thanksgiving break. I've been procrastinating. Considering, you know, the *ordeal*, as Mom refers to it.

I'm sure most colleges don't get many *I survived two fires and my mom's boyfriend's attempt to murder me and now I've learned to carpe that diem* kind of essays.

My eyes dart to the headline.

PENN STATE ALUM CONFESSES TO THREE
MURDERS AND ONE ATTEMPTED MURDER OF
VALLEY HIGH STUDENTS

Mark's mug shot is right underneath it. I have to look away. Something my body does to protect itself.

Robbie's hand finds my back. I relax into his touch.

I told the journalist I was just glad it was all over and that the Morenos, Ebensteins, and Crestmonts finally had answers.

John takes a sip of his gingerbread latte. It's his staple this time of year. We've been getting coffee together every morning, the three of us, before school. It's been nice, having a routine. A ritual. After everything's been so fucking chaotic and surreal.

"Did you read it?" I ask him.

John fiddles with his nose ring. "Once to take it in. A second time to take notes. And a third for critique," he says. "Overall, they didn't leave much to the imagination."

"Mark thought he'd have time on his side," Robbie says bitterly. "Cocky piece of shit."

"Yes," John says. "The DNA on Victoria's top was pretty degraded, but they had so much evidence against him for your case, Lauren, that they leveraged that to get him to confess."

I think back to the letter Mark typed. Trevor's "suicide" note. How even in that letter, when he was pretending to be someone else, he only admitted to killing Vic. He couldn't admit to Jess.

It's obvious to me now. Jess was his daughter's best friend.

And maybe that's why, if Jess suspected Mark of murdering Vic, she was waiting until she had more proof to tell

Trevor or Ainsley. She wanted to be sure. It was something she'd never be able to take back. Accusing her best friend's dad of murder.

I think of Ainsley. I can't even imagine what she's feeling right now. She texted me a couple of days ago.

I have to give my phone back soon, but I just wanted to say I'm glad you're okay

Thank you. I hope you're doing okay too.

I'm glad I'm in California. Don't think I would still be alive if I wasn't

"Guess who'd been commissioned to do the security camera upgrade to the all-digital system at Valley High the week of the pep rally?" John says.

I bite my cheek and tell myself to let go. I'm not doing that anymore.

"Horizon Networks," I say.

Robbie flips the paper over. Like he can't look at Mark anymore.

"He drugged Trevor at the barn and waited until he could drop him off without being seen in the Valley High parking lot," he says. "He knew how to stay out of frame so that he could leave Vic's top at the stadium."

Mark made everyone think Trevor killed himself because

he was guilty. Suicide is already so stigmatized. He robbed Trevor of a real memorial. He robbed the Crestmonts of truly being able to grieve.

"Ben had just started looking into Mark when I called him from your house," Robbie says. "Mark used to oversee private home security installations before he was promoted to the commercial side of things. One of the installations he oversaw was the Morenos', which is probably when he started getting obsessed with Vic. The other was our lake house. Ben also looked at the email exchanges between my dad and Mark. He said my dad wanted the install complete by Fourth of July that year, but Mark said that weekend wouldn't work. Our security cameras weren't live until the weekend after."

The weekend after Mark killed Vic. Which proves that everything was premeditated.

"He'd been abusing his access privileges for a while," John says. "He used fake security updates to disable customers from using their cameras so he could get remote access."

He turns to me. "Which is probably how he was able to get Vic's top off the boat after you found it, Lauren. He even got caught hacking cameras once, but Horizon just gave him a slap on the wrist."

Robbie picks at the cracked finish on the library table. "My dad's suing them. If they'd fired him . . . maybe Trevor would still be alive." His eyes find mine. "He could have been caught before he tried to hurt you."

I take in a breath and it hurts.

The doctor said I might feel fragile for a while. Mom immediately corrected him. *Fragile is what you call a vase*, she'd said. *Not your patient.*

My new phone lights up with a text. I swipe it open. Ready for a momentary distraction. My theory is that my old phone is at the bottom of the lake.

It's not the only thing of mine missing. The necklace Mom gave me, that I'd retied onto my key ring, is missing, too. Mark likes to keep things from his victims, I've learned.

This place looks cute.
Should I book it?

A photo of a boutique hotel in Manhattan is attached, right near the New York Public Library.

Let's do it!

Mom and I decided to move up our trip and spend Christmas in New York next month. Neither of us can stomach spending it at our house.

After I got home from the hospital, Mom took the rest of Mark's things, the things the police didn't want, and put them in a box. Then we took it to the dump. We celebrated by getting ice cream at the Creamery.

"I think I'm going to sell the house," she told me. "Once you're in college."

I set my spoon inside my empty bowl.

"We don't have to wait that long," I told her, meeting her eyes.

I see his face every time I climb our staircase. I picture him on the landing, smiling as he waited for me to collapse. A moment he'd been eagerly awaiting for months.

Mom rubbed her left ring finger. She's been doing that a lot lately.

I decided I'm going to get her a ring for Christmas. A fake ruby. Her birthstone.

"I can't believe I fell in love with a monster," she said.

SIXTY-ONE

Two days after Thanksgiving, I ask for a booth in the back of
the Corner Room. Before I can descend into a spiral of worry,
he's here.

I don't know how to do this. I don't even know how to
breathe right now.

Somehow, I get to my feet. He towers over me. The smile
I used to love lights up his face.

"Lauren," Clint says. "It's good to see you."

Hearing his voice still makes my heart skip a beat.

Both of us stand there like fish out of water. Then I go for
it. I'm hugging him. He smells like home. Like all my memories. I fight to keep my emotions in check.

I can't believe he actually agreed to meet me here.

We pull away from each other and slide into opposite sides
of the booth. His hair is shorter than it was in his last Instagram
post. There are a few shiny bald spots where it will never grow
back. The multiple skin grafts he received on the left side of his
face have settled in. There's less and less scarred skin. Except for
on his jawline and his neck. Where he was burned the worst.

A lump forms in my throat. I sip my iced tea until there's nothing left.

"I can't imagine what you've been through," he says.

His voice is my comfort.

After I texted Clint, he told me he'd seen the news about Mark on TikTok, since this case eclipsed the *Centre Daily Times*. I knew he'd be coming to Penn State sometime this fall to meet with their lacrosse coaches. I asked if he'd meet up with me whenever he was in town. That is, if he hadn't already come here. Luckily, he hadn't.

Now I'm sitting across from him and I'm as nervous as I was on our first date.

"We never said bye before you moved," he says.

"I thought that's what you wanted," I say finally. "I was trying to be respectful."

The words feel wrong as they come out. I know the truth. I sigh out, "I was ashamed to tell you I was leaving."

He rubs the edge of the booth with his fingertips. "I think you assumed a lot," Clint says. "But I know my family didn't make it easy."

My cheeks burn.

I think of the last time we were alone, when he was in the hospital. I'd held his hand until I couldn't anymore. I didn't want to cry in front of him. I didn't want him to feel like he had to be the one to comfort me.

When I finally left his room, his mom stopped me. She'd been waiting for me, her ear pressed to the door.

She put her hand on my shoulder and looked at me with the same eyes as her son.

I'll never forgive you. Stay the hell away from him.

"Can I get you anything else?"

The waiter's voice is a jolt to my system. Clint orders coffee and a stack of pancakes. Somehow, I get the words out for another iced tea.

Then he's gone and we're alone again.

We'd both been drinking that night, the night of the fire. I needed Clint to be drunk. I needed him to leave me to my own devices, not check up on me like he always did. Because he had a heart of gold. One I'd destroy by the time the night was over.

I needed Donovan to be shitfaced. That way he couldn't stop me.

The three of us were at Donovan's house, at his party for the lacrosse team. It was quickly turning into a rager. I took a shot with the boys like I always did, and then another, to start them off on the right track. But after that I was cutting myself off. I poured myself a drink and pretended to sip it throughout the first round of beer pong. I cheered Clint on, like I always did. But after he won, Jake, his partner, went to hook up with the girl he'd brought and Clint wanted me to fill in.

"Babe, come on," he said.

"I suck at beer pong."

"I just want to play with you," he'd told me, grabbing my hip and pulling me close.

Every time he touched me, he still made me blush.

"Okay," I told him.

I sucked, as I predicted. I ended up chugging cup after cup of beer. By the time the game was over, I was full-on drunk, not just the little bit tipsy I intended to be.

I found Donovan after the game of beer pong. He was reconnecting his phone to Bluetooth for the music. He saw me and the clearness of his eyes told me it wasn't time. Yet. I wanted his eyes to be bloodshot.

"Do a shot with me," I told him, grabbing him by the hand.

He licked his lips. He followed me to the kitchen. I grabbed the nearest bottle and poured us both a shot.

I handed him the red Solo cup.

"To new beginnings," I said.

"I always knew you were cool, Lauren."

Fuck you, Donovan.

I downed my portion and watched him down his.

He's at least six deep by now. Just a few more and he'll be close to his limit.

Before I could walk away, he grabbed the strand of hair coming loose from my half-up, half-down waves.

"I'll see you later," he whispered.

Let him think that.

"Maybe," I said, and then I watched him fix himself a new drink, emboldened by the prospect of hooking up with me behind his best friend's back.

Donovan would never touch me again.

I danced with Clint. I played another round of beer pong. I waited until I saw Donovan's eyes become red-rimmed. And then, when Clint was in the bathroom, I snuck into the backyard. Donovan always kept the key to the guesthouse under the rock next to the pot of succulents.

I swiped it, unlocked the door, and slipped inside.

I used my phone flashlight and made my way toward the guest bed. It smelled like cheap perfume. I tried to remember where I had seen Donovan put the photos. I searched under the bed first, my cheek rubbing up against the worn, rough carpet. I found nothing except a shoebox filled with childhood trophies, and an old pair of slippers.

I stood up and went to the nightstand next, pulling each drawer open and finding only loose pens, breath mints, and a couple of expired condoms.

The excitement I'd had was gone. If I didn't find the photos, my entire plan was going to fall apart.

They have to be in here.

I grabbed ahold of the soft comforter and lifted up the mattress of the bed.

Donovan was never the smartest. There they were. Small piles of photos, spread out around the center.

There were dozens.

Dozens of girls.

One was a sophomore girl I recognized. I flipped the photo around. I didn't need to violate any of these girls again by staring at their photos any longer than was necessary.

But I had to make sure mine were there. I flipped through them as quickly as I could until I glimpsed one of my own face. The confirmation I needed.

I gathered all the photos into a pile and stuffed them into my purse. I shut off my phone flashlight and peered out of the guesthouse window. I waited until the two lax guys sharing a joint had their backs turned. Then I snuck outside.

The thump of the bass pounded in my head. I was giddy and drunk. I stumbled toward the side of Donovan's house. I took the photos out of my purse and chucked them in the garbage. Or, I tried to. But my aim was shit and they scattered all over the ground.

I remember scrambling to pick them up. I saw things I never wanted to see. Faces I didn't want to remember.

Then my eyes found another one of mine.

There I was, sprawled out on the bed. Barely clothed. I looked terrified.

That's how he wanted me to feel.

Something came undone inside me in that moment. I threw the photos into the garbage but it was no longer enough. They needed to be destroyed. Incinerated.

I took out my lighter. Click. The flame came to life. I remember thinking how beautiful it looked. A flash of indigo building into golden orange.

Then I picked up the photo of myself and kissed it to the flame. The image began to blur away.

I tossed it on top of the others in the garbage can. Hearing them bend and warp and crackle gave me something I had seldom felt. I felt powerful.

I swayed on my feet. The heat was getting stronger. I took a step backward, almost colliding with the fence. The flames grew, propelled by alcohol-soaked Red Solo cups and the dry brush overflowing from the green waste container. It was like my own private wildfire. I watched in awe as the flames licked the side of the house.

"What the fuck are you doing?!"

I was too drunk to move quickly. Donovan was there, grabbing me by the shoulders.

"Get OFF me!" I yelled.

But he wouldn't. Then I yelled for the only person I knew there who could hear me.

Clint.

By then the fire had caught on to the house. The heat was unbearable, like standing in an oven. I was pinned against the fence until Donovan finally let me go.

"Look what your idiot girlfriend did!" Donovan screamed. He was trying to put out the flames with garbage can lids, but this was no longer a small fire that could be smothered.

This was out of control.

Clint grabbed my hand, yanking me toward him. I stumbled forward, coughing ash.

I flick my gaze down to the table. A dribble of maple syrup has dried into a tacky amber blob.

I will never forget the sound of Clint's screams. They were

sounds I'd never heard from him before. Sounds I'd never heard from another human before. Sounds I will hear for the rest of my life.

The hanging planter box had caught fire. Clint had walked right into its path when he was trying to guide me away from the flames. That's when it fell on top of him.

"I thought you hated me," I tell him.

"I tried texting you and calling you," he says. "After enough times, I figured you changed your number."

I look at him, at all of him. His freckles only decorate half his face now. The rest are buried underneath new skin.

"Maybe, if you knew the truth, you wouldn't have tried to reach me."

Clint rests his fork on the edge of his plate. He reaches for his napkin and brings it up to my face, gently blotting my tears away.

I reach for his wrist and hold it midair. Making him stop.

He gently lifts my chin up to meet his gaze. "It was an accident," he says. "You were smoking. You were drunk."

I take a deep breath, and then I tell him the thing I've never been able to.

"It wasn't an accident." I hold my gaze steady. "What everyone said was true."

The softness in his eyes is gone. He retreats from me.

"What do you mean?" he says, his nostrils flaring.

"I couldn't . . ."

"You couldn't what?" Clint says, his eyes locked on mine. His voice is a hair away from shaking.

It's still so painful to admit.

"Donovan had all kinds of photos. Of all different girls."

Clint clenches his jaw. "Donovan."

His voice is filled with disgust.

"Including me," I say.

Clint grabs ahold of the table like he's bracing himself.

"What do you mean he had photos of you?"

"He kept them in his guesthouse and he used them to get me to do . . . what he wanted. Grab me whenever. Touch me wherever."

I remember the homecoming dance. I remember the shock. His fingers slipping under my dress.

I can't say these things out loud. I need to forget they ever happened to me. "Even if you were standing a few feet away."

"How did he get photos of you?" Clint asks.

He can't even look at me as he says it.

"I was drunk one night. He . . . used it to his advantage."

"Where the hell was I?" Clint asks, exasperated.

"You were out of town. Looking at lacrosse programs. Donovan made it seem like you would never believe me. I did what he told me to do."

Clint takes a sip of his water. He sets it down and it clatters against the table. He hugs his arms around himself and I watch as his short nails sink deeper into his biceps.

"He humiliated me for months," I say. "I saw an opportunity at the party. I stole the photos. Then I set them on fire."

The words make my throat sore, the way it felt when I was still in the hospital. I keep talking to fill the silence from his side of the booth. "I hurt you in the worst possible way."

His hands slide down from his biceps, down to his elbows. He finally looks up at me. "I wish I would have known."

"I'm sorry," I say. Two words that are not enough and will never be enough. "I'm so sorry for everything."

The light from the window outside makes his blue eyes seem turquoise.

"I was at a party this past summer," he says. "You had already moved. Tara came up to me."

Tara, one of my old teammates. Our sweeper. "She'd drunkenly said that maybe Donovan had been one of the reasons why you moved away. I didn't understand what she meant. I texted her the next day and she never responded. It's been eating away at me since. Now I get it."

Maybe he had photos of Tara, too.

She would have never said anything to me. Because she didn't know I burned them. That I'd gotten rid of them. For all of us.

Clint looks at me. "Donovan got caught drinking with a fourteen-year-old and word got around the Division One circuit. I don't think he'll be playing in college." He shakes his head. "My former best friend is trash."

"He is."

Clint relaxes his shoulders. I remember the way I used to wrap my arms around him. Just then, his face loosens and his expression grows surprisingly warm. "I didn't think we'd ever see each other again."

"I've thought about you almost every day I've been here," I tell him.

His mouth breaks into a small smile. "I just wanted to know that you were okay," he says.

I remember the way we were. The way I loved him. It feels like it's finally part of the past now. And I can feel the two of us letting what consumed us go, together. A welcome ease enters our conversation as we talk about what's next for us.

When we say goodbye, I feel lighter. I squeeze him tight. One last time.

SIXTY-TWO

It's agony, sitting on the bench when I should be on the field. It's even harder not to scream my face off when Mara scores the goal that breaks our tie with less than one minute left in the game. We're headed to states.

Coach loses it. I've never seen him happier.

Sometimes I have to forget that I considered him our prime murder suspect. Although I still haven't necessarily figured out if he ever crossed a line with Gwen or any other girl from Valley High.

"You'll be able to play a few minutes in our first game. I know you will. Just keep resting," he says before he's bombarded by the entire team. I'm passing out waters to everyone as they come off the field. Everyone's careful not to hug me too tight, because my ribs and lungs are still healing. My doctor hasn't cleared me to play yet, even though I was released from the hospital three weeks ago. I'm praying that by later this week, I'll get the okay.

"You're a fucking beast, O'Brian," Andrea says, squeezing my forearm instead of my torso.

Then I reach for her, and I pull her into a hug. She buries her face into my shoulder and I rest my head against hers.

She visited me on my second or third day in the hospital, when I was still hopped up on pain meds. And maybe that's what finally gave me the courage to tell her the truth about Labor Day weekend. That day on the boat. Finding Vic's top and the call from Mark that came after it. Discovering Ainsley was the one behind the troll account.

I'm done keeping secrets.

Before she left, she had said those same words.

You're a fucking beast, O'Brian.

"We're winning this year. States, I mean," I whisper into her hair. "For Vic."

"For Vic," she says. Then she's jogging toward her mom, and I realize for the first time how cold it is tonight.

My ears sting, and I pull on a winter headband. I'm not used to the lack of a sweat blanket I usually have coating me after a game. I don't even have a bag to sling over my shoulder. I'm still not supposed to be lifting anything heavy. My recovery feels like it's been an eternity.

When I turn to walk off the field, I see someone. Walking toward me.

Robbie. Holding a bouquet of dark flowers.

"These are for you," he says.

"For what?"

"Congratulations on heading to states."

"Thank you."

He hands them to me and twists the moonstone ring on his finger. Something he does when he's nervous. Is he nervous right now?

"I asked your mom if it'd be okay if I took you to dinner tonight. But only if that's something that you'd be down for."

I stare at him, my whole face feeling hot.

"Like a date," I say.

"Yeah," he says, running a hand through his hair. "I know that wasn't always in the cards for us. I wanted to give you time . . ." His cheeks are flushed. "But it's the full moon in Gemini tonight. I thought I'd go out on a limb. And I'm hoping, maybe, it's working in my favor?"

I like seeing him like this. A little self-conscious.

It's the real him. It was always there, hiding underneath the version of him I met in the storage room. Hiding to protect himself from getting hurt.

I did the same thing. Because if I never loved someone again, I could never hurt them. Maybe it was safer that way. But it was miserable, too.

"I met up with Clint," I say quickly.

Robbie's gaze is curious more than anything else.

"He was in town for a lacrosse thing," I explain. "He'd heard about . . . you know. Everything."

"How'd it go?"

I exhale. "It made me feel like I could finally move on," I say.

"Like closure," he says.

"Yeah. Something like that."

"I don't think I'll ever feel at peace," Robbie says. "And I don't know what I would have done if . . ."

He doesn't have to say it. Because I know. Because I can feel it, the energy between us. Because I've always felt it, and I've tried to deny it. Because girls who set fires have to punish themselves.

But being on that boat with Mark changed things. It changed everything.

It made me realize how much I had to lose. That I actually had things to lose.

My second chance gave me everything I thought I never deserved. Including the person standing right in front of me.

When we kiss this time, I relax into the way his lips feel against mine. His one hand lingers behind my ear. The other finds my back.

But then I'm trembling because I don't remember how to do this. How to kiss someone and mean it.

It's terrifying, to care this much.

Robbie must sense I'm a mess inside because his lips leave mine. "If this is too soon—"

"No." I squeeze his hand. I'm determined not to ruin this moment. "It's just . . ."

I think back to when I first moved to Happy Valley. When those Saturdays were just for us.

I say the words I've kept locked inside for months.

"It was you all along," I tell him, watching the way his entire face lights up.

ACKNOWLEDGMENTS

I am beyond thankful to everyone who has helped me publish my first novel.

I have the great pleasure of working with two incredible agents, Kristin van Ogtrop and Stephen Barbara. Thank you for taking a chance on me and championing my work. Your guidance, your energy, and your votes of confidence keep me going. I'm very lucky to have landed at InkWell. I'd also like to thank Lyndsey Blessing for helping this book reach more readers, and Sidney Boker for all of your work behind the scenes.

Ann Marie Wong and Mark Podesta, my amazing editors: I have had so much fun working on this book with you. Our vision for this story has always felt aligned, and you took it to new heights. Thank you for believing in this manuscript and for your deeply thoughtful questions, edits, and words of encouragement. You have challenged me in the best possible way.

Thank you to everyone at Henry Holt Books for Young Readers and Macmillan who has helped bring this book to life, especially Jen Besser and Jean Feiwel.

Aurora Parlagreco: Thank you for designing the perfect cover. I will forever be obsessed.

Alexei Esikoff, Allene Cassagnol, and the entire production team: Thank you for shaping this book into the polished story it is. I am in awe of the work you do.

Jen Edwards, thank you for championing this book on the sales side.

To Molly Ellis and Tatiana Merced-Zarou: Thank you for your

publicity talents, and your enthusiastic outreach to help this book reach its audience.

To Mariel Dawson, Gabriella Salpeter, and Naheid Shahsamand: Thank you for your marketing prowess, and for bringing Lauren and her haphazard investigation to even more readers.

Thank you to Elishia Merricks, Maria Snelling, and Drew Kilman for all of your work on giving this book a home in audio form.

Thank you to my first readers, Maya Eckhardt-Polanco and Amber Viera. Your unwavering support and enthusiasm for this project and my writing has propelled me forward.

Thank you to Ally Abrams for telling me you couldn't wait to fill your bookshelf with my books someday. *Rebecca* forever.

Special thanks to the 2024 debuts for sharing your wisdom and kindness with me.

I'm grateful to the teachers who encouraged me, especially Mr. Marshall, who fostered my love of story, and Professor Fae Myenne Ng, who taught me how to cultivate my writing sanctuary.

There are many people who show me such kindness in this life. Thank you to all of my friends. I love you!

To my family, especially my parents: Thank you for encouraging me to follow my dream. Your support and love mean everything to me.

Colt, thank you for being the most supportive partner, for reading new drafts of this book while we had a newborn, and for helping me find the time I so desperately need to write.

A, thank you for being my little writing companion. I love you!

My final thanks go to you, dear reader, for picking up this book.

I wanted to share a couple of additional resources in case the topics mentioned in this story resonate with you. RAINN.org is a great resource for understanding consent. If you are struggling with a drug or alcohol use disorder, you can call 1-800-662-HELP (4357) to speak to someone who can help. Take care.